"I'm your best bet if you want to survive this little adventure."

"Open the portal that'll take us home." Vicki Nelson gave Ren points for looking in the right direction but, given her rising panic, didn't wait for a response. "You can't, can you? Not from this side."

"We weren't going to go back." Ren waved a trembling hand at the corpse and the scavengers and the sky of red stars. "It wasn't supposed to be like this!"

"Yeah, well, surprise." A scavenger with more appetite than survival instinct tried to take a piece out of the top of her head; Vicki crushed it almost absently, wiping her hand on her jeans as she watched the circling birds. Some of them were flying fairly high. They'd be visible as silhouettes against the night to anyone—or anything—with halfway decent vision. It reminded her of lying on the sofa with Mike, soaking up his warmth, and watching television.

"They're going to draw other scavengers. The way vultures do. Maye other predators. We have to find cover."

"How do you know that?"

"Animal Planet."

"But you're a . . ." Even though she was clearly fine with poking holes into other realities, Ren couldn't seem to say it.

This was neither the time nor the place for denial.

"Vampire. Nightwalker. Member of the bloodsucking undead." Vicki frowned, trying to remember the rest and coming up blank. Three would have to do. "I have cable. And I'm your best bet if you want to survive this little adventure."

—from "No Matter Where You Are" by Tanya Huff

A
GIRL'S GUIDE
TO GUNS AND
MONSTERS

edited by Martin H. Greenberg and Kerrie Hughes

DAW BOOKS, INC.

DONALD A. WOLLHEIM, FOUNDER

375 Hudson Street, New York, NY 10014

ELIZABETH R. WOLLHEIM
SHEILA E. GILBERT
PUBLISHERS

http://www.dawbooks.com

First Printing, February 2010

1   2   3   4   5   6   7   8   9

ACKNOWLEDGMENTS

CONTENTS

INTRODUCTION

My favorite stories have a common theme: a girl, a gun, and a monster to defeat. It stems from a life filled with monsters disguised as humans. I'm certainly not the first person in life to be beaten, abused, and raped, and sadly I won't be the last. I see it in the news every day—children kidnapped and murdered, animals tortured, the mentally ill abandoned to their own madness. And then there's war; is there any monster bigger than war and the atrocities committed during it?

A person could go crazy obsessing over the injustice of it all. Is it any wonder addiction is the main way to anesthetize one's self from the fact that at any time and in any town any one of us can be the victim of a stranger in the dark or your ex-lover in the light? I spent years being bitter and angry over the idea that most monsters never pay for their crimes, and the one that hurt me got to walk away free and easy. Or was that simply a lie I told myself? When I stopped dwelling in the past, I found out that most of my tormentors were in jail for other crimes or had created a personal hell for themselves with alcohol, drugs, and self-loathing.

I also found that I could become one of the most hated monster slayers of all time, an agent of change. So I learned how to be a survivor and then how to teach girls, and sometimes boys, to fight monsters. I do this by working at a rape crisis center in my hometown. Every time I answer a call to go to the hospital and let a victim know their rights, and that they not only have the power to survive, but to fight back against the monster who attacked them, I feel like Buffy slaying a vampire. A conceit I formerly only knew in the plots of really good books featuring a girl, a gun, and a monster.

In this anthology I was pleasantly surprised to find that the stories I received could be put together in a chronological order that starts in the Old West and ends in outer space. The order is particularly apt, since monsters have existed for thousands of years, and will also exist in the future as well. I was even more pleased at the range of ages of the heroines represented. The best surprise was the variety of monsters and how they each meet their demise!

I hope you enjoy them as much as I have. Feel free to friend me on Facebook and share your favorite story, or maybe how you have learned to slay monsters yourself.

Kerrie Hughes, Monster Slayer

THE DRIFTER

Jane Lindskold

Prudence Bledsloe rode into town on a big buckskin stallion. She was on the trail of trouble, and it didn't take much to see she'd found it.

She was accustomed to attracting stares when she arrived in a new area. It wasn't just that she traveled alone. In these modern times, women did that all the time, but usually by stagecoach or train rather than on horseback.

It might have had something to do with the rifle in her saddle boot or the six-guns on her hips. It might have had to do with the fact that she wore trousers. It might have had to do with the message that every inch of her long, lean body and the direct stare of her yellow-brown eyes projected: "Don't mess with me. I'm more trouble than you can handle."

But today, as she rode through the central town plaza, Prudence sensed that none of the usual reactions were behind the stares. The stares she knew were usually long, disapproving stares or sidelong shocked stares. These were scared stares, fast and quick, checking her out, making note of her and then reacting.

What were they feeling?

Prudence took Buck to the rail in front of the general store and dropped-tied him. She'd had to make too many fast getaways ever to tie her horse. Anyone who tried to steal Buck, well ... they'd learn that messing with the horse was as bad an idea as messing with the rider. Buck would mind the pack horse, a tough, wiry tricolor paint gelding Prudence had christened, with a rare spurt of imagination, "Trick."

"I'll be back in a moment, guys," she said softly. "Then we'll get you out of all that tack and comfortable."

Prudence had one boot on the wooden sidewalk when it hit her what she had seen in the eyes of the locals. Fear, yes, but fear mixed with something else, something she never expected.

That something else was relief. Relief that Prudence wasn't whatever it was that had them so deeply concerned.

If they were that scared, she'd probably come to the right place, but could she get folk to talk to her? That was the biggest problem about going it alone. When Jake had been around, he did the talking to strangers. Now, bridging the gap was up to her.

Riding boots echoing on the boards, Prudence strode over to a shop that the neatly painted sign over the door announced was Eli's Mercantile.

A round-faced man with a fringe of graying hair and a neatly trimmed beard looked up too fast from where he'd been counting stock. A round-faced little girl, fair-haired, probably no more than ten, jerked back behind the counter, then peeked around, her blue eyes wide as the western sky. Her rosebud mouth was working slightly. She smelled of peppermint.

"Afternoon," Prudence said conversationally. "Mr. Eli, I need some supplies."

"We've got 'em," the man said, acknowledging his name with a slight dip of his head. "Grub over there, blankets there, ready-made clothes there."

As Mr. Eli mentioned each category, he jerked his bearded chin in the general direction where the stock was shelved or stacked.

The shopkeeper gave Prudence and her unusual ornamentation a long look, then added, "Ammo and gun supplies are behind the counter. If you're needing reloads I think I have what you'll need. Looks like you're carrying a .32 Smith & Wesson."

Prudence nodded. "You've a good eye. I've a .56-.50 Spencer rifle out on my saddle. Could use reloads for that, too."

"Got 'em, and you're welcome to 'em."

Prudence spent several minutes stacking items on the worn but lovingly polished wooden counter. Casually, she made certain that Mr. Eli caught a glimpse of her weighted coin purse, just to reassure him that she could pay. He'd been more polite than many she'd met, even when Jake was still around.

There'd been that about Jake that made people give him and Prudence service, even as they dripped disapproval.

The little blond girl watched intently as Prudence asked for coffee, bacon, and beans. For new socks. For a little bag of peppermint drops. Prudence ventured a smile. The little girl vanished behind the counter again.

The child had fair skin to go with her fair hair. She was surprisingly untanned for one who lived under the punishing southwestern sun. Prudence took a second look when the round face peeked out again. No. This child hadn't always been kept away from the sun. Her fairness was that of tan fading, not of one who had always been kept inside or with her face ruthlessly shadowed by a sunbonnet.

That meant the little girl's parents—Prudence took a look at Mr. Eli, now stiffly climbing a ladder behind the counter to reach something on an upper shelf—her grandparents must watch over her carefully.

Prudence felt her face tighten, remembering a time she had not watched carefully, a time she had failed, and someone else had paid the price.

When her purchases were spread on the counter, they dickered a bit over the prices. In the end, when Mr. Eli threw in a couple of cotton bandanas to sweeten the deal, Prudence felt that the mood was such that she could ask a few questions.

"Any news of the road?"

"What sort of news?"

"Trouble someone traveling alone should avoid," Prudence said. Watching the shopkeeper carefully, she added, "Things like sheep being killed. Cattle, maybe, too, but definitely sheep or smaller domestic animals. Maybe a person or two going missing, especially a young person. Maybe a very old person, but more likely someone young."

And fat, and tender . . . Prudence thought, but didn't say aloud.

Mr. Eli went tense. The little girl looked flat-out scared, but there was something else in her expression, something about the set of the chin that Prudence noticed.

Neither said anything. That lack of answer was almost as eloquent as a speech would have been.

Prudence gathered up her purchases. When Mr. Eli bent to help her with one of her bundles, Prudence slipped a bag of peppermint drops to the little girl.

"I followed a stream into town," Prudence said as Mr. Eli was helping her load her purchases into Trick's saddle bags. "Anyone mind too much if I camp there?"

"There's a stand of cottonwood," Mr. Eli said, not quite answering her questions. "When folks come in for market and don't want to stay at the hotel for one reason or another, they often camp there."

"Thank you," Prudence said. "Good afternoon."

She swung into the saddle, but didn't head directly to that stand of cottonwoods. Instead, she found a reliable-looking livery stable and arranged to have Buck and Trick cleaned up and fed.

"I'm going for some grub," Prudence said, sliding her rifle out of the saddle boot.

"You may leave your saddlebags here," the hostler said. He was a short, thickset man, and his words were flavored with the music of a Spanish accent. "I will watch them for you."

"Gracias," Prudence said. Buck was a good judge of character, and the stallion was already lipping the hair on the hostler's arm. Her bags would be safe. "I should be back in a couple of hours."

"If you go to the hotel, ask for my niece, Maria," the man said. "She waits tables there and does some of the cooking. She'll set you up real good if you tell her Ricardo sent you."

"I appreciate it," Prudence said. "Let me get a few things from my bag. They'll like me better in the dining room if I don't have trail dust on me."

Ricardo smiled a short, humorless smile. "They'll like having you. Business, it has been slow."

Ah, Prudence thought. *That explains the welcome. Ricardo must have seen Mr. Eli helping me with my purchases. I bet the old man only does that for a cash customer. Good*

*as a written reference then. When times are tough, even a
woman in trousers is welcome if she can pay her way.*

Ricardo turned to the horses. Prudence went over to
the hotel.

A weary-looking young woman met her at the entry
to the dining room.

"Ricardo told me I should ask for Maria," Prudence
said as the young woman escorted her to a good table.

The young woman smiled. "I am Maria. I will take
good care of you here. The stove is a little cold, but I
can do something with fresh eggs, bacon, tortillas, maybe
some beans if you can wait just a little."

"Is there a place I can wash up while I'm waiting?"
Prudence asked.

"Oh, yes, if you don't mind coming back to the kitchen.
The boss is resting, but he wouldn't mind, probably."

Prudence pumped her own water and carried it to
a little room off the kitchen. A short while later, face
washed, braids coiled into a loose bun rather than looped
at the base of her neck like she wore them on the road,
dusty shirt and vest replaced with a clean blouse, she
looked almost respectable—as long as no one looked
under the table.

When Prudence re-emerged, Maria was doing something wonderful-smelling with not only the promised
eggs and beans, but with onions, chiles, and cheese. Prudence nodded and went back to the dining room. There
she chose a seat where she could overhear the conversation in the adjacent bar.

As Ricardo had indicated, there weren't many cus-
tomers. Except for Prudence, the dining room was
empty. In the bar, three men were playing a lazy game
of cards. The bartender was chatting with a fat man with
printer's ink staining his fingers.

They all noticed Prudence when she took her seat, but after she pulled out a Bible and began to read, they went back to their other activities.

Jake had taught her the Bible trick. The Bible wasn't the kind of reading matter a "soiled dove" would favor. Nearly as good as having crossed eyes or spotty skin to keep the men away.

Jake . . .

This time the Bible didn't work. Prudence smelled printer's ink. Then a shadow spilled over the pages. The fat man was standing beside her table.

"May I join you?" he asked, and slid out the chair across from her without waiting for her reply.

He had the mellifluous tones of a professional preacher, squint lines around his eyes as if he did a lot of reading in poor light, and nothing of the unctuous manner Prudence had come to dread from the hucksters who went from town to town, pretending to be holy men.

"Mr. Eli at the mercantile said you were asking some mighty strange questions," the fat man said.

Maria came in and set Prudence's plate of eggs, bacon, and beans in front of her. She gave the fat man a fleeting smile.

"Coffee, Reverend Printer?"

"Yes. Black as night, sweet as sin," the man answered, rolling his words with gusto, "and hot as hell . . ."

Maria giggled. Prudence guessed this was an old joke between them.

She rolled some of the bacon, beans, and eggs into a flour tortilla and took a bite. Heavenly. She ate another bite.

Maria looked inquiringly at Prudence.

"If this is what you do on the spur of the moment," Prudence said, "I'm coming back when you're ready. I'll join the gentleman in a cup of coffee, and put his on my bill."

"I thank you," the man said, when Maria had left, "for your hospitality. I started poorly. Let me introduce myself. My name is Gerald Holman. I am an ordained Lutheran minister, but I am also the editor of the local newspaper."

"Thus the nickname," Prudence said.

"As you say. As editor of the local paper, I was interested when a prominent local citizen told me a curious tale."

"Did he bring it to you?"

"No. I stopped in for some supplies. Eli was still trying to figure you out."

Prudence smiled. "Good luck to him. I'm Prudence Bledsloe, by the way."

"Of?"

"Currently, that stand of cottonwoods down by the stream, if no one objects."

Reverend Printer's eyebrows rose. Prudence knew her choice of doss would create comment, but comment was what she wanted.

"No one should object," Reverend Printer said. "Now, Eli said you were asking about . . ."

A loud, almost human scream from outside interrupted him. Prudence's table was next to a window. They leaned forward as one to get a better line of sight.

A muscular, stocky man was walking down the middle of the street, leading two pack ponies. Or rather, trying to lead two ponies.

One pony had apparently been struck by a rock and was now trying to bolt. Only the handler's considerable strength kept it from doing so. A laughing group of men on the porch of the saloon across the plaza made amply clear where the rock had come from.

Despite being dressed in jeans and a button down shirt, the man now quieting the frightened pack pony was obviously an Indian—Navajo or Apache, Prudence guessed. He wore his dark hair to brush his shoulders, beneath a high-crowned hat that shaded the sculptured lines of his face.

"Nathan Yaz," Reverend Printer said quietly. "He's courting Maria—the woman who cooked your lunch."

"He doesn't seem overly welcome," Prudence said.

That was an understatement. None of the several people watching Nathan Yaz's ordeal were coming to his aid. A tall man wearing a sheriff's star pointedly turned and walked into the nearest building.

"We've had Indian trouble lately," Reverend Printer said, pushing back his chair and heading for the door.

Prudence thought about joining the minister, but decided that the appearance of a woman in trousers might only make matters worse.

She settled for easing open the window and resting her rifle barrel on the sill. She was a good shot, and if those rock-throwing drunks threw another rock, a warning shot might make them think twice.

But there was no more trouble. Reverend Printer escorted Nathan Yaz around the side of the hotel. There was a sound of angry voices from the kitchen. When these quieted, he returned, bearing the coffee pot.

Prudence had already slid her rifle back under the table, but kept it where she could get to it quickly.

When Reverend Printer had filled her cup and resumed his seat, she asked quietly, "Indian trouble?"

"Sheep killed—messily. Cattle stolen. In a few cases,

cows were found mutilated. Worse, a little boy who lived on one of the outlying ranches disappeared. Later, a little girl, not more than three, also went missing. Her mother—a reliable woman—claimed the child had been stolen out of her bed."

"And folks are sure it's Indians?" Prudence said.

"Who else?" Reverend Printer's tired voice said that he knew there were other options, but also that in a case like this people took sides along race lines pretty fast. "Rustlers would sell cattle, not butcher them. Still, until the children vanished, it could have been rustlers. When the children started going missing, well ... Everyone knows that the Indians keep slaves."

"So did white folk," Prudence said softly, "not that long ago."

"I know. I know."

"So that's why Nathan Yaz got such a warm welcome?"

"Not so long ago the Navajo were the enemy," Reverend Printer said. "Never mind that they've been re-located to lands where it's a full time job keeping body and soul together. People don't forget."

"Neither have the Navajo, I bet," Prudence said. "They're going to be saying things like, 'Look. We live peacefully, and still they blame us. Why should we stay peaceful? What is there to gain?'"

"So you can see why I wondered at you coming to town as you did, asking questions like you did," Reverend Printer said. "As editor of the local paper, I've been exercising a little censorship, playing down the sensationalism, but people do talk."

"And you wondered if I came following that talk?" Prudence nodded. "In a sense. I'll assure you, though, I have no desire to stir up further trouble."

She didn't say more, and she guessed something on

her face told the fat man that she wasn't going to do so. He sipped the last of his coffee and rose.

"Pleasure meeting you, Miss Bledsloe."

"Pleasure," Prudence echoed, and meant it.

After Reverend Printer had left, Prudence sat thinking over what she'd learned. She didn't think it was Indians causing the trouble, but if she told Reverend Printer her suspicions, it wouldn't help. No one would believe her. No one who hadn't lived through what she had.

The dining room was cool and pleasant compared to outdoors, but if she was to pitch her camp she should get moving. Prudence found Maria in the kitchen, rolling out what looked like pie crust.

"I've come to settle my bill," Prudence said.

"No bill," Maria said firmly. "I saw your rifle on the windowsill. I don't think you would have shot Nathan. Come back tonight. I am making peach pie."

Prudence put her coin purse away. "Thank you, and I just might."

She collected Buck and Trick from Ricardo. The horses's coats and their tack gleamed. Buck nibbled with sleepy contentment along her arm, telling her he'd been treated very well indeed. Prudence paid what was asked without dickering and added a tip besides. Then she rode for the cottonwoods.

It was a nice stand, plenty shaded, with a pole corral and stone fire circle already in place. Prudence pitched her tent, then built a fire, going a bit afield to gather something other than cottonwood. Cottonwood burned hot and messy, tending to flare out of control.

Like some folks I know, Prudence thought.

She didn't go into town for dinner, but sat by her small fire. If anyone had been watching, they would have seen her taking the single piece cartridges she had bought from Mr. Eli and methodically changing the lead bullets for some she took from a box she took out of her own gear. These bullets shone brightly as she inspected each in the firelight . . . shone like silver.

Prudence had banked her fire to dull coals and settled her head against a rolled blanket when she heard stealthy footsteps approaching. She was reaching for her six-shooter when she smelled peppermint.

"May we come in?" came a hushed, female voice.

Prudence hadn't heard this voice before, but she knew who it must be. She didn't put the gun aside, but she did ease her finger off the trigger.

Two small figures came into her camp and stood where she could see them, but where they would not be visible from outside the camp. One was the little girl she'd seen in Eli's mercantile. The other was a Navajo boy just slightly taller. He smelled of wood smoke, mutton, and sage, spiced with peppermint.

Interesting, Prudence thought.

"Welcome to my fire," she said. "Coffee?"

"No, thank you," came the girl's voice. "And thank you for the peppermints. They're my favorite, but Grandpa only gives me a few at a time."

"Good for the digestion," Prudence said. "I don't see any harm in them."

"Your name is Prudence Bledsloe," the girl said, rather as one confirming a fact, not asking a question.

"It is. And you are Miss Eli?"

"Miss March. April March. April. My mama was an Eli. This is my friend, Vernon Yaz."

Ah-hah! One mystery solved.

"Pleased to meet you both. Does your grandpa know you're out, Miss March?"

"I . . . well, no. I piled up the blankets in my bed, though, and he and Grandma are well and truly asleep."

"Still, you shouldn't stay out late, just in case. I think you and Hosteen Yaz have something to tell me?"

The boy laughed softly. "Hosteen" was a Navajo title of respect, roughly translating as "old man." He had caught her joke and appreciated it.

"You were asking questions," he said. His words were flavored with the accent that marked a Navajo speaker: *t*s and *d*s blending, *g*s vanishing, vowels elongated. The syllables were run together, as if the speaker was accustomed to much longer words. "I heard Maria telling Nathan—he's my mother's brother—what Reverend Printer told you, but Reverend Printer doesn't know it all. April said you should hear this."

"So there is a Navajo side to the trouble, too," Prudence said. "I thought there might be."

"We have lost sheep. We don't have cattle, but the peaches have been ruined on the drying racks. And our children—three little ones—have been stolen. There are whispers that a witch is at work."

"Tell me more."

Vernon did so, going into great detail. Prudence listened carefully, making little noises to indicate that she had understood, but otherwise not interrupting. She needed to hear what Vernon had to tell, but if children were disappearing, the last thing she needed was to have these two found in her camp.

Vernon's story matched what Reverend Printer had told. The thefts showed a level of malice beyond what rustlers or simple thieves would commit. Goods had been spoiled. Misery, not gain, had been the goal. And no trace had been found of the missing children.

"When did these things happen?" Prudence asked.

Vernon told her. His way of giving dates didn't follow the Gregorian calender, but he had a firm awareness of phases of the moon. That was good enough. With
his permission, Prudence took out a scrap of paper and
made notes.

April was less certain when the white children had
been stolen, since they didn't belong to the town community, but she did know when her grandparents had
started watching her more carefully, keeping her from
going outside to play.

"I have a new pony," she explained. "Vern and I were
practicing for the races. Grandma and Grandpa hadn't
minded, then all of a sudden they did."

"And they'll mind," Prudence said firmly, "if they find
you out of bed. I'll walk you back to your house. You
staying in town, Vern?"

"Nathan," the boy said, his smile flashing in the dark,
"is visiting Maria. I am supposed to be sleeping off very
much peach pie."

"I'll walk you both back," Prudence said firmly.
"Buck, mind the camp."

The stallion snorted and shifted his weight from side
to side.

After April and Vern were delivered to their respec-
tive beds, Prudence hurried back to her camp. She tried
to sleep, but memory warred with conjecture, keeping
her awake long after the coals of her fire had guttered
into ash.

The next morning, Prudence broke camp and headed
out toward where Vern had told her the worst of the
"witch trouble" had occurred.

Most white folk thought of the Indians—when they
bothered to think about them at all—as living the life of

hunters and gatherers. To some whites this was living in savagery. To others the Indian way was the ideal of the noble savage. In the case of the modern Navajo either image was also completely false.

Although the Navajo were not town dwellers, as were the various tribes the Spanish had dubbed "Pueblo" Indians, neither were they tepee-dwelling migrants as were many of the Plains tribes. The Navajo built houses—most commonly the various styles of hogan—kept flocks of sheep and herds of horses. Some even maintained orchards, favoring peaches and other stone fruit. When Kit Carson had wanted to drive out the Navajo, he'd burnt their trees.

But Prudence's route didn't head toward the stream beds or river bottoms where those orchards would likely be, nor did she turn toward where flocks of sheep and goats grazed on the sparse summer vegetation. She set Buck's head toward the hot, dry, rocky reaches, a land of majestic stone cliffs and vegetation closer to grey than green in color. The trail they followed once they left the town and its outliers was merely the suggestion of a trail, a path of least resistance rather than one that indicated frequent travel.

As Prudence journeyed away from the town, she thought about what had brought her to these hot, dry lands, so far from where she'd grown up, and with nothing but two mustangs as companions.

Prudence Bledsloe had been born in the Smokey Mountains of Tennessee, in a tangled green hollow well away from any of the towns listed on any map. The Bledsloe clan had been part of a small community of a dozen or so families, all of whom were descended from a group of immigrants who had come to the New World from Eastern Europe.

Those original immigrants had been lured by the promise of unsettled land. More importantly, they longed for a degree of tolerance toward different creeds and ways of life that was impossible to find even in the most isolated parts of Eastern Europe.

The Bledsloe clan had consisted of Prudence's parents, her elder brother Jake, and a couple of younger cousins who had moved in with them after a sickness took their own parents. Sometime later, a return of that sickness had wiped out Clan Bledsloe along with much of the community. Most of the survivors had resolved to rebuild. Jake and Prudence had decided to head West.

The two remaining members of Clan Bledsloe hadn't had much, but they were adaptable. The skills they needed merely to survive in the Smokeys had served them well on the trail. Sometimes they'd linked up with a wagon train, but most often they traveled alone.

Prudence thought about those long days on the trail, eating dust on foot at first, later eating more dust on horseback. Those hadn't been precisely happy days— shelter was often scanty, and Prudence and Jake both mourned those who had died of the sickness. They'd done all right for food, though, both being skilled with various weapons. And they'd had hope, hope of finding a place where they could settle, raise cattle, and maybe someday forget.

Buck snorted and shifted uneasily. Prudence shook herself from the dangerous distraction of memory. Pulling her rifle from the saddle boot, she swung down to get a look at what had disturbed the big mustang.

She found it within a few yards of the trail: a sheep, one of the hardy, four-horned *churro* breed that the Navajo favored. Telling much more was pretty near impossible. The sheep hadn't just been killed; it had been flayed open. The guts had been pulled out and much of the meat had been stripped from the carcass. The hide had been left intact, but many of the bones were splintered and sucked clean of marrow.

Flies buzzed over what remained, their wings making enough noise that Prudence knew she should have heard it from the trail. The carcass stunk, too. She should have smelled that.

Prudence scanned her surroundings, resolving that no matter how compelling the past was, old memories had to wait on the present. That is, unless she wanted to give up all hopes of a future.

A new thought hit Prudence, making her catch her breath.

Did she honestly care if she had a future? The future had been taken from her twice: once when the Bledsloe clan had been wiped out by disease, once when Jake had been taken from her.

She'd been drifting since then, drifting west, drifting after rumors that might lead her to . . .

Prudence forced herself to think about what she was seeking, forced herself to accept.

To lead her to what Jake had become.

Standing under the hot sun, hearing Trick shift nervously under the packs, Prudence faced the memories.

She and Jake had gotten wind of a town where cattle buyers were congregating. She'd never been quite sure whether the buyers had come because the cattle were being driven there or whether the cattle were being driven there to meet the buyers. What she did know was that for a couple of weeks there was plenty of work, even for a couple of scraggly drifters.

Prudence had gotten work washing dishes and

chopping stuff in the kitchen of the railroad hotel. Jake—
who dreamed of owning a ranch someday—had gotten a
job keeping the gathered herds in order. After weeks in
the saddle, the cowhands were eager for the delights of
civilization, even as offered by a rough-edged nowhere
town like this one.

That their delights included women was a given, so
Prudence kept back in the kitchen. Days had passed.
The buying and selling ended. The loaded trains rattled
back toward Chicago.

The cowboys, their pockets fat with severance pay,
remained, wilder than ever. Jake's work, however, had
evaporated when the cattle were shipped out, so he and
Prudence decided to move on.

Had the cowboys tracked them or had the meeting
been chance? Prudence didn't know. Her memories
of that terrible night began with waking to the sound of
coarse laughter, the smell of tobacco and whiskey. Of
Jake's voice, superficially tough and angry. Trembling
beneath the anger was a thread of fear.

Prudence had been jerked from her bedroll by a
rough hand. Still half-asleep, she'd staggered, trying to
catch her balance. Instead, she'd fallen into the arms of
the man who had pulled her up. He started pawing at
her breasts, pushing aside the fabric of the loose cotton
nightshirt she wore for sleeping.

"Leave my sister alone!" Jake had shouted.

The cowboys had only laughed. Prudence fought to
get loose, froze when she realized her struggles only excited her captors.

And Jake . . . Jake had lost control. The moon was full,
and but for that they might both be dead now: raped,
anonymous corpses, if ever they were found.

There was a reason that the Bledsloe ancestors had

immigrated to the New World. There was a reason that once they got there, they moved to lands at the fringes of human habitation—lands the white man didn't want, but the red man had been driven away from.

There was a reason, and that reason was that the Bledsloes were not entirely human.

All across the world, legends tell of those who can take on the forms of animals. In Europe, that animal is most often a wolf or bear. Werebear met with some toleration, even respect, but werewolves met with none at all.

Jake had changed. He had not become a wolf all at once. With almost human hands, Jake had grabbed the six-gun from a man who had been laughing at him a moment before. With almost human hands, Jake had shot that man dead.

But there had been five men there. Even if the gun had been fully loaded, even if Jake had been able to make each bullet pay, several of the men were clustered so close to Prudence that Jake could not fire at them without risking harm to her. Instead, he had sprung forward, more and more a gigantic wolf with every moment. He had leapt, torn, and bitten.

He had swallowed human blood and eaten human flesh.

Prudence had been too involved in her own battles to interfere. In her the wolf also rose, but in her case—perhaps because she had no fear for Jake's safety—the impulse that carried her was one of flight.

A slim, grey she-wolf had torn through the flimsy nightshirt, had run for safety. As dawn was greying the eastern sky, a frightened girl, naked but strangely unscratched by the brambles she pushed through, had made her way back to the camp.

Jake was gone. Five dead men lay in their camp. Blood splattered everything.

As she gathered what she could salvage of their gear, Prudence had remembered one of the earliest lessons her mother had taught her.

"At no time ever, even if you are starving—especially if you are starving—should you eat either the flesh of a wolf or that of a human. The one will rob you of your ability to become human, but the other will be worse. It will rob you of your sanity."

Later, Prudence had learned other things. Depending on the phase of the moon, a werewolf—even in human form—gains tremendous strength, including immunity from most physical injury, although not from disease. When the moon is full, only blessed weapons or silver can harm a werewolf.

Prudence had tested this herself, as had, she supposed, nearly every werewolf child. She had liked running as a wolf, enjoyed feeling invulnerable. Perhaps her name influenced her, though. She was prudent. She did not care for the lack of control, for the tug of the moon on her sensibilities.

Jake, though . . . Jake had liked being stronger. That was one reason he had been determined to go west. He knew that he was stronger than average. He didn't want to hide when he could win a place where what he did would be above question.

And Prudence, ever prudent, ever responsible, had gone with him. Yet, in the end, she had been the reason catastrophe had come to her brother.

"Jake . . ." she sighed aloud remembering, sorrowing. To her astonishment, she was answered.

"Hello, Pru."

Jake's familiar voice came from the shadow of a dark

red rock. Prudence turned to face it, shading her eyes with her left hand.

"I can feed you on something better than rotted sheep," the voice, clearly Jake's, continued. "Come along. I'd love to show you my place. I've settled here now."

Prudence let her right hand drop to the gun on her hip. Jake laughed.

"I don't think so, Pru. I can smell the silver from here. That's something the folks never told you, did they? They said we go insane. There's a little of that, at first, as you adjust. Then . . ."

Jake stepped out into the sunlight. He wore battered jeans, frayed from mid-calf on down and a cowboy hat. Nothing else. His feet were bare and his skin, although sun-bronzed, showed no signs of burning.

"Then you're stronger than ever. The moon's power is with you all the time. What they call insanity is just the body adjusting to sharper senses, to the ability to claim the wolf at any time, to becoming something pretty close to a god."

Prudence took an involuntary step away from her brother. Jake looked healthy, but not quite the same. His shoulders were broader, his body hair a bit thicker. His eyes—once a pale brown much like her own—were yellow. He wore his hair longer, touching his shoulders. Something about the way it grew and caught the light reminded Prudence of fur rather than hair.

"You've settled here," she echoed, catching on something safe to say.

"I made a friend and he convinced me this was the place for me. I knew you'd been tracking me, figured you'd catch up. Heard Nathan Yaz saying something last night, and knew you were here."

"Nathan Yaz?"

"My friend is Navajo. He's what they'd call a skin-walker, a witch. That's why he hasn't introduced himself to the locals. The way the Navajos treat those they figure are witches makes what the Salem folk did seem mild. In Salem, at least, a witch got a trial."

Jake smiled a slow, easy smile. Were his teeth whiter, the canines a bit sharper? Prudence thought they were.

Jake made a wide, inviting gesture. "Come along, Sis. Gather up your horses. I've a place for them out of the sun."

Prudence went. She'd been seeking Jake. It seemed foolish to leave when she'd finally found him, but she sure wasn't certain what she was going to do now that she had.

She'd expected to find Jake raving mad. In her thoughts Jake had already been good as dead. What she'd been doing was going to put down a mad dog—or wolf. Again, her mother's words came to her.

"We're responsible for our renegades. We alone know their weaknesses. Alive they soil the reputations of both our communities and those of the wild wolves. We must put them down lest they do more harm."

But this . . . Prudence didn't know what to think of this Jake. He seemed much like himself, but improved.

Jake's new home was in one of those surprising little canyons that crop up even in the badlands: an oasis of scrub growth and tall grass. The grass was drying with late summer, but still succulent enough that Buck whickered appreciatively.

"Surprised the sheepherders haven't found this place," Prudence said, trying to sound conversational. If Jake's sense of smell was as improved as he claimed, he'd smell her apprehension, but she had her own self-respect to consider.

A male voice spoke from the shadows. The cracked notes of old age did not disguise the Navajo accent.

"The Navajo will not come here," the old man said. "Not only is there no good grazing between here and their sheep camps, but it is said that a witch lives in these rocks."

From under a jutting ledge, the speaker emerged. His browned skin was deeply lined and his hair iron grey. He wore what was rapidly becoming Navajo traditional dress. Trousers, shirt, vest, and round-crowned hat might have been worn by any cowhand, but the wide sandcast silver and turquoise concho belt and the broad squash-blossom necklace were too large and gaudy for most American women, much less for an American man.

Prudence swallowed a derisive snort.

Your partner guards himself with silver, Jake. Have you noticed, or is this skinwalker hiding his armament in plain sight under the guise of "native dress?"

Jake paused and made a waving gesture with his hand, as if making introductions at some society function.

"Prudence, meet my partner, Clyde Begay. Clyde, this is my sister, Prudence Bledsloe."

"Pleased to meet you, Mr. Begay," Prudence said politely.

The old man narrowed his eyes as he looked at her. His response was much more ambiguous.

"Your brother has spoken much of you, Miz Bledsloe."

Jake cut in. "Pru, bring the horses over here. That sun's too damn hot."

Prudence obeyed. The space under the ledge provided good shelter for the horses. Behind it, a wide-mouthed cave sighed out cooler air.

Buck and Trick were happy to settle into a pole corral

under the ledge. There was no evidence that Jake kept horses of his own, but he'd cut fodder and built this corral, another bit of evidence that he had indeed expected her.

Jake led Prudence into the cave. He motioned around, pleased as if he was showing her a mansion.

"Not bad, huh? This time of day the light from outside does us fine. We use the space under the ledge sort of like you'd use a porch in a house. For night we have both lanterns and candles."

The cave wasn't bad, especially when compared to some camps she and Jake had shared. Bedrolls were stacked neatly to one side. Water dripped from a seep. A pottery basin collected the precious fluid. Jars lined up nearby showed that the occupants stored the excess.

Jake offered Prudence water. Prudence opened up her pack and brought out some of the grub she had brought. While beans were warming, Jake started in on his tale.

"After that night, you know the one I mean, I got to admit, I didn't feel so good. I was worried about you, but my head was going six directions at once. I cut and ran until I couldn't run anymore. Days went by. I guess I hunted along the way, but it was a while before I could think straight."

Prudence nodded. This part matched her own deductions. She'd trailed Jake by the tales of a rabid wolf slaughtering sheep or other small domestic animals. Once a child had been killed, a boy of about ten, who'd been sent out to look for a wandering heifer.

"After a while," Jake said, "I started being able to think again. I was scouting out a place where I could settle in and figure out what to do when I met Clyde. Now, Clyde was a prominent warrior during his people's wars with the white man. He's never come to terms with their eventual surrender. Clyde showed me this cave and shared with me his vision for the future."

He paused. Prudence asked the expected question.

"Vision?"

"Clyde wants a world where the Navajo are again mighty. For that, we need war. War suits me just fine. When people are fighting each other, they don't have time for chasing spooks."

He looked at her, seeking approval for this bit of wisdom. Prudence made a noncommital noise. Jake went on.

"Me and Clyde work well together. Clyde has been studying the folk around here, white and red. He gives me suggestions as to who I can attack in order to create maximum tension and distrust.

"The Navajo's fear that there is a powerful witch among them keeps them from coming after me. It also creates division within their own community. The usual thing is to seek a witch among your own people. Since Clyde and me are outsiders, they're chasing shadows.

"Meanwhile, the white men are eager to blame the Navajo. Some of that eagerness is fear. Some is greed. There are those among the Navajo, like Nathan Yaz, who have aroused envy by doing too well. He not only has orchards and sheep, but the love of a beautiful woman."

Jake gave a hoarse, barking laugh.

"I honestly don't care whether they act out of fear or greed or a sense of justice. What matters is that the whites will eventually break their treaty with the Navajo. When they do, the Navajo will fight back. Other reservation Indians will hear about the treaty breaking. There is a good chance that widespread unrest will follow."

Jake spread his hands. "And then, sister, people like you and me will have a refuge. It will be far better than holing up in the Smokey Mountains, jumping at shadows. In the midst of chaos, no one will notice our comings and goings. Only in settled times and places are we endangered. On this frontier, surrounded by war, we will thrive. And we will be in a position to spread the chaos, to maintain the war."

"For a time," Prudence agreed. "Then it will be for us as it was for the Indians. More and more white men will come from overseas, eager for new lands, willing to fight for those lands. We will be defeated."

"I've thought about that, too," Jake said. "Take a look at the beginnings of my new army."

He gave a whimpering call. From a darker place at the back of the cave, five little shadows resolved into five little humans, five little humans who smelled of rotting meat. Two were white, the other three Navajo. They emerged from what must have been a sub-cave, blinking sleepily at the light.

"You thought I had eaten them, didn't you?" Jake said proudly. "I have not. I'm turning them into werewolves just like you and me."

"But those who are turned die or go insane!" Prudence protested.

Jake grinned happily, looking over at the five little monstrosities as if they were his own children. "The skinwalker helped me. His traditional magic involves changing shape—changing his skin—but he can only do so for a short period of time. He was fascinated that not only can werewolves take on the wolf form, we can pass the ability on to others.

"After hearing my story, Clyde had a thought. He said that since I had gained new abilities after I had eaten human flesh, perhaps the eating of human flesh would help these little ones to stabilize their new abilities.

"We made mistakes at first. My first project was a boy about ten. Even after I had gifted him with my breath, he refused to eat the meat, not even when we starved him. After that we chose younger children. They had far fewer scruples. They will be the new Clan Bledsloe, Prudence. With them we will win a part of the west to be our own."

Prudence knew what would come next. It was written in the cynical twist of the Navajo witch's smile.

"I'm offering you a chance to join us," Jake said. "We've always been close. You're smart. You're determined. You'd be an asset."

"You know I'm carrying silver," Prudence said, "and you know what that means."

"You came looking for me," Jake said, "thinking you might need to kill a crazy werewolf. Now, though, you see I'm not crazy."

"Easy as that you'd trust me? Let me join your pack?"

"Not quite," Clyde interrupted, "that easy. There must be a test. When skinwalkers initiate one into our secrets, we demand they prove their sincerity by killing someone. That is what we ask of you."

Prudence nodded, trying to hide the creeping dread that chilled her entrails.

"Kill someone, like some trail drifter?"

Jake laughed, a warm, friendly sound. "Oh, no, Pru. We don't just kill at random. I told you. We have an agenda. I think it would be good if you killed someone whose death would stir up trouble between the whites and Navajo. Maybe Reverend Printer. He's a popular man."

"I have a better idea," Clyde said. "Kill the girl, April March. Later, kill the boy, Vern Yaz. One death would be seen as vengeance for the other."

"Beautiful!" Jake said. He looked at Prudence and added generously, "You can just kill the girl. I'll kill the boy. Better he be shot and a white man's prints seen in the area. The girl, though, she should be torn up. Savages mutilate their victims. Every white knows that, but the Navajo will feel unjustly blamed. Damn, Clyde, you're smart."

"I am old and perhaps have gained a little wisdom," the Navajo said.

Prudence swallowed a surge of bile.

"When?"

"Moon's rising full," Jake said thoughtfully. "Be easier for you to make the change then. Why don't we set it up for as soon as can be?"

Prudence thought about silver bullets and full moons.

"All right," she said. "How do we get that girl out at night?"

Getting April March to come out proved to be almost too easy. Clyde Begay went into Eli Mercantile ostensibly to trade for a blanket. When Mr. Eli's back was turned, Clyde slipped April a note written by Prudence, asking the girl to come to the stand of cottonwoods down by the stream that night, and not to mention the meeting to anyone.

"It won't matter if she talks about it. If she does, she's sure to mention an old Navajo brought the note. All fuel for our fires," Jake chortled.

Jake seemed boisterous and ebullient, but he wasn't so far gone as to forget to make sure Prudence took the silver bullets out of her guns, and that she left those guns behind.

"You won't be needing them," he said, "not on a full moon night, not when your prey is a mere child."

And Prudence had to agree.

She shifted shape and they ran shoulder to shoulder in the direction of town. It was a glorious experience. The summer night that had seemed hot and clinging to her human form was alive with such interesting smells and sounds that she hardly noticed the heat. The loneliness that had been her lot since Jake had vanished, dissolved. Wolves didn't talk as humans did, but she was keyed to his mood through his scent.

Glorious in all his enhanced powers, Jake was supremely alpha. Running beside him, dropping back a pace or two when some obstacle presented itself, Prudence felt a contentment she'd forgotten could be hers. Someone else was in charge. Her job would be to follow orders.

The note had told April to come out at midnight. When the two werewolves arrived about eleven, there was some activity around a few of the saloons, but everything else was dark and quiet. They had hardly quenched their thirst at the stream when an owl flew soundlessly into the grove.

A moment later, Clyde Begay's flat, Navajo-accented voice said, "The child is coming."

Jake shifted back to human. He stood, naked and very male, looking down at Prudence.

"We'll fall back now. Just in case you have some fancy ideas, remember I'm here. I can kill the child, too. If I do it, I'll make her dying last, and I'll make it ugly."

Prudence shivered in her skin. It took no feigning at all for her to roll over on her back, then display her belly and throat in submission. Jake laughed softly and rubbed her belly fur with his bare toes.

"Good, Sis," he was saying when Prudence struck.

There is one type of weapon other than those made of silver or blessed by a suitably devout priest that can harm a werewolf—the fangs and claws of another werewolf.

Prudence twisted and sunk her fangs into Jake's bare ankle. She bore down and felt the bones twist, then crack and break. Jake started to bellow in pain and anger, but swallowed the sound.

Yellow eyes glowing bright with fury, Jake bore down on his mutilated limb. Prudence felt his weight, felt his blood hot on her belly fur and in her mouth. Almost as quickly, she felt the bleeding slow, felt the stream in her mouth dry to a trickle, felt the torn skin begin to knit.

There was a reason for their clan name. All werewolves have strengths: some can tap the moon's power farther away from the full, some can control wild wolves, some can hear the thoughts of their fellows.

The Bledsloe's strength was that they healed far faster than normal, even in human form. When the moon's power was upon them, even a normal Bledsloe healed quickly—and Jake was far more powerful than normal.

But Jake was in human form. Of the werewolf's three shapes, this was the weakest.

Prudence knew minutes would be needed for those broken bones to knit. Jake might choose to ignore the pain, but he could not make a crushed ankle carry him.

She rolled from beneath the pressure of Jake's foot, heard him stumble. As he stumbled, she wheeled around. Launching herself from a crouch close to the ground, bringing all her weight to crash into his chest, Prudence knocked Jake flat onto his back. She leapt to hold him down.

The breath whooshed out of Jake's lungs as he landed, whistling around teeth that were already turning into fangs. Prudence knew that Jake would choose the man-wolf form. If he made that change, he would have the advantage over her. She must act before ...

There was no time for thought, no time for planning. An errant breeze brought Prudence the scent of fresh bread, honey, and peppermint. April March would be here soon.

Hands already tipping with claws grasped Prudence around her ribcage. Claws ripped into fur and through muscle, seeking her lungs. Jake was smiling grimly, his expression already triumphant.

Prudence feinted as if to go for his eyes. When Jake flung his head to one side to avoid her darting muzzle, he exposed the right side of his neck. Without hesitation, Prudence bit into the corded muscles. The prickly guard-hairs of Jake's budding man-wolf coat offered no protection against her fangs. She bore down, tasting salt and sweat, then blood. She ripped into meat, shaking side to side, tearing an enormous hole.

Blood flowed, then gouted. Jake's last breath gusted out with it. In the sudden silence, Prudence heard April's footsteps cracking over the brittle cottonwood twigs at the edge of the grove as she tried to make a stealthy approach.

A moment, a moment, and all would be ...

Prudence threw back her head and howled, howled with sorrow and misery, howled for a brother dead and a family forever gone.

April March did not hear the grief. She heard only the cry of a wolf, dangerously close. She ran as if the wolf was on her trail. Near the center of town a rinkytink piano stopped in mid-note. Then someone laughed and someone else made a coarse comment. The music resumed.

Prudence raised her wolf's head and saw Clyde Begay staring at her in fascination.

"I do not think," the skinwalker said, "you will be my ally as your brother was. I will leave this place. Soon, I think, you will lead others to our cave and I do not wish to be there."

He moved his hands and sang a few words in Navajo. In a moment, a scrawny old wolf, tail clamped between his legs, stood where the man had been. He paused, assessing her once more.

Prudence growled and the old wolf ran.

Warily, Prudence changed back to human. With the moon's strength in her, she lifted Jake's body up and carried it at a trot to the badlands. She buried him under a fall of rocks where no one would ever find his corpse, nor wonder at the manner of his death.

Then she sought out his cave. Five shabby wolf puppies played in the deep grass of the canyon, but they stopped hunting grasshoppers and mice as soon as they caught Prudence's scent. They came for her with a very unfriendly look in their yellow eyes.

Prudence dealt with them as she had her brother, wondering if her heart would ever stop weeping. She forced herself to watch as five little wolf cubs turned back into five scrawny children. In the front of the cave, she buried the bodies of those Jake had hoped would be his new family.

The next afternoon, scrubbed clean, her six-guns at her hips, her rifle in the saddle boot, Prudence rode into town. There she sought Reverend Printer and told him an edited version of events.

She ended by saying, "I'll draw you a map, so you can find the cave and the children's bodies. Their deaths will be sad news for the families, but sometimes sorrow is better than hope."

"So you think the trouble is ended?" Reverend Printer asked.

Prudence snorted. "As long as humans are humans there will be trouble. All I'm saying is that one madman is dead."

"Fallen down a cleft in the rocks."

"That's what I said."

Reverend Printer nodded. Prudence could tell he didn't believe her, but also that he wasn't going to push it.

"And you came here why?"

"He was my brother. Mama always told me we shoot our own dogs. We don't leave the job for someone else."

Then Prudence Bledsloe, last of the Bledsloe were-wolves, mounted her big buckskin stallion and rode out of town.

OUR LADY OF THE VAMPIRES

Nancy Holder

"**Y**ou won't go hungry here," my mother told me, as she set my suitcase down and rang the bell of our Lady of the Angels Home for Girls. Night was falling. Her face was so thin she looked like a skeleton, and I tried not to show my fear. For her. Of her. If she ever died, I would die, too.

It was December 23, 1929, and everyone was afraid. The stock market crash, the bank runs ... overnight, our world had blown up, and we were not very good survivors. We were fragile females, used to being catered to and doted on. My mother had lived like a queen—like the Queen of Los Angeles—and I'd been my father's princess, and he took care of everything. My mother had never touched a paper bill or a coin in her entire married life. It was a bargain ladies made with society— we would barely exist in the world, and in return, men would love us.

But my father hadn't loved us enough. On Halloween, he had leapt from the ledge of his office window in the Crocker Bank Building on Santa Monica Boulevard.

36

They are vampires, he had written in his suicide note. *They have sucked the life's blood from this country.*

We didn't know who "they" were. The industralists he played golf with? The glamorous movie stars who made deposits in his bank at two in the morning? We didn't know, and so we couldn't protect ourselves against them.

I couldn't understand how one day we had servants and cars and pantries bulging with food; and the next, our Los Angeles house was gone, and so was our apartment overlooking Central Park. And so was my father. But it was all gone, as if sunlight had burned it up. As if we had awakened from a long and beautiful dream.

Now we had less than nothing, and I was hungry for everything I used to have, for my future, for my life. We tried everything, but we simply had no money.

We began to starve. We didn't even know how to buy food; and I think the greengrocer and the butcher cheated us, because they thought we were still rich. We didn't know how to haggle or bargain. We'd had people to do all that.

And so, my mother took me to the orphanage, where they had people.

I was only fourteen but as we stood before the door, I felt as tired as the woman who had dragged herself down the palm-lined avenues of our exclusive neighborhood up in the hills. We had seen her many times since the crash. She was once quite beautiful, but her desperation stole her beauty from her day by day. Wrinkling and aging, she sold apples on some days, pencils on others; and all her jewelry after the apples and pencils got no takers. I didn't know who she was, but the sight of her somehow pleased my mother. She would laugh rather crazily, watching the woman from the window of the home that soon would be gone.

Once, as the woman stumbled along the street, my mother turned to me and said, "You can never trust other women, Bess. Remember that. They will want what you have. Your husband. Your home."

Then she stared at the woman with pure hatred on her face.

I called her Our Lady of the Vampires, because vampires had killed my father, and ruined us, and I sensed that once upon a time, she had been a threat.

"You won't be hungry," my mother whispered, her voice breaking, as we waited at the door of the orphanage.

As the door to Our Lady of the Angels Home for Girls creaked open, the same dried-out woman glowered down at me, or so it seemed. But this woman was different—older, thinner, and dressed in the black and white habit of a nun.

By the watery light of a ceiling lamp surrounded by the motionless blades of a fan, the withered old woman glared at the two of us as if she hated us. I began to panic, and I grabbed onto my mother with both hands.

"Please, no," I begged. "Mother, don't leave me here."

My mother burst into tears, and I did, too. She clung to me, and ground out in agony, "How could they do this to us? How could *he* do this?" and I hugged her so tightly I thought her pencil-like spine would crack.

My stomach growled.

"Come now," said the nun, grabbing my forearm. "Stop that. This is difficult enough for your mother without your dramatics."

As we entered, I heard more sobbing.

And when my mother left, still more.

*   *   *

A girl named Annabelle had been found dead in her bed the morning of the day that I went to live at Our Lady of the Angels. I could still hear the wailing and sobs as the ancient nun, whose name was Mother Mary Patrick, directed me to lug my beautiful crocodile hide suitcase down a labyrinth of passages to my dormitory room.

"Whatever is in that, you won't be needing it here," Mother Mary Patrick said, as I set it down and wiped my brow. Then she handed me a uniform—baggy blue dress, white pinafore—that looked like something out of a Victorian novel. My suitcase contained everything I owned in this world—several smart outfits including my lovely silk pajamas; my silver brush and mirror; my fox stole; and my bride doll, Angelique. Draper, our former driver (now let go) had tried to persuade my mother to sell all my clothes and trinkets, but she had refused. Now I wondered if I was about to lose them anyway.

"Here's number four, your bed," she said, still holding my suitcase.

I stared in disbelief at the metal cot in the center of double rows of eight—sixteen of us in a long, drab room with a creaking, dark wood floor and a crucifix made of what appeared to be olive wood hanging over each bed. There were no sheets on the thin, padded mattress or the equally thin pillow. All the other beds were unmade, and the pillow of the bed directly across from mine—number twelve—lay on the floor. The bed of the dead girl, then. Annabelle had been found at sunrise, white as a sheet, eyes glassy and half-open. I'd been only minutes at the orphanage, and I had already heard all about it.

My hair stood on end. I didn't want to sleep anywhere

near that bed. But it seemed I was to be given no choice.

"Put on your uniform and come to my office," Mother Mary Patrick ordered me. Then she looked hard at me and said, "You're quite old enough to be on your own. I only took you in as a courtesy."

To whom? I wanted to ask. She wasn't courteous in the least.

"Please, miss, I mean Mother, where should I put my suitcase?" I asked her.

She looked confused for a moment. Her eyes were milky, and I wondered if she had trouble seeing. If maybe that was why she kept glaring and squinting at me.

Then she said, "Under your bed, I suppose. Hurry and dress, then come to me."

I tried to do as she asked, but my tears made everything hazy, like her milky eyes. I had never dressed myself alone before; I'd always had a maid, and then my mother had helped me. I was helpless.

The room swam; shaking, I lay down on the bed that was directly across from the dead girl's bed, and cried.

Two hours later, after I had washed and swept untold numbers of floors, I was sent to dinner.

I staggered down a hall, so hungry, tired, and frightened I could barely move. The din in the enormous room buffeted my ears as over seventy girls sat down to eat. Some girls were still crying over the death of Annabelle. Others were laughing and chatting. I missed my mother. I wanted her arms around me, holding me against her bony chest. I would rather have that than the watery soup and pieces of unbuttered bread being served by six young girls wearing all-white habits to orphans seated at six plain wooden trestle tables, a dozen to each table.

Then I forgot my longing as I caught sight of a tall, uncommonly thin girl seated at my table. She looked to be near my age and was wearing my fox stole around her bony shoulders.

"Look at me, lahdidah, the new girl," she announced, grinning at me, swirling the stole around her shoulders. A couple of the other girls at the table—my new dorm mates, I supposed—grinned as they gazed from her to me, watching to see what I would do.

"You went in my suitcase," I blurted; then I realized she'd done something even worse. My suitcase was locked, and I wore the key around my neck, beneath my pinafore.

"What about it?" she asked, dangling the end of the stole over her steaming bowl of soup, as if she meant to dip it in and ruin it. "Who cares? You're not rich any more. Can't lord it over us any more."

Her followers chuckled and nodded. Their eyes gleamed like the eyes of predators.

"I only just got here. I've never seen you before in my life," I told her. She was so tall and skinny and mean-looking that I stayed rooted to the spot instead of walking past her and taking my seat at the far end of the table.

"You've never seen any of us," she said, picking up her spoon. "We were your stupid servants and the coarse, low-class girls your parents would never let you talk to. And now . . . this place is ours, and you aren't welcome." She narrowed her eyes at me. "Annabelle thought she was too good for us, too."

I sucked in my breath.

She lifted her chin. "And so did Sarah."

The other girls at the table blinked and shifted uncomfortably. "Now you've gone too far," said one of them, thin-faced and freckled, with a single wheat-colored braid down her back.

Then all heads turned as Mother Mary Patrick swept into the room with a tall young man who was dressed in priest's black, wearing a priest's white collar. His hair was the color of a tawny, sun-kissed lion, and his eyes were dark and deep set. He gazed around the room without speaking, and then his look lit on me. I swayed a little; then, as if somehow he had emboldened me, I reached forward and grabbed my fox stole from around the shoulders of the girl.

"Oh," she said. The young priest looked at her. Really looked. She paled, crossed her arms, and turned back around.

"What is that you've got there? What are you doing?" Mother Mary Patrick asked me sharply.

The room grew silent. Everyone was looking at me. I gathered up the stole and clutched it against my chest. If I lost it again, I would die. I felt it as strongly as hunger.

Weeping, I turned and ran out of the room; I stumbled down the dark passageways, meaning to go to my dormitory, grab my suitcase, and leave. Instead, I found myself in the chapel. I had no idea how I had wound up there but I ran inside, claiming sanctuary.

Annabelle's coffin sat before the altar. It was a simple pine box, not an elegant ebony coffin with gleaming hinges like my father's. Large white candles on either side of the altar cast flickering light on a lid. A spray of pink roses and a shiny silver cross were arranged on the lid. Unnerved, exhausted, I pulled out the kneeler and folded my hands, threading the stole through my fingers like a rosary.

I closed my eyes and prayed for her soul. I prayed for my own, and I prayed for help, and for food. It had been stupid of me to leave the dining room. I was so hungry I could barely stand it.

Hail Mary, full of grace ...

A soft scratching sound interrupted me. I figured it for a mouse and tried to resume my prayer. I concentrated on the soft fur of my stole, remembering days when my mother and I would dress up in our furs, gloves, and hats, and meet friends in tea rooms and at bridge parties.

The sound was louder this time, scritch, scritch, scritch ... *was it coming from the coffin?*

"Annabelle?" I cried, but my voice was a dry husk. I jumped to my feet and raced to the coffin, moving aside the cross and the roses and setting them on the altar. I leaned over it, spotting a brass handle, and realized what I was about to do. As the candles flickered, I gazed at the entrance to the chapel, then back down at the coffin lid. I should fetch someone; I should call for help ...

Instead, I wrapped my fingers around the handle and yanked back the lid. The wood let out an awful creak. Chills ran down my spine and I flinched and looked away, then back ...

... at nothing.

The coffin was empty.

I blinked, not understanding, looking in again. Footsteps rang on the stone floor and I half-expected to see a young girl—Annabelle—laughing as she came toward me, telling me it was all a joke. The footfalls grew louder. I shut the lid and replaced the flowers and cross, then scooted back to my pew, where I sat unsteadily down. I didn't know why I was being so secretive. Why I was shaking even harder. There were reasons why the body would not be inside the coffin—perhaps she'd died of a contagious illness. Maybe she had begun to smell ...

"Hello," said a voice. I turned, to see the young priest standing in the doorway, holding a bowl of soup. I got to my feet again, holding on to the back of the pew as I turned to face him.

"Sorry," he said, walking toward me. Steam rose from the bowl; I smelled meat, barley, carrots, and potatoes and nearly screamed. "I didn't mean to startle you." He held out the bowl with one hand and touched my face with the other. "Poor Bess."

I stared at the soup as if I had forgotten how to eat. It was thin, and there were no vegetables or meat. Maybe I had only imagined their bouquet.

"Annabelle. She–she's gone."

He blinked. Studied me.

"Her . . . she's not in there," I tried again. My mouth was watering.

"No. She's not," he said. "We've already buried her. There was some concern about contagion." He took me by the arm and sat me down, gesturing for me to eat.

I slurped the watery soup, trying to eat like a lady, unable to stop making so much noise. I sounded like a dog lapping up water.

"We didn't tell anyone about Annabelle," he said, watching me with mingled pity and amusement. "However, to set your fears at rest, a doctor examined her and declared her to be free of disease."

"Then why not put her back in her . . ." I couldn't even say the word "coffin." It sounded so ghoulish. I began to lose my appetite, and I panicked and kept eating.

"Timing," he replied. He played with the end of my stole. "The girls had already been through so much, and the replacing of the body would too traumatic."

I imagined a girl my age in the cold, cold ground, and shuddered. "Is there a graveyard here?"

"Yes. I presided over her burial myself."

He gestured to the food. "Eat. Drink."

"Why did she die?" I asked him.

"She had a weak heart," he said, his voice dropping. He sounded sad and troubled. My own heart went out to him. I took several more spoonfuls; still hungry, I laid the spoon in the bowl.

"I want my mother," I told him. I was dizzy, and I could barely keep my eyelids open. "Why couldn't she stay here, too? She could earn her keep."

He lifted my spoon to my lips. "Unfortunately, there are too many mouths to feed here as it is. Now listen, Bess—that's your name, isn't it? Others sacrificed so that you would be nourished. Not well-nourished, I'm afraid," he added.

"I'm so tired. I'm too sleepy," I said, which astonished me. Five minutes ago, I wouldn't have believed I could say such a thing, but my eyes were closing.

"Come now," he prodded. I didn't answer. I was half-asleep already. "I'll walk you to your room, then," he said. "You shouldn't be in the hallways alone."

I wanted to ask him why. This was a convent, a holy place, wasn't it? We were safe.

I couldn't form the words. I felt as if I were dreaming as he took my hand and helped me to my feet. I imagined that he would carry me, like a princess. He was too handsome to be a priest.

That's sinful, I thought, sighing.

"You're troubled?" he asked me, as the walls of the dormitory floated past me.

"Everything ... is troubling," I said. "Who was Sarah?"

"Another girl. She passed away six months ago." He paused. "There was a washerwoman, too. A young Irish

woman. The girls seemed to have forgotten about her."
He crossed himself.

"That was before the crash." I stumbled; he steadied
me, but I began to fold up, like the accordion our old
priest at Sacred Heart used to play, like a tired, wan survivor. "How did she die?"

I knew he answered, but I didn't hear him. Then
hands came around me ... was he undressing me? Was
someone else? I couldn't seem to see anything. I remembered that my bed was unmade, yet now I lay in
starched, bleached sheets. They made my skin itch, and
my eye water as they closed ...

... and I woke up suddenly, my lids half-opening, as
whispers wafted through gloomy half-light:

"This is the one." It was Mother Mary Patrick. *"Such
a troublemaker."*

"Perfect." The young priest.

I opened my eyes. My head was at an angle; light
from the hallway spilled into my room, and a shadow
fell across my face. With terrible effort, I slowly turned
my head and raised it off my pillow, almost grunting.

Their backs to me, Mother Mary Patrick and the priest
stood at the head of the bed beside Annabelle's. They
were gazing down at the occupant; then Mother Mary
Patrick pulled a piece of white cloth from the sleeve of
her habit and handed it to the priest. He draped it over
the crucifix on the wall.

They turned, facing me, and I shut my eyes tightly.
I could feel them moving past my bed; and my heart
skipped beats as they stopped.

"She didn't eat all her gruel," the priest said. "She was
too upset."

"You don't think ... ?" Mother Mark Patrick replied,
sounding anxious.

"No. She's asleep." He snapped his fingers. "Bess?" he whispered. "You see? It's fine."

"Poor lamb, poor lamb," Mother Mary Patrick murmured, her voice far kinder than I had ever heard it. "All my poor lambs."

"It's for the best," the priest replied. "You know that."

Then they left the room, shutting the door, taking the light with themselves. I tried to get up, but I couldn't force my eyes open again. I was trying to puzzle out what I'd seen and heard. Had they put something in my soup to make me sleep? What had they been doing in our room?

It was too hard to think. Time passed; I drifted; and then a penetrating cold spread through my body, like someone injecting ice into my veins. I was so cold I hurt; and I thought I might be dying.

Trembling, I lay as still as I could; then I heard a little sigh, and someone whispering, "Hush."

I forced my eyes open. A strangely glowing, bluish mist wafted around me, illuminating the room. Shadows were thrown against the ceiling, and there was nothing on top of me. Ever so cautiously, I raised my head and looked across the room.

Two figures in white gowns were bent over the bed to the left of Annabelle's. The feet of the person lying in the bed kneaded the sheets, as if she were struggling. As if the two were hurting her.

Before I knew what I was doing, I sat up and half-crawled, half-fell out of my bed. Swaying, I crossed the room, advancing as quietly as I could, aware that I could barely stay on my feet.

"It's done," whispered one of the girls—for they were girls—in the white gowns. I saw now that the fabric of the one who spoke was tattered and moldy; spider webs and moss clung to the long sleeves. The dress of the girl beside her was lovely and fresh.

The tattered one straightened and turned around.

Her eyes were large and very blue; her face was a pale oval. Her blond hair, coiled in a braided chignon, was covered with cobwebs. And her mouth was painted with fresh blood.

I gasped; she held up a warning hand and the second girl—the one in the nicer dress—looked at me. Her mouth was bloody, too. She wore her black hair pulled from her face; her dark eyes widened as she stared at me, then at the blond girl—the *vampire*—at her side.

I tried to scream but I was too stunned. The two advanced; and as I backed away, they both stopped and held up their hands, as if shading their eyes from a light that was too bright. Then the blonde grabbed my arm and covered my mouth with her hand. Her skin was so cold it burned me, and I nearly fainted.

She dragged me out of the room. No one else stirred. The sleepers were drugged. I was certain of it. There had been something in the gruel, and I hadn't drunk enough.

And I was about to die.

The moon shone overhead as the vampire pulled me down corridors and out into the chill night air. The little brunette followed behind, silent.

My bare feet sank into moist earth. I couldn't see where I was going; the vampire in the tattered gown had clamped a hand over my mouth, and her hair was hanging across my face. She smelled like wet earth and rose petals.

I whimpered once and she said, "Shut up or we'll rip your throat out."

Then she jerked me to a stop. "Listen, you. You know what we are, Annabelle and me. And what you are. Food, see? So if you scream we'll eat you up."

"Sarah, please, don't be so mean," the dark-haired vampire protested. I knew she was Annabelle. Newly risen from her grave, and taken by the older vampire to our room, to drink blood.

"Why were you awake?" Sarah demanded of me. "Did Father Mark put you up to something? Did he tell you to attack us?"

I was at a loss. I began to cry.

"He wouldn't do that," Annabelle said, smiling kindly at me. "He's a good man."

Sarah laughed. "There are no good men. He gave *you* to me, Annabelle. And picked out Maria for you to kill."

I remembered the cloth over the crucifix. It had been a signal . . . for murder.

"No," I gasped. They both turned to look at me, almost as if they'd forgotten I was there. I arranged my fingers in the shape of a cross, and Sarah's lip curled. Annabelle looked stricken, and kept her distance.

"Maria was a horrible little troll. A beast," Sarah said.

I kept my fingers in the cross-shape, backing into something cold and hard. It was a gravestone, but the cross that had been atop it had been broken off, and lay half-buried in mud. There were no crosses anywhere in the graveyard.

I glanced to my right and saw a newly turned mound of earth. Roses were placed upon it.

"That's my grave," Annabelle whispered. "My resting place."

"We have a bargain, see?" Sarah told me. "The vampires of Los Angeles. We want new kin. And they want food."

"They . . ." I said.

"The humans. Father Mark and Mother Mary Patrick. Human food," Sarah elaborated. "Bread, apples, whatever we can get."

"But . . . it's not enough." Annabelle glided toward me and ran her fingers down my cheeks, and it was not unpleasant. "There's not enough in the world any more to feed all of you."

I began to heave. Weak, terrified . . . I bent forward, dry retching, and Annabelle put her arm around my shoulders. She cooed, holding me, and I felt her lips brushing against my neck.

"I agreed," Annabelle told me. "Sarah, Father Mark, and Mother Mary Patrick. They asked me to become what I am now, and I consented. I wasn't well."

She stroked my cheek again. "You came to the chapel. You prayed for me. I was watching."

I remembered the little scratching noise.

"I would have died, and so will you," she said.

I shuddered, hard, wobbling on my feet. She held me up. I was going to be sick or faint. "Why–why will I die?" I asked her.

She stroked my hair. "You're too delicate. You were taught to allow people—men, servants—to take care of you." Her voice was mournful. She pitied me. "But no one will."

"No one will," Sarah concurred. "No handsome knight in shining armor. No government. No one is coming to save you." She waited a beat. "Or your mother."

"No," I whispered.

"Your mother is beautiful," Annabelle said. "But the world will be too much for her. Humanity has shown its true face. Men don't care for widows and orphans. They care for money. Gold. And they dare to call *us* monsters."

"We are what God intended," Sarah said. "Born to new life, through the blood."

Together the two vampires gazed rapturously toward heaven. Moonlight washed down on them; the alabaster beams bleached their foreheads, the hollows of their cheeks. Blood was drying on their lips.

"Who did you kill tonight?" I asked Annabelle.

"Maria. That horrible girl who took your stole," she replied. "We were watching. We saw everything."

"They'll eat you alive here," Sarah said. "You're too soft. *We* can save you."

"Yes, please," Annabelle urged, "be our sister. You will never die, or be hungry." She smiled at Sarah. "And the feeding is most pleasant. It's like a holy thing."

Sarah smiled back.

I burst into tears. Annabelle gathered me into her arms, holding me, comforting me, as no one had since my father's death—my mother had been too shellshocked, too undone, to do anything but lock herself in her room. To watch Our Lady of the Vampires roaming in the hot sunlight, withering, dying inch by inch. I had had no one. Annabelle held me, and rocked me, and I began to forget that there was blood on her lips.

Someone *was* coming to rescue me. Someone had come: two vampires.

Two angels.

"We should do it now," Sarah said, "before it's light."

"No. Please, let her consider," Annabelle murmured,

cocking her head at me. "Do for her what you did for me, Sarah. Give her some time to think."

"She'll tell." Sarah glared at me in the same way that Mother Mary Patrick had. I was a threat.

"I won't," I promised. "I swear I won't."

"Tomorrow night, then, give us your answer," Annabelle pleaded sweetly. "We can change you, and take you away. You don't have to feed here, among the girls. We can find you someone else. Somewhere else."

"You'll never be hungry again," Sarah said. "You can take the starving, the hopeless. It's a sort of mercy."

"Maria felt nothing," Annabelle assured me.

I frowned. "Her legs kicked—"

"A reflex." Annabelle crossed her arms over her chest, posing like a dead girl. "I promise." Then she took her hands. "We'll teach you everything. Crosses burn us. Wooden stakes through the heart destroy us. You'll learn to be cunning. And strong." She glanced at Sarah. "So I have been promised."

"You will," Sarah assured her.

"And if I say no?"

Sarah blinked as if the thought hadn't occurred to her. But Annabelle stepped forward. "We will let you go. If you leave this place and tell no one, we will not harm you. I give you my word."

I swallowed hard and looked at the other vampire, the one who had been dead longer. She lowered her head in assent.

Sarah said, "We'll let you go."

Go where? I thought, as they escorted me back to my dormitory room, and watched as I climbed into bed. *To the streets, to starve?*

Did I have a choice?

I drew the sheets up. The two vampires stepped into the hall, and closed the door. There was still light in the room: through two high, arched windows, the dawn was coming.

I saw then the statue of the Blessed Mother at the far end of the room. I hadn't noticed it before. She looked very young. I had been taught that the Virgin gave birth to Jesus when she was fourteen.

I was fourteen.

The Blessed Mother's world had been filled with turmoil—her people were slaves under Roman rule; she had nearly been stoned to death when her pregnancy became apparent. She was unmarried. Her husband had spoken for her, telling the rabble and the priests of a dream, a holy vision.

My mind raced; my heart thundered. I rolled on my side to face the statue and clasped my hands in prayer, sliding them beneath my pillow. I tried to pray, but mostly, I cried.

My fingertips brushed something beneath the pillow. I jerked my hands away, then sat up and lifted it up.

In the hollow sat a folded piece of paper. On it was written: *BESS (THE NEW GIRL)*.

I unfolded it, and read.

> *Dear Bess,*
> *Im sorry I took yor fox stole. I aint had much and i thought it would be better hear at Our Lady but its not. Its just as hard. So I was mad when you come cause its hard as it is without new girls. But it would be easier if we was friends instead of enemys. Will you be my friend?*
> *Sorry agin,*
> *Maria*

Maria, who was dead. I could never tell her now that yes, I would be her friend. Yes, it would be easier. I remembered the nameless Irish woman who had also died. My father used to talk about the Irish problem— too many immigrants, taking the jobs of the "real" Americans. Stealing the wages of men who'd been there first.

Vampires.

I looked at the statue of the Blessed Mother. I looked at the drugged girls, who were as hungry and frightened as I was.

I reread the note from Maria, and kissed her name.

Then slowly, unsteady as a lamb, I stood on my bed and turned around. I stared at my wooden crucifix. I remembered that Father Mark and Mother Mary Patrick had covered the one over Maria's bed so that the vampires could approach. That they had shied away from the cross over my bed as they'd dragged me into the graveyard.

I took a deep breath, and laid my hand on the cross. I took it off the wall.

We can make a garden, I thought, looking at the sleeping girls. *We can grow our own food. We can work together. We can be sisters. And I'll find my mother and Our Lady of the Vampires, and they can live here, too.*

Then I broke the cross in two, as if I were making a wish on the turkey wishbone at Thanksgiving. The edges were very jagged.

Two pieces.

Two stakes.

We'll learn how to kill them. To fight them.

To take care of ourselves.

I slipped them under my pillow.

My decision, my bargain, was made.

When darkness fell, I would lead these girls out of the land of the vampires.

We would have a table—ours—in the presence of our enemies.

And the world would call us blessed.

BEST FRIENDS

Lilith Saintcrow

"You can't be serious." I pushed my bangs back fretfully, I hadn't had a trim in ages. I wanted to wriggle out of my damp bikini top, but I hadn't brought a T-shirt. "He's just your stepfather. Or going to be, anyway, since your mom's . . . well."

Kate sighed, a sound of sharp metal frustration. "Look, do you think I'd be telling you if I wasn't sure? I'm not crazy, Becca."

I eyed her for a long critical moment, sucking on the straw. Finished my chocolate milkshake, set the paper cup down, and slid my shades down the bridge of my nose. We both smelled like chlorine and sunscreen, because you can't ever wash pool-smell out of your hair in the showers at the Y. Kate's blond braid dripped, soaking a dark patch through the shoulder of her Frexies T-shirt. Her burger was half-eaten. She hadn't even touched her fries.

It was unheard-of. Usually, Kate finished her potato products first, and a healthy helping of mine as well, world without end, amen. But today she had a few lone survivors on her spread-out cheeseburger wrapper.

She hadn't been eating much lately.

It was a ninety-plus day, but I shivered. "Okay. So what are we gonna do?"

Kate's face crumpled. For a moment I was sure she was going to cry, so I looked down at the ruins of my lunch, to give her some privacy.

But Kate just picked up a napkin and blew her nose. A hot breeze from the Tasty Freeze parking lot made the tattered umbrella over our table flap. Everyone else was inside enjoying the air conditioning. Sitting outside on a day like this could fry your brain.

"He's awake sometimes during the day, even if he never goes outside." Kate's voice was small, as if she was six again. "He hates garlic, too. And at night he's just bouncing off the walls. Mom thinks it's cute. They're really into each other since she brought him home."

It was what she'd said before. But my gaze came up and fastened on Kate's hand. She'd taken to wearing that fashionable buckled leather cuff everywhere, even into the pool. Now it lay on the table, getting lighter as it dried. The two marks on the pale underside of her wrist where she hardly ever tanned had worn, white-looking edges. Their centers were dark and angry, though. Scabbed over.

Right where they taught you to take the pulse in First Aid.

Kate made a restless movement. "I thought he was just creepy. But he ... God."

"He just comes in your room while your mom's gone, right?" That was important, though I couldn't say just why. "Is she ... acting weird? I mean, weirder than normal?"

"She's tired a lot." Kate hunched her shoulders. "He's

got money, says she doesn't have to work. She's about ready to agree. Her shifts are pretty long."

"Yeah." I sucked on her straw thoughtfully, making a weird bubbling noise. "But if she's home more often . . ."

"She's so *tired*." Kate's eyes came up, and she stared significantly at me. "You know?"

As tired as Kate looked, probably. Dark circles under her eyes. Worn out.

Drained.

The sunshine was hot, but it didn't touch the ice inside my stomach. "Okay," I said again. The exact same way I said it every time Kate had a problem. "Don't worry. We'll figure something out."

School was out, but the sharks were still swimming. I walked on the road side of the pavement, as usual, and as soon as I heard the engine behind us I knew it was trouble. They were driving too slow, whoever it was.

Kate cast a quick glance over her shoulder, fine golden curls drying and unraveling at her temples. "Asshole alert," she muttered. "Great."

The car slowed down with a brief squeal of brakes. I had a quick vision of the brake cable snapping, failing somehow, and the whole merry crew of them driving off a cliff.

"*Leeeeeeezz*-bians!!" It was Nathan Bardsmore. "Look at the *leeeeeezzzzzzzzz*-bians!"

A familiar ball of red-hot anger settled right behind my breastbone. You'd think summer vacation would turn out better than this.

"God." Kate's flipflops made snapping sounds as she stepped. They were only a block from home and safety. "I wish he'd just die."

I stopped. Lifted my head and stared at the red Ford Escort. Bardsmore was hanging out of the passenger window, waggling his tongue like a four-year-old. Only he was doing it between a V made of his left-hand fingers, and troll-like laughter poured from the other rolled-down windows along with a throbbing beat of rap music.

Nathan was one of the rich-jock set. Big, blond, broad-shouldered, and with an allowance that was probably more than most people's parents made. He was just a symptom, really. The whole world was rotten.

The heat crawled up from my chest, made a lump in my throat, and stung my eyes. It was a familiar feeling, ever since the first day of middle school. Kate's fingers touched my wrist. It was warm and comforting, and before I knew it I'd grabbed her hand.

We thought we were being so careful, but everyone knew.

"Go fuck yourself!" The yell bolted free of my lips, and more troll-like laughter echoed in response. Kate's fingers were sweating, and stuck to mine. But she didn't pull away, and the Escort sped up and bumped down the street. It made a hard right down near old man McAllister's house, and the heartbeat of rap bass faded.

"He'll be back." Kate sounded tired all over again. "You should just ignore him, Becks."

The idea burst inside my skull, along with the hate and the anger. My stomach turned over hard, and I wondered if I was getting heatstroke. "Let's get inside. I want some lemonade."

"You're so lucky." But Kate didn't sound like she thought it was lucky at all. She just sounded sad. "Your mom's home all the time."

The pool bag bumped against my back as I shrugged.

"She's probably getting her hair done. But there's lemonade and we can watch Judge Judy. You want to stay over tonight?"

The hopeful smile breaking over Kate's face made the anger simmer down. "You sure? I mean . . . yeah."

"Of course I'm sure." I took a tentative step forward. Swung our linked hands together, like we'd done in private a million times before. "I've got an idea."

"What kind of idea?"

"About your problem."

"Okay." We walked on, the liquid shade of an elm tree swallowing us whole. "So . . . what?"

I stopped again. Our hands stayed linked. My bikini was already dry under the sarong; the heat was that fierce. Scarves of pollen on the breeze were as golden as Kate's hair. I thought it over one more time, making sure it was all clear in my head, and spent the next couple minutes laying it out.

Kate chewed her lower lip for a little while. "You believe me?" Like she hadn't realized I would.

"I believe you." What I didn't tell her was, well, I kind of didn't. But those marks on her wrist were awfully persuasive. And the circles under her eyes. And how she'd lost a bunch of weight since school let out. Her hipbones stuck out, and so did her ribs.

And how her stepfather, Edgar, made me feel, like I'd swallowed a sack of greasy snakes.

"We'll get caught," she whispered, her eyes big, blue, and round.

The urge to put my arms around her and kiss the soft hot part where her shoulder met her neck almost made me shake. "No we won't. Not if we're careful."

*   *   *

I had Mom call Kate's mom and make the invitations, figuring that was the best way to make it impossible for Ms. Cooke to refuse. The ploy worked, since Mom's one of those saccharine-polite people that you absolutely, positively cannot say no to without feeling like a total asshole. I would hate her for it, but then, that's the only way she can deal with Dad. It's the only way anyone can.

"Keep a lookout," I whispered, and left Kate at the top of the stairs. She stood there, rubbing the top of one bare monkey-toed foot against the other, holding onto the railing. Mom's voice floated up from the kitchen— *how nice for you! Congratulations! . . . Well, Kate is always such a pleasure, so well-behaved . . .*

So on, so on, so forth.

I stepped carefully into their bedroom. Breathed in the talcum powder and Tabu, the French cologne Dad wore, the close still scent of them in the same room. Two twin beds, their floral coverlets pristine and military-tight. Mom made their beds every morning, probably to cover up the fact that Dad slept more often on the huge overstuffed couch in front of the TV, turned down all the way and glowing like a fourth alien member of the family.

I was in luck. Dad's closet door was open. I knelt down on blue carpet, vacuumed religiously every two days, and felt around. His suits, ranked in a neat row, brushed my head. The slice of carpet lifted away, I keyed in the code and braced myself for the heavy safe door.

Folders of important papers, like birth certificates and passports, a stack of hundreds in their neat paper rings, and the thing I was looking for. It was heavy metal,

I took it carefully. It wasn't near the end of the month, so he wouldn't be opening this up to look at his cash pile soon.

I stared at the money for a long few seconds, the way I did every time. Then I hurried to close it up, because Mom's voice from downstairs rose in that particular way people have when they're saying good-bye. I had everything sealed up and the carpet brushed to get rid of the indents of my naked knees by the time Mom said "Cheerio, then!" and dropped the phone back into its charger.

"I think she said yes," Kate whispered as I beckoned her toward my room.

My heart was banging against my ribs, and my red bikini was damp again. "Of course she did." We made it to the safety of my room, and I shoved the heavy metal as far back as I could reach under my own pink-fluffed, curtained daybed. I was taking my sarong off in the bathroom when Mom tapped at the door and peeked in, her careful brassy-blond coiffure lacquered in place.

"Your mother says it's all right, Catherine." She has a wide toothy grin, my mother, behind carmine lips. "My goodness, you look tired! It's so dreadfully hot out there. Would you like a snack before dinner? Some cookies and lemonade?"

"That'd be great, Mrs. Robins." Kate gave her a winsome smile and I imagined my mother melting. The bathroom door hid Mom, but I could see Kate lounging on the bed, in what she called her come-hither pose. A black one-piece swimsuit, a rhinestone buckle between her shallow breasts, against all that pink. She was unbraiding her hair and it sprang back in tame waves against her paleness.

I was pretty sure Mom wished I'd been born blonde to match the room she kept decorating for me.

"I'll be back up with a tray. Did you girls have a good time?"

"Superlative," I drawled through the bathroom door. "What's for dinner, Mumzers?"

She trilled her brittle little laugh. "Oh, very simple— chicken breasts with lemon, angelhair pasta, some vegetables. I just have no *time* for anything fancy. I'm sure Catherine doesn't mind, do you, dear? You're one of the *family* by now."

"It's always good, Mrs. Robins." Kate's smile stretched and I was pretty sure she was thinking of something to whisper to me as soon as Mom was out of earshot. "Thanks."

But Mom lingered. "Is your mother not feeling well? She sounded . . . not quite herself."

I half-closed the door and wriggled out of the bikini.

"I think she has a summer cold. And she's working really hard." Kate kicked at the poolbag, discarded on the Pepto-Bismol rug.

I stepped into jeans, yanked a T-shirt down. "Mom, can I take the car after dinner and go pick up Kate's stuff?"

"Oh, certainly, sweetheart. Cookies and lemonade coming up!" She bustled away down the hall, staggering slightly on her heels.

Gin at three in the afternoon. If it was any more of a cliché she'd be wearing pearls while she scrubbed the spotless oven.

"Is she okay?" Kate's forehead creased.

"Just kind of drunk." I stepped out. "Bathroom's all yours."

"We don't have to go to my house. I can just—"

"We'll just be there for a couple minutes to pick up your stuff and take a look at things. Okay? It's part of the plan."

She nodded, chewing at her lower lip, and I wanted to kiss her. But I put my hands behind my back as she heaved herself up from my bed and slid past me. All my nerve endings felt her, like the weight of sunshine on already-burned skin. She stopped right in front of me. "Becks?"

"Yeah?" My fingers knotted together. The pink bed pulsed with a secret under it. The first time we'd made out in the middle of the night had been on that bed.

She pressed her lips to mine. Sunscreen, chlorine, fresh air, and the faint biscuit odor she carried everywhere, all around me. We melted into each other for a long time until my mother's footsteps sounded in the hall again. Kate untangled her fingers from my damp hair, I let go of the sweet curve of her waist. She vanished into the bathroom while Mom brought in a crimson lacquered tray piled with cucumber sandwiches, sugar cookies, and a pitcher of lemonade.

I knew Mom wouldn't see how I was blushing. She just gave me a swift booze-fogged glance, checking for loose threads or zits, and breezed right on out.

The Cooke house was a small brown ranch number three streets over, where the neighborhood went from genteel to shabby. The yard wasn't mowed, and the juniper hedges were straggling. Both grass and bushes were turning a weird yellow. We had the windows down, and her mom's car wasn't in the driveway.

Edgar's maroon Lincoln Continental crouched there instead, its pristine paint job shimmering under golden evening light. Its windshield was a blind, dark-tinted eye.

I set the parking brake and we both eyed the house. Kate let out a nervous, jagged little laugh. "He's here."

"You knew he would be." I blew out between my teeth. Sweat sprang out all over me. Even for just a few streets with all the windows down, Mom's black Volvo was a furnace inside. There was no breeze. "It's daylight, remember? We'll be okay."

"Sometimes he's up during the day. And it's late."

"But he's always half-asleep and slow, right? You just go in, get your stuff. I'll talk to him." I kept my fingers away from my throat with an effort. The little gold Communion cross I hadn't worn since I was twelve felt unfamiliar. "Don't *worry* so much, Kate. It'll be okay."

All the blinds were pulled. She let us in with the key, yelled, "I'm here to get my stuff!" and bolted down the hall to the left. I peeked around the wall to my right, into the dark frowsty cave of the living room.

The television was on but muted, a baseball game going on. Edgar lay on the ratty brown couch, his slick black pompadour almost crushed under the weight of a meaty arm flung across his eyes. "Hello, Mr. Black," I chirped.

He grunted. So he *was* awake. The sunshine coming in through the front door didn't do much to penetrate the living room, but I was suddenly sure he hadn't been watching the game before we pulled up. Just what he'd been doing was anyone's guess, but I would bet money he hadn't been on that couch.

The idea of just walking into the room and yanking one of the ancient curtains aside did occur to me. But Kate came flying back down the hall. "Bye!" she yelled over her shoulder, and I watched Edgar twitch. His skin was an unhealthy pasty color, like a mushroom left in the cellar. There was a faint sour odor, too. A sharp breath of rotten potatoes, when they start weeping that weird fluid and fuzzing up with white.

I followed Kate out into the heavy honey evening. She headed for the car like dogs were after her, but I stopped and peered at the windows.

No crack between the curtains. But I thought I saw one of them twitch.

Huh.

I walked slowly back to the Volvo, jingling my car keys and feeling someone staring at my back. Just like school.

In the middle of the night she curled up into a little ball and cried against me. I hugged her hard, faint moonlight edging in between curtains I hadn't pulled all the way shut. Stroked her long silky hair, kissed her until her mouth opened like a flower and she kissed me back. We rocked together on the little ship of my bed, and when I saw the black paper cutout shape of a man's head in the window I just held her tighter, my wrist aching a little as I finished the movements that sent her over the edge. She shook and shuddered in my arms, and I stared at the window. Two bright specks of red stared back, but my bed was lost in shadows. By the time her hot little mouth was at my cheek and her clever little fingers were sliding between my legs, the shadow in the window vanished.

I closed my eyes.

"Kinky." Kate giggled, a high hard flush rising in her cheeks. I rolled my eyes, pushed the two twenties wormed out of Dad this morning across the counter, and ignored the way the pimpled clerk was smirking. He didn't go to our school, but when two teenage girls in bikini tops and jean shorts wander into a military surplus shop—you get the idea. It's not pretty.

"Anything else, ladies?" If the kid was any smarmier he'd leak oil.

I scooped my change out of his hand and grabbed the bag. "Nothing *you* can sell."

Kate went into more hysterical giggles at this, and I dragged her out through the automatic doors. Before they closed behind us, I heard him mutter *bitch*.

Of course.

I swiped my bangs out of the way as we headed for the car. "Stupid fucking minimum-wage jackass."

Kate half-choked on laughter. I waxed indignant for another minute or so before unlocking the Volvo's door. There were only three cars in the parking lot. It was another fry-an-egg day.

"What do you think he thinks we want this stuff for?" She hissed a little as she dropped onto the leather seat, her shorts riding up and pale sunscreen-drenched legs sticking with a faint tacky sound.

I shrugged, twisted the key in the ignition. "Doesn't matter. It's legal to buy it."

"What if he knew? Jesus." She rolled her window down. It was useless to turn on the air conditioning right away. It would just blow out oven-hot air.

"He wouldn't do anything if he knew. He was too busy having little whack-off fantasies about us anyway." I sounded a little more savage than I felt, and grabbed for the can of Coke in the cupholder. Beads of condensation clung to its sides. We hadn't been in there very long—I had a List, and I know how to shop. It's the one useful thing Mom taught me. "One more stop, and then we can go to the pool or something. Or go home for lunch."

"What are we going to get now?"

For a moment I was irritated, but then I popped the parking brake off and reminded myself she was always like this. "Big dowels. Remember? And rope."

"Oh yeah." She grabbed for the Coke; I gave it up. "Becca?"

I hit the turn signal, checked both ways on Vane, and stamped the accelerator. Hot wind poured through the open windows. "What?"

"Thank you." She gulped at the Coke as we bounced out across a few lanes of traffic. "I mean, you know. Yeah."

My heart made a funny quivering movement inside me. "No problem, kid." And I polished her bare knee with my palm.

Kate hung up the phone, her cheeks flour-pale. Checked the fall of sunshine outside the window. "She's due at work in twenty minutes and she didn't call in sick, so she must have left."

"Good." I slid the very last thing into my pool bag, checking it twice. "Which means he's probably there in front of the TV again. Waiting for you to come home."

She shivered and rubbed her wrist against her jeans. "Are you sure this is going to work?"

I wasn't. But how could I tell her so? "Remember fifth grade, and the Ex-Lax in the teacher's lounge?"

That got a faint smile. "Yeah. They never did figure out where that pan of brownies came from."

"This is just the same."

"It's not. It's . . . you know what he is."

"I know what he's going to be." I zipped up the bag. "Kate, just trust me, okay? You're gonna be okay."

But nothing ever goes exactly according to plan.

* * *

We got there all right, walking through drowsy heat and bands of golden drifting pollen. There were undercurrents and eddies of cooler air, and long breeze-borne stretches of the weird sour odor of old concrete and a type of spiny bush that smells like old-man pee on hot days. Her house looked just the same as it always did, except the grass was a little yellower. Edgar didn't go out with a sprinkler the way my dad did. Some of Mrs. Cooke's boyfriends had been into lawn care—but none of them stayed around long enough for it to matter.

Edgar had already beaten most of them by hanging around for three months.

The maroon Lincoln Continental crouched, gleaming and poreless. Kate held my hand, bruising-tight. We got up to the front door and she jangled her keys. I gave her a meaningful look, unzipped my bag, and dug out the pepper spray.

The door opened. "I'm home!" Kate squeaked, and I stepped in.

"Anyone here?" I peeked around the corner and saw the same thing I'd seen yesterday. Edgar on the couch, arm over his eyes. This time he had a can of beer in his other hand, resting on his taut stomach. He was muscular, in a thick greasy sort of way. You could see why Kate's mom had brought him home. "Oh, hi, Mr. Black. What's up?"

He grunted a little. Kate left the door open and bolted, scrambling, across the living room.

The dumb bunny. I'd told her to do it casually.

Edgar jerked into motion, his arm dropping from his eyes and the beer can flying. I dropped the pool bag, inhaling the weird sour-yeasty odor Kate's house had taken on recently, and brought the pepper spray up. The tab depressed, and the jet of it hit him right in his open, snarling mouth.

And if I hadn't believed Kate before, I did now. Because the instant the spray hit him, he *changed*.

Strong, champing ivory teeth, fangs curving to sharp points. Hellfire burning in his swelling bruised eyes, his aquiline nose instantly running with snot and pepperspray. He made a sound like a freight train crashing into the side of a skyscraper, and I almost dropped the spray. My fingers froze, I started shouting every bad word I knew and pressed the tab down *hard*. The spray fizzed and spurted. He got a whole mouthful of it and dropped off the couch like he'd been hit on the head with a sack full of hammers.

Kate finally got the curtains jerked open. Someone had fastened them with duct tape, and the sound of it ripping away from the wall was like pants ripping down the back when a fat teacher squats. Light flooded the room, direct sun pouring in. Edgar howled, the inhuman sound bubbling through a mess of snot and blood on his face.

I began to feel dizzy. The Communion necklace burned against my skin, a thin curl of steam drifting up.

He convulsed against the carpet, hitting the couch and making it thump solidly back. Kate let out a half-scream, half-sob. The sunlight ate at him like acid, and the plan was for me to get close enough to snap the handcuffs on him. We could have asked him some questions before I hammered the dowel through his chest with the deadblow hammer filched from my dad's never-used shop bench in the garage. And if that didn't kill him, there was the thing I'd taken from the safe. Dad had told me never to mess with it, never to touch it, never never never.

He'd said that about boys too. Would he be happy that I'd listened? Probably not.

I stared at the smoking thing on the floor. It stopped howling and spasming, twitching instead. It had long translucent claws that sliced at the thin carpet. Bits of bubbling stuff ran out of it.

I dropped the pepper spray. Bent down and cautiously dug in my pool bag. The yeasty smell crawled along the back of my throat.

The gun was heavy. There wasn't any safety. I pointed it at the steaming, bubbling, hissing thing.

"Becca?" Kate whispered.

"Just stay cool." I sounded like I had something stuck in my throat. The thing jerked. "Just stay right where you—"

The thing on the carpet screeched and scrabbled up, leaping for me. Bits of bone peeked through its rotting skin. His pompadour was melting, sliding down his face in long runnels.

The first shot went wide, plowing through the wall between the living room and kitchen. The thing that used to be Edgar moved faster than it had any right to, and I fell over backward, the gun skittering away and his teeth clicking shut like heavy billiard balls smacking each other. I got an arm up, rugburn crawling up my left calf as I screamed and crab-walked back too slowly.

His teeth sank into my forearm with a meaty sound and I screamed again. Kate yelled too, our voices rising in weird harmony. A bolt of sick fire raced up my arm, jolted my shoulder; he growled and shook his head the way a dog will try to shake a bone. My necklace flared with heat, a *shhhhhh!* under all the noise, like bacon slapped on a hot griddle.

Kate was screaming my name. I was just screaming,

the way you will in a nightmare. I fell back into the hall, into a square of golden light. Edgar made a ratcheting sound deep in his rotting throat.

A *gulping* sound.

The gun roared. I squealed, losing all my air at the end of a scream as something burned along my leg. Edgar flopped senselessly aside in the long rectangle of evening sunlight.

Kate stood there, both hands clumsily bracing the gun, and shot him four more times. I got in a whooping deep lungful. Someone was mowing their grass somewhere, and the fresh green scent cut briefly through the yeasty rot.

My lungs hurt. Short sharp breaths. Sweat slicked me all over. I made a small baby sound and Kate stepped back, still with the gun pointed at him. "OhGod," she husked. "OhGod. God."

"Goddamn," I rasped. Blood slid down my arm, hot wetness. I hadn't thought to pack a first-aid kit.

Right now, that was the least of my problems. "Get a dowel." My throat felt like it was on fire. "And the hammer. Hurry."

She dropped the gun. I managed to get up on my side. My arm hurt if I put any weight on it and my Communion necklace dropped off, the cross a molten twisted blop plopping on the carpet. I crawled forward a little, listening for sirens. Did anyone hear the gunshots? Jesus.

The smoking ruin that used to be Edgar lay on its back, arms wide and charred lips pulled back to expose violently-white, killing-sharp teeth. Kate stumbled back and dropped the dowel.

I got to my knees, watching him in case he twitched again. "You'll have to hold it, I'll hammer."

She nodded, lips clamped together. If I thought she was pale before she was almost transparent now. Sweat slicked her face and her cheek twitched a little right under one of her blue, blue eyes.

She held the rough point I'd chipped on the dowel to the left side of his chest. I hefted the hammer in my good hand. My arm throbbed, and it was a good thing I didn't have to stand up. I didn't think I could.

The first blow skittered off the end of the dowel. Kate jumped and squeaked. I swallowed hard, set my jaw, and waited for her to resettle the point against the crackling, blackened skin.

We wrapped my arm with an old kitchen towel and some duct tape. Kate wanted to spray some Bactine on it, but there wasn't any. I took one look at the ancient bottle of hydrogen peroxide and said no way.

"You might get infected." Kate bit her lower lip, rubbing her left wrist against her shirt. The leather cuff scraped T-shirt material, and she darted a quick glance at my face. "Or something."

I shrugged. My hair fell in my eyes again. I swiped it away, irritated. I was sweating and everything smelled bad and I *really* wanted a big dish of cherry ice cream.

The phone rang. I would have told Kate to ignore it, but she picked up before I could stop her.

"H–Hello?" A short pause. "No, she's not. I thought she was there." She sounded honestly shocked. A longer pause, and her forehead furrowed. "Um, okay. No . . . uhn–uh." She shook her head violently, as if whoever was on the other end could see her. "I will, sure. Okay. Bye."

Then she hung up, her eyes big as saucers. There were bruised-looking rings underneath them.

"Kate? You shouldn't have answered ..." I swallowed, hard. *Oh fuck.*

"My mom." It was a tiny breath of sound. "She's not at work."

We found Ms. Cooke sitting in her blue Mazda in the garage that used to be full of boxes and crap. I guess Edgar had been cleaning it out when we thought he was just laying there watching baseball. Her legs were out the driver's side door and the dome light was on. She stared sightlessly through the windshield at us, her blue eyes clouded like weird Jell-O. Two neat little puncture wounds glared in her neck, one with a thread of dried blood trickling down.

Kate buried her face in my neck and started crying. I just stared, numb and dry-eyed, and tried to figure out what came next.

The cops never came, so I guess nobody heard the shots. We sat in the kitchen, my throbbing arm crusted with dried blood, and I drank a couple glasses of water. The puncture wounds were ragged, two on the top and two on the bottom, right in the meat of my forearm. There was bruising, too. Once I washed the blood off it looked like I'd slammed my arm in a car door or something.

Kate stared at the counter. Once in a while she'd pick at it with her fingernails. It took her a long time to say anything.

Finally, though, she raised her head. Her hair was lank with sweat, almost as dark as mine. "Do you think she's dead?"

"Right now she is." I took another gulp of water. "But when it gets dark ... I dunno."

"What are we going to *do*?"

A bolt of white-hot anger shot through my head. "Just hang *on*, Kate. I'm *thinking*."

She shut up. I stared at the toothmarks on my bruised arm. The crease along my leg where the bullet had burned throbbed dully as well.

Hammering a dowel through Edgar's chest was one thing. But Ms. Cooke ... that was another thing entirely. I couldn't count on Kate for that. It was her *mother*, for Chrissake.

And if Edgar wasn't dead, maybe Kate's mother would keep him busy for long enough to ...

... to what?

"Do you want to ... to do the same thing to her?" Kate whispered finally.

I took a good look at her. She was shaking, and there were big bruised circles under her eyes. Decided. "We'll get cleaned up. Go back to my house." I swallowed so hard my throat clicked, dry despite the tepid water. "Spend the night. In the morning we come back and see if either of them have moved. If they have we know how it works, how it happens. If they haven't we go out, call the cops from a phone booth, and lie like hell. Say we were never here."

She chewed at her lower lip. "What about the gun?"

"I don't know." I shifted back and forth on the stool, stared out the kitchen window at the overgrown back yard. Shadows ran over long grass and the window, the pines soughing as the evening breeze picked up. "I'd better take it home and put it back. If Dad swears it was in the safe ..."

"They have ballistics." But she subsided when I stared at her. "Sorry."

Why was she fixated on *that*? We'd have bigger problems either way. "Dad will get a lawyer if he has to." I stared at my arm. "I need something long-sleeved to cover this up. And a pair of jeans. If we can get into the house without my parents noticing us . . . we'll just say we were walking around or something."

As plans went, it sucked. But Jesus. What else could we do?

That night we lay in my bed, stiff as boards. I knew she was still awake, she knew I was, and we just . . . lay there. And sweated in the air-conditioned coolness of my house, while outside the night breathed.

In the darkest, deadest time of night, right around three AM, I heard a faint scratching, scrabbling noise. My arm gave a heavy, heated throb, and my head turned on the pillow.

The shadow in the window bobbed. Twin red sparks winked out, came back up.

"Sweetheart." A soft, sibilant whisper, audible even through the glass. *"Sweetheart, it's Mommy."*

My heart gave a leap like it intended to jump out of my chest. Now we knew how it worked. Mostly.

I clapped my hand over Kate's mouth before she could scream. "Shut up," I whispered fiercely. "Shush."

"It's so warm and soft," Mrs. Cooke crooned. *"It is. Let me in."*

More scratches. Kate's eyes rolled. She was no longer a board, she had turned to hot frantic flesh that hugged me tight. Her spit slicked my palm.

"You'll be like us soon, sweetheart. Mommy will help you. Let me in."

Waves of heat slid down my body. The bite on my forearm was hot and hard. Kate's hair brushed it, and a scorch slid through me.

"Shhh," I whispered. "It's okay, Katie. It's okay."

She moaned against my palm. We held each other while her mother prowled outside, and after a little while the sounds went away. Kate hugged me, twitching.

I peeled my hand away from her mouth.

"Becca . . ." She shook, and we were both sweating again.

"Don't worry." My voice dropped into the dark. "It's okay." The punctures on my arm beat an invisible tattoo in the dark, nerves pulling on the bones. I could almost feel the infection spreading.

Maybe I should have let her pour peroxide on it. But then I'd miss how my teeth were tingling. And I'd miss Kate nuzzling at my throat. She made a little mewling sound as her fangs scraped my skin, and I jumped a little. She froze.

I wondered how long she'd be able to go out in the sunlight.

Probably just long enough.

"I'm so thirsty," she whispered apologetically. "I don't know what to do."

"Katie." My arms tightened around her. I tipped my chin up, cupped my hand at the back of her head. Guided her face into my throat again. "Don't worry. I know what to do."

"Good morning, sleepyhead!" Mom chirped. I tried to summon up a grin, scratching at the back of my neck under heavy hair. I really needed a trim. "I'm just about to go to the stylist's. You're a late bird!"

"Mmmh." I spotted the coffeemaker. My throat was on fire, I blinked at the light falling through the kitchen window. "What's for dinner?"

I didn't care, but if she thought I'd be here, it was all to the good.

"Spaghetti bolognese!" Mom swept a hand back through her freshly washed hair. The morning sunlight was harsh. Even foundation couldn't hide the deep cracks in her face. "Listen, Becky, did you hear anything last night?"

My heart about stopped in my chest. I covered it by stamping for the fridge and opening it up. Cold air bathed my feverish skin. "Nope. Other than Kate snoring. Why?"

"Your father swears he heard a prowler last night."

My heart leapt up into my burning throat. I wished she'd go so I could pull the blinds. It was too goddamn bright in here, even though the sunlight dimmed. "Really?"

"I told him he was being ridiculous. But he swears. Be sure you keep the doors locked, okay?"

"I will." I got out the orange juice and shut the fridge door. "We might go to the pool today."

"It's hot enough. They say there'll be thunderstorms this afternoon, though. It's already cloudy. Well, *ciao,* darling! You should get your hair cut, you know."

Just like Mom. I muttered an agreement, and she pranced out.

As soon as the garage door closed and the sound of the Volvo's engine faded, Kate peered around the corner into the kitchen. I rubbed at my throat. "She's gone." I didn't have to work to sound tired. "Get ready to go."

"Are you sure?" Blue eyes wide and luminous, she blinked furiously. I didn't blame her, it was bright as hell in here. The sunshine dimmed still more as clouds moved across the bright sky.

"Of course I'm sure. Take a shower and put on something with long sleeves." I thought about it for a second, then yanked the fridge open and dropped the OJ back in. "I'll find us some shades."

Edgar's body was still a slimy, stinking mess. The dowel in his chest had been wrenched out, but Ms. Cooke was nowhere in sight. I didn't stick around, just grabbed the car keys from the coffee table and headed back outside.

The Lincoln Continental's interior smelled like baby powder. It started with a swift sweet purr and I backed out, nosed down the street to a patch of deep shade under a cedar tree. Kate was there, in a long-sleeved thermal shirt and jeans. The sunglasses were blank holes on her pale face. Behind my own shades my eyes stung furiously, and thunder rumbled in the distance. The weird green-yellow bruiselight of a storm approaching made the maroon paint on the car look diseased.

I popped the trunk and Kate piled our bags in. I leaned over to unlock the door, and a roll of cash in my right pocket dug into the inside crease of my hip. The rest of the money from the safe was in my purse, thrown on the floor in the back.

The gun was under the driver's seat. I took the extra bullets too. You never know.

Kate dropped in and slammed the door, mopped at her sweating face. "Thirsty." An angry red flush had crawled up her cheeks from the sunshine. But the windows were tinted, and the light didn't hurt from in here, even when the clouds pulled back a little and the street melted under the weird flat illumination right before a storm really hits.

My throat was a furnace. It made my voice husky. "Me too. We'll drive for a while. Tonight we'll find something. To, um, drink."

It stood to reason that soon we'd start sleeping

during the day. Sleeping like the dead. I'd figure something out then. I was sure of it.

"You sure?" She rubbed her pale wrist against her jeans. Under the thermal's cuff, the puncture wounds had vanished. The ones on my arm were closing up, and the ones on my throat looked days old instead of fresh. I'd tried a swallow of Coke this morning and almost threw up. I knew what I wanted, and I knew we'd find it.

"Yeah." I reached over and grabbed her hand. She slid her fingers through mine. Even though we were both sweating, her fingers were marble-cold. Pretty soon mine would be too. "I've got it figured out."

I didn't *entirely,* not yet. But I had enough of it. Two girls, one as pretty as Kate? We wouldn't have any trouble. We could get money if we needed it. And there were all sorts of things we could do without parents and school and all that shit.

"Becca?" She pushed her shades down a little, leaned over. Her mouth met mine, and the sharp edges of her fangs brushed my tongue. "I love you," she said shyly, when she pulled away.

All of a sudden I couldn't wait to stop for the night. I dropped the car into drive. It moved smoothly forward when I touched the gas, and I found out I could take my sunglasses off. Edgar had known what he was doing when he had the windows tinted.

I licked my lips. My teeth tingled, and I swiped my bangs out of my eyes. "I love you too, Kate."

Soon I'd have fangs too.

I couldn't wait.

ELIZABETH AND ANNA'S BIG ADVENTURE

Jeanne C. Stein

This story is dedicated to The Tot—Anna's youngest fan.

My name is Elizabeth. I'm eight years old and I've already had an adventure.

My mommy and daddy tell me I shouldn't think about it. They say that because they think it makes me scared when I do. But I don't mind thinking about what happened. My Aunt Anna is the bravest person I know and she says I should always remember because we saved each other's lives and that makes me as brave as she is.

Here's how it happened.

My Uncle David was supposed to babysit me last Saturday while my mommy and daddy went to a party. But Uncle David has another new girlfriend and she wanted him to go with her to a party, and I guess spending the night with what my daddy calls a "hottie" was way better than spending the night with me.

Anyway, he sent another babysitter to take care of me. Her name is Anna Strong. She's not really my aunt but I call her that because she likes it. She works with Uncle David. They're cops, sort of. They go after guys

who try to get away instead of going to trial. Daddy calls
them bounty hunters. And he knows about stuff like
that. He works in the District Attorney's office.

I've met Aunt Anna before. Mommy was surprised
when Uncle David said she would stay with me because
she's not really the babysitting type, (I'm not sure what
that means since she's always been nice to me) and that
she must owe Uncle David a big favor. I didn't know
what that meant either.

So Aunt Anna came over with popcorn and Three
Musketeers bars (my favorite) and two movies. She's
pretty but not like a movie star. She has light brown
hair and green eyes. She was dressed the way she always
is. Jeans, a T-shirt, a jacket she never takes off. Even in
summer. Mommy says she must have poor circulation
because she's skinny and so she's probably cold all the
time. Daddy says she looks like a runner, lean and hard-
muscled. He gets a funny smile when he talks about her
that makes Mommy punch him in the arm.

Mommy and Daddy left for their party and we got
ready to start the first movie. *Princess Bride*. Aunt Anna
said it was her favorite movie but made me swear not to
tell anyone—especially Uncle David.

I don't think this counts.

Aunt Anna went into the kitchen to get us drinks. I
heard her cell phone ring and she answered it so I put
the movie in the TV and sat back on the couch to watch
previews. I can't do this when most adults are around—
they use words like inappropriate and violent. Funny
since when we watch "Animal Kingdom" there's lots of
stuff that goes on there that seems pretty inappropriate
and violent to me.

The doorbell rang right in the middle of the first preview: *The Witches of Eastwick*. I stopped the DVD, lis-

tened for Aunt Anna to tell me she was going to answer it. I don't think she heard it since I could still hear her talking on her phone.

So I did.

I'm not tall enough to look through the peephole. I asked, "Who is it?" through the door and a woman's voice said, "A coworker of your dad's. He left some papers at the office and asked me to bring them by."

It's happened before. I opened the door.

There was a man and a woman standing there. They were dressed all in black and had masks on their faces. The kind of masks you wear to ski when it's really cold. The kind that cover your whole head and have holes for your eyes and mouth. I started to scream for Aunt Anna, but the woman grabbed me, put a hand over my mouth, and carried me inside.

My heart was pounding so hard, I thought it would burst. Then I thought I would suffocate since her fingers were over my nose and mouth and I couldn't breathe. I kicked and tried to hit her, but she was too big and too strong.

The man said, "Take it easy. We don't want the kid dead."

She bent down so her eyes were looking right into mine. "If I let you go, do you promise not to scream?"

Her eyes were big and black and serious.

I nodded.

She loosened her grip and led me over to the couch. Then she shoved me and I sat down, hard.

The man sat down beside me. He put one hand on my head. In his other hand he had a gun.

"You are a very pretty little girl. What's your name?"

I was trying very hard not to look at the gun. I clamped my lips together. I don't talk to strangers.

"How old are you?" he asked then. "Eight? Nine?

You must be the result of the congratulatory screw your momma gave your dad after he sent me to prison."

The woman shushed him. "You don't have to be so crude. None of this is her fault."

He smiled. Not the kind of smile that's friendly. He was staring down at me again. "Your daddy told you not to talk to strangers, right? Too bad he didn't tell you not to answer the door."

He looks around. "Where is your daddy? Upstairs?" He tilted his head as if listening. "It's a good bet you're not here alone."

I listened, too. I didn't hear Aunt Anna anymore. I didn't hear anything. Something wiggled in my stomach. She didn't leave me alone when she heard them, did she?

The man got up and headed for the stairs. I heard him clomping around up there, going from room to room.

The woman pointed to the TV. "What are you watching?"

She picked up the remote and the DVD flickered on. The preview this time was *A Nightmare on Elm Street*. "I can't believe they let you watch this stuff." She tossed the remote on the couch beside me. "Where are your parents, kid? We know they wouldn't leave you alone."

The man came back. He shook his head. "He's not up there. I'll try the kitchen."

"They're next door." The words seemed to come out by themselves. "At the neighbors. They'll be right back so you'd better get out quick."

They smiled at each other. The woman said, "You do have a tongue. Good. When will they be back?"

They both stared at me. I bit my lip. "Soon. They just went over to see the new baby."

The man quirked a finger at the woman and they

moved away and whispered at each other. When I looked up, I saw Aunt Anna peeking around the kitchen door. She put her fingers to her lips and nodded. Then she stepped back out of sight.

My stomach was not wiggling so much now. When the man and the woman came back to stand near the couch, the man had a phone in his hand.

"Call them. Tell them to come home."

He pushed the phone into my hand. I knew the neighbor's number but I was afraid to call it. I started to dial and the man stopped my fingers and pushed a button. "Speaker's on, kid, so don't fuck around."

Now I was really scared. When the neighbor answered, the man would know I lied. Just then, our telephone rang. The man snatched his phone from my hands and bent to look at the caller ID. "Who's Anna Strong?"

Something told me just what to answer. "She's the neighbor."

He handed me the receiver. At the same time, he pulled the gun from inside his jacket and pointed it at me. "Tell your daddy to come home now."

He looked around the phone for the speaker button but couldn't find it so he put the gun next to my head. "Tell them just to come home. Nothing else."

I picked up the receiver. "Hello?" I tried to keep my voice from shaking.

"Elizabeth. Listen closely. You're doing great. Say, 'I'm fine. But I need you to come home.'"

I did. The man nodded at me.

Aunt Anna said, "Say, 'I can't get the TV to work.' Like they're asking you why."

I repeated what Aunt Anna said, then added, "'Hannah Montana' will be on in ten minutes. It's my favorite program."

"Good girl. Now say good-bye. I'm watching. It will be over soon."

When I hung up the phone, the man put the gun back in his jacket and patted my head like I was a baby. "Nice work. You're a born liar. Like your dad."

The way he said it made me mad. "My daddy is not a liar. You'll be sorry you said that."

He looked at the way my fists curled up in a ball and he laughed. "You are a feisty one. Maybe when this is over—"

The woman slapped his arm. "Forget it, Jake. We're not hurting the kid."

Quicker than I can take a breath he slapped her, hard, across the mouth. "You fucking idiot. You used my name."

She fell back onto the couch and rubbed her cheek. Her eyes got big and shiny, like she was trying not to cry.

He looked at his watch. "How long does it take to walk fifty fucking feet?"

He went over to the window. "Which house?"

I wasn't sure what he meant so I asked, "What?"

He came back to the couch so fast, it made me jump. "I said, which house?"

I start to shake my head because I still didn't understand what he was asking me.

The woman put an arm out in front of me. "Don't you touch her," she said. "We agreed. We want the kid's dad. No one else."

The way his eyes looked made me think he wanted to hit her again. Or me. I tried to make myself small but he pushed the woman's arm away and reached for me anyway. He grabbed my arm and gave it a shake. "Right or left. Which house?"

I tried to think. His fingers hurt my arm but I wouldn't let him see that. I wish I knew if either of the neighbors was home tonight. "Left," I said, crossing my fingers.

He went back to the window. But he was there only a minute before he turned to look at me. "There are no lights on in that house."

His eyes were angry again. "If you tricked me with that phone call, there is going to be trouble. I want your daddy. But I'll settle for you." He smiled. "In fact, you might even be better. More fun for me. Clearer message for him."

He came toward me and the woman sprang up at him. "I said leave her alone."

He didn't even stop. He raised his gun and hit her. She fell so hard, I was sure she was dead. He was almost at the couch. I grabbed the remote and threw it at him as hard as I could. It just bounced off his chest and he laughed but it gave me a chance to crawl away under the coffee table.

He grabbed the corner of the table and lifted it up. "Come out, come out wherever you are," he said. "Come on. I won't hurt you. Much."

"Get away from her."

There was a blur from the kitchen. A *blur*. Like when a cartoon character moves really fast. Only it wasn't a cartoon character.

It was Aunt Anna.

She tackled the man before he could raise his gun again. She hit him so hard they both fell back against the wall. But Aunt Anna, her face was *different*. Her eyes flashed, and they were greenish-yellow, like a cat's. Her mouth was open. Her teeth were funny, too—pointy with two long fangs.

I looked and looked. I'd seen people like this before.
A long time ago, in a movie I wasn't supposed to watch.

They were called vampires.

Aunt Anna?

She grabbed the man and shook him like he was a doll.
He was looking at her face and screaming. He dropped
the gun but Aunt Anna didn't let go. She had his face in
her hands and she pulled him toward her. She stripped
off the mask and put her mouth right on his neck.

Then she looked at me.

Something changed in her face. She stepped back
a little, nodded at me, and swung her fist. The man's
jaw kind of moved sideways. He dropped just like the
woman had when he hit her with a gun. Only Aunt Anna
just used her fist. She grabbed his gun and stuck it on top
of the television.

Then she ran over to me and scooped me up. "Are
you all right?"

She was hugging me so hard, I thought I might break.
Where our cheeks touched, her skin was very cold. After
a few seconds, she held me away from her. Her face was
normal again.

"He didn't hurt you, did he?"

"No. You are *very* fast."

She looked at me the way adults looks at each other
when they have something serious to discuss. She
brought me to the couch and we sat down together.

"What you saw me do—what you saw me become,
I'm sorry if I scared you."

I shook my head. "That man scared me more."

Her lips turned up, like she wanted to smile but
shouldn't. "I know. But I have to ask you to do something that you may not understand. I wouldn't ask you
at all if it wasn't so important."

I sat very still and put my hands together to show her I was listening.

"I have to ask you to keep what you saw me do a secret—between the two of us. No one else can know. Not even your parents or Uncle David. Can you do that?"

Just then we heard lots of sirens coming down the street. Aunt Anna looked toward the door and then back at me. "I don't have time to explain why right now. I will soon though, I promise. Do you trust me?"

I nodded my head. "You saved me. I trust you. You can trust me, too. I promise not to say anything."

And I did the best thing I could do to show her how serious I was. I crossed my heart and held out a pinkie finger. "Pinkie promise."

She linked her pinkie with mine and we sealed the oath.

There were lights flashing outside by now and someone banged on the door.

Aunt Anna went to open it and lots of policemen in uniform burst in. Right behind them came Mommy and Daddy. They practically knocked Aunt Anna down to get to me. There was a lot of hugging and kissing and asking if I was all right.

The man who broke in was beginning to wake up. A policeman put handcuffs on him and hauled him to his feet. Another policeman did the same to the woman, but she was bleeding from the back of the head and they weren't so rough with her.

As soon as the man saw Aunt Anna, he began to yell. "Look at her. She's a monster. She has eyes like a cat and she tried to bite me. I think she's a fucking vampire."

He must have seen the movie, too.

Of course, Aunt Anna didn't have eyes like a cat

anymore and she was sitting quietly on the sofa so the policemen just rolled their eyes at him and told him to shut up.

Daddy came to sit with Aunt Anna, Mommy, and me on the couch.

"Who is he?" Mommy asked Daddy in her you-have-some-explaining-to-do voice. She still had her arms tight around my shoulders.

Daddy looked sad and angry at the same time. "His name is Jake Halloran. He and his brother, Frank, shot a convenience store clerk nine years ago. I was the prosecutor on the case. Jake wasn't the trigger man, so he did his time and was released on parole."

"Why did he come after you?" Aunt Anna asked.

"We heard that his brother was killed in prison. A week before *his* parole hearing. I guess he holds me responsible."

"And the woman?"

"Frank Halloran's widow."

Daddy turned to Aunt Anna. "I can't thank you enough for calling us. And for saving our little girl. I don't know how you did it. He had a gun. David was right when he said you are one hell of a woman."

The man in the corner starts to yell again. "She's not a woman. She's something else. Her teeth are pointy and she has fangs. Tell her to open her mouth. She has fangs. I'm telling you, she's a vampire."

Aunt Anna smiled at him. I guess to show how normal her teeth were. Then she said to my daddy, "It's Elizabeth who is one hell of a woman. She never got scared and she never lost her head. If anyone deserves credit for what happened here, it's your daughter."

I was really proud. No one ever called me a woman before. Even Mommy and Daddy were looking at me as if I wasn't a little girl any more. I scooted over to hug Aunt Anna and she hugged me back.

The police were ready to take the man and woman away. He was still screaming that Aunt Anna was a monster and they should be arresting her, too.

Aunt Anna and I looked at each other and I knew she could tell what I was thinking.

There are monsters in the world. I know it for sure now. That man would have hurt Daddy and me ... or worse. There *are* monsters.

But my friend Aunt Anna isn't one of them. She's brave and strong and didn't even need a gun to get that bad guy. I can't wait for her to tell me how she did it. If becoming a vampire is the secret, I want to be just like her when I grow up.

LUPERCALIA

Anton Strout

A lot of people had walked through the doors of New York's Serendipity on East Sixtieth Street over the years, but it was doubtful that any had come in with a crossbow strapped across their back. In that respect, Leis Colchis was singular. Her roommate, Helen Leda, certainly didn't have one on her. Helen hadn't even realized Leis had one until she took off her winter cloak in the restaurant.

"Is that what I think it is?" she whispered. "I'm pretty sure our R.A. would tell us that we're not allowed to have one of those in our dorm room." Although no one was paying attention to the pretty, long-haired blonde with the weapon yet, Helen figured it was only a matter of time.

Leis turned to her. "Good thing we're not on NYU property then," she said. Leis dropped her cloak onto a bench by the front door and released the crossbow's strap.

Helen grabbed Leis's arm. "You're not going to hurt anyone, are you? I know you're pissed with James and everything . . ."

Leis pulled away from her dark-haired roommate
with ease. Helen's grip wasn't strong enough to hold on,
and for once the petite girl wished she was a little stronger so she could restrain her friend.

"Relax," Leis said. "I'm not going to hurt anyone who
doesn't deserve it . . ."

Before Helen could ask her what the hell she meant
by that, Leis strode into Serendipity's dining room. It
was packed to the gills, full of seated couples and families
doing the tourist thing. The ceiling was white pressed tin,
and just below it hung the restaurant's famous Tiffany
glass structure that was a mix of pop art, twisted wires,
and glass butterflies. Helen thought it stood out against
the whitewash of the surrounding walls like a wrecked
car on the West Side Highway. Red hearts of all shapes
and sizes were stuck to every wall.

As Helen watched Leis walk through the crowd, a
few heads turned. Helen shook her head. Leis was stubborn over simple stuff, like policing who ate what food
in the common room fridge. God only knew what she'd
do if she found James in here . . .

Helen watched the crowd fall silent as Leis wandered
through the tables. The waitstaff didn't quite know what
to do about a woman with a crossbow in the shop. They
just stood there, holding large cut crystal chalices filled
with their signature frozen hot chocolates, an iced slush
of chocolate topped with a mountain of whipped cream
drizzled with even more chocolate on top. They were so
huge a small child could probably bathe in one of them.
Helen looked closer at the tables around the room.
Practically every table had one or two of them on it.

Never having tasted one, Helen was curious, but
turned back to Leis, who was looking at one particular couple a few tables away where she had caught the

eye of the man sitting there. Leis dashed over to it and grabbed the well-dressed man by his tie, pulling it tight. The woman he was sitting with started to stand, but Leis pointed her crossbow at her and used her foot to kick her back into her seat.

"Hey!" the woman shouted.

Leis shot her a look over the crossbow that killed any further outbursts.

The man cleared his throat. "Do . . . do I know you?" he asked, looking confused.

Leis tightened her grip, not giving the man an inch of wiggle room. "What's your name?"

The man looked perplexed, his mouth hanging open, stuttering. "D–D–Darrin."

"Darrin *what*?"

"Darrin Georgiou."

Leis searched his face while Helen watched in horror. Something in his eyes told her that there was nothing but fear behind them. Leis let go of his tie, and he slumped back in his seat, not daring to move.

"It's not him," Leis said. She straightened, her shoulders relaxing.

"Ya think?" Helen asked. She looked around the room, the eyes of everyone burning into her. "I could have told you that wasn't James. Can't you identify your ex? I know you've dated a lot, but it would probably help if you could at least remember their faces." Helen's gaze met the woman's at the table and she smiled weakly. She could imagine her later telling the cops all about the attractive, leggy blonde and her shorter, less attractive companion. "Sorry about that. I think my friend is tripping. C'mon, Leis. Let's get out of here."

"We're not leaving," Leis said. She scanned the sea of faces. "Listen up! I'm looking for a guy."

Most of the crowd was silent, but one of the men at a nearby table still managed to snicker. Leis turned on him, leveling the crossbow.

"Funny," she said. "Aren't all us girlie girls, right?" With the business end of a crossbow pointed at him, the man fell silent. Leis turned from him to address the room. "Not sure what he might look like right about now, but he probably goes by one of several names. James Valens, John Dearly, Jason Love, Jeffrey L'Amour . . . he gets a kick out of all those names. Me? Not so much. Anyone heard of him?"

The crowd looked back at her with blank faces. Helen thought that if this had been a less touristy kind of place—more true New York, maybe—someone would have been telling them to shut up and sit down by now, but instead the room remained quiet.

"Fine," Leis said. "Have it your way. *Don't* talk."

"Great," Helen said, feeling a bit relieved. "Your ex isn't here. Can we leave now?"

Leis shook her head. "He's been here, though."

"How can you tell?" Helen asked.

Leis took a deep breath and scrunched up her face. "Love," she said, tapping a finger against her ear. "It's in the air. Listen."

Helen concentrated, listening to the sounds of the room. There was now a low whisper among the crowd, but Helen was sure no one dared raise their voice enough to catch Leis' attention. Above it all was the sound of tinkling glass . . . from above. Helen and Leis both looked up. The crazy mobile was rocking back and forth, pieces of metal and glass brushing up against each other with the gentle sway. Three small, humanoid *things* moved in and out along the structure. Helen's heart raced—she had never seen anything like them in her life. The leathery-winged little beasts clung to the art piece with sharp talons, looking like some perverted form of monster children with greasy little mops of hair. At the moment, they were trying to undo the couplings holding the structure to the ceiling.

"What the hell are those?" Helen asked, not quite trusting her eyes.

Leis circled another table to get a better view. "I'm not sure exactly," she said, unfastening what Helen imagined was some kind of safety on the crossbow, "but they don't look like anything I'm familiar with. But at a best guess? Cherubim."

One of the gnarled little creatures looked down at Helen. Its eyes widened and its lips pulled back as it emitted a shrieking hiss, causing the crowd to erupt into chaos as they leapt from their seats screaming. The beast stayed focused on Helen as it leapt into flight. Helen dove under a nearby table as it passed overhead.

Leis hadn't even moved. She tracked the creature in its flight across the room using the shiny metal tip of the crossbow bolt as her guide. Aiming slightly ahead of it, Leis pulled the trigger. The bolt flew over the crowd and hit the creature square in its chest, cutting through its leathery skin like it was paper. The creature curled in on itself, falling from the air and slamming into the lap of a stunned little girl a few tables away. She let out a scream that was far worse than the one the creature had made. The little girl shoved the monster off her lap and burst from her chair, her shrill screams breaking the spell over the dumbfounded remains of the crowd, sending the last of the patrons running double time to clear the place.

Helen's table had been overturned in everyone's rush for the doors, leaving her curled in an exposed ball out in the open. Leis grabbed Helen by the arm, and lifted her to her feet.

"Get up," Leis said, "before you get trampled."

"Sorry," Helen said, shaken. She pulled her arm from Leis and stared at the dead creature on the floor not too far from them. "You sure this is a cherub? I thought they were supposed to be, you know, cute chubby little kids."

"Doesn't look that way to me," Leis said, already pulling back the crossbow's drawstring and notching another bolt. "That's what you get for studying for your history of art final on Wikipedia."

Leis turned back to the other two creatures still high overhead. The closer of the two was hitting one of the restraints holding the mobile in place, causing the structure to sway back and forth precariously.

"Stop them," Helen shouted. "Before they destroy it!"

"That doesn't matter," Leis said, firing off a second shot. "All that matters is that they die."

The bolt blurred through the air, but the mobile was swaying far too much to get a clear shot at the second monster. Instead, it smashed through one of the panes of glass and kept going, tearing a hole in one of the creature's wings before lodging in its arm. With a screech, the monster started to fall, flapping wildly to no avail. It caught one of the metal bars along the bottom of the structure, flipping over and dangling in midair.

"Crap," Leis said, running underneath the struggling monster. The creature's feet flailed over her head as she jumped up and caught it by a bony ankle. The mobile pitched wildly, but the creature's grip broke and it came free. Leis used its momentum and slammed its body straight into the floor. In an instant, it rolled like a cat trying to right itself, but Leis' foot was quicker and she pressed her boot into its neck.

Helen looked on in horror. "Jesus, Leis, when did you become such a killing machine?"

Leis twisted her foot until the creature's neck snapped. The winged beast thrashed once more, then lay still. "All's fair in love and war," she said.

Exasperated, Helen shook her head. "Leis—"

Leis cut her off. "Don't 'Leis' me," she said, but didn't get any further.

A cacophony filled the room, and they looked up to see the mobile crash down on them. The last of the creatures rode down with it, cackling maniacally like a "Gremlins" version of "Doctor Strangelove." There was nothing to do but cover their faces and hope for the best.

The mobile hit the floor with a thunderous crash, pinning them both underneath. Glass and metal was everywhere. The Tiffany butterflies had shattered, their once beautiful wings now jagged shards that hung from broken twists of wire. Helen's lower half of her body was caught in the tangle and she looked over at Leis to see if she was okay while she cautiously tried to free herself.

Leis was dead center under the mess of it all and looked dazed by the impact, but a second later, she was fighting for her freedom. Pinned, Leis heaved upward and the mobile moved a little, allowing her to lift it. Getting to her knees, Leis repositioned herself to support the broken structure's weight, then carefully stood and started to work her way out from under it. Helen was impressed by her friend's strength, but it was a fleeting feeling amidst the chaos of the situation, especially when she saw the last creature climbing up the side of Leis's body.

Its sharp talons were digging into Leis' shirt, but Leis didn't seem to notice. She looked too busy concentrating on the tangle of broken mobile all around her. Helen was too winded to even call out to her. It wasn't until the creature dug its talons deep into the flesh on Leis's left side and a small stream of blood began running down her shirt that she even seemed to notice. She flinched and finally looked down at the little monster hanging there with grim determination on its twisted face.

Helen knew that she herself would have been screaming by now, but not Leis. She looked both horrified and repelled, but remained quiet. She let go of the mobile, its full weight dropping onto her shoulders. She teetered under the force of the blow, but remained upright.

With ferocity on her face, Leis grabbed at the monstrosity and pulled. It was reluctant to let go, but in the end, there was no contest. Leis tore it free from her shirt, the creature writhing in her hands. She adjusted her grip, taking it by its wings, making it impossible for the creature to get a good swipe at her.

Helen could see Leis tiring from the struggling creature's ferocious movements. With the weight of the damned mobile still crushing her, there was little Leis could do other than maintain her current position. Helen had to help her and quick.

"Leis!" Helen called, finally able to move now that the mobile was resting on Leis' back. She rolled out from under the mobile toward one of the large glass vessels of frozen hot chocolate that had fallen on the floor nearby. Remarkably, its contents were still intact right down to the mountain of whipped cream topping it. Helen wrapped her left hand around it. She pulled her arm back then slid the whole thing forward, launching it across the floor toward Leis. The contents threatened to spill out, but the chalice's weight and speed helped it bowl any obstacles out of its way. It slid to a stop at Leis' feet.

Leis dropped back to her knees. The mobile crushed down on her, pushing her down to the restaurant floor, but thankfully not before she got her free hand under her.

The creature was able to get its feet under it as well, giving it a bit of leverage. The creature twisted its gnarled upper torso, pulling its wings free from Leis' hand. Turning, it pulled back its lips, revealing dangerous rows of tiny teeth. The monster lunged for the hand that had been holding it, but Leis was faster. Her hand flashed behind its grotesque head, grabbing the stringy patch of greasy hair and forcing its face into the frozen drink.

Unable to breathe, the creature went wild trying to free itself, but Leis didn't let up. The drowning monster thrashed around, flapping its wings like a bug caught in a zapper. Leis held it there until the strength ebbed from the creature as the fight went out of it, and after one last, convulsive effort, it went limp. Leis let go of it and it remained face down in the dessert, unmoving.

Helen worked her way over, lifting the fallen mobile up to help her friend out from underneath. Leis stood after first recovering her crossbow. Helen looked around as she waited for Leis. The shambles of a restaurant was empty, with the sound of sirens rising in the distance, growing ever closer.

"We should go," Leis said.

Helen dropped the mobile. It fell to the floor of the restaurant and the last of the Tiffany glass fell from it, sounding like an angry set of wind chimes. Helen dusted whipped cream and glass off her clothes. She looked over at Leis. "Go where? He wasn't here, remember?"

Leis was already walking off toward the door, grabbing the wintery cape she'd left by it. "But he *had* been here," she said. "Or didn't you notice the little winged beasties?"

Helen held her arms out as if showcasing the debris around them like some kind of crisis-oriented Vanna White. "We came. I saw. You conquered."

Leis laughed, despite what had just happened.

Helen smiled back. "So if your ex isn't here, where is he then?"

Leis held the door open, waiting for Helen to cross the room and join her. "He's moving downtown," Leis said. "And I think I know where."

Helen gestured out the door. "Lead on, McRough."

On the street, Helen had to practically run to keep up with her much taller roommate. For mid-February, it was uncommonly warm. Helen wondered how Leis could stand it under that black fashionista cloak of hers, but she guessed if you wanted to hide a crossbow and who knew what else, it was a small price to pay. Even with all that extra bulk, following Leis was still no easy task.

"Slow down," Helen called after her. Leis paused, but only long enough for Helen to catch up before she took off again. Helen followed, this time keeping pace. "Leis, this is starting to get a little ridiculous. We've been all over Manhattan. We checked the carriage rides in Central Park. You spooked the horses. Then it was The Cloisters. You spooked the tourists. Then the skating rink at Rockerfeller Center. I'm pretty sure you spooked someone there, but it was hard to tell, given the spastic way everyone was skating."

"Can't blame me for that last one," Leis said. "If you don't like it, go back to the dorm room."

"I am *not* sitting alone in my dorm room on today of all days," Helen said, "and I'm sure as hell not going to any of the NYU mixers. I'm not that hardcore of a loser quite yet."

"Give it until senior year," Leis said.

"You're so jaded," Helen said. "That's what you get for studying both cultural *and* social anthropology at the same time."

"No," Leis said, stopping and spinning around. "That's what I get for giving my heart out wholly and getting it diced up and handed back to me time after time."

"So . . . what?" Helen asked. "Because you had a few bad relationships, you're going to take out Love?"

"Not just a few bad relationships," Leis asked. "Try thirty-six of them in three years. That's messed up."

"Okay, fine, but gunning for Cupid? I think that's going to piss a lot of people off."

Leis eyes were dark and she gave Helen a dark, bitter smile, shaking her head. "Gotta love a cultist," she said.

"Huh?" Helen asked. "How is Cupid a cultist?"

Leis wrinkled her nose. "Well, he had a cult, anyway. Back then, he was considered one of the most powerful gods because he held sway over everything—animals, the dead, even the gods of Olympus. A god who could control the other gods? That's pretty powerful, if you ask me."

Helen's face went white as the gravity of it all hit her. "And you still think this is a good idea, trying to take him down?"

Leis nodded. "I'm not interested in humiliating my exes or arguing with any of them all over again," she said. "They're really just middlemen in all this. I'm cutting to the root of the problem. And for your information, it's not Cupid that we're after."

"So . . . who then?" Helen asked. "Saint Valentine?"

"Not exactly," Leis said. "Hell, they're not even sure who Saint Valentine really was."

"Really?" Helen asked.

"Really." Leis nodded. "There were at least three possibilities. One was a bishop in what the Italians now call Terni, another was a Roman priest . . . hell, the last one wasn't even in Italy. He lived somewhere in Africa. This creature that I'm looking for isn't any of them. We're dealing with something completely different. Something older."

"Is this from one of your classes?" Helen asked. "I didn't know NYU dug so deep."

Leis shrugged. "Some of it," she said. "The rest came from a lot of research time spent in the older parts of the main library. I spent hours looking through it all, trying to find out what I could."

"Yeah, well, maybe *that's* why you have so much trouble with dating. You ever think of that?"

Leis turned and glared at Helen, who threw her hands up in the air. "Just saying."

Leis turned and started walking off again. Helen hurried after her. "Go on," she said. "Please."

"I was studying up on my target," Leis said, continuing to get her nerd on. "Call him Cupid, call him Eros, but call him the god of love either way. The Greeks and the Romans have similar stories about him despite their cultural differences, but he predates those pantheons. Even the Christians sucked him into the Valentine Day's mythos, but that's a sham too."

"Wait," Helen said, confused. "Now you're saying Valentine's Day isn't Valentine's Day?"

"Far from it," Leis said, stopping again. "The whole saint construct of the holiday was just a whitewash by the church they concocted when they wanted to convert others to their beliefs. They took the dates that were important to a culture and superimposed new traditions over them, hoping that their ways would be adopted in place of older pagan rituals. For instance, ever hear of Lupercalia?"

Helen shook her head.

Leis grabbed her face and squeezed her cheeks. "See what a good job your Catholic upbringing did at overwriting it!"

Helen brushed her hand away. "Knock it off," she said. "What's Lupercalia?"

"According to legend, it was an ancient pagan ritual that focused both on purification and fertility. Its roots were in honor of the she-wolf that cared for the tossed-aside infants Romulus and Remus. As part of the celebration, they'd wheel out the Vestal Virgins and have them do a blood sacrifice of a dog and two goats. Then two young men would happily run through the city striking women along the way with strips of hide from the goat. These supposedly purified any women touched or helped barren women become fertile again."

Helen winced at the thought of a blood sacrifice. "Sounds like a party," she said.

"The Christians didn't think so," Leis said, with a dark smile. "They replaced the whole festival with one honoring one of their saints instead. Valentine, the patron saint of lovers. People would pull the names of a saint out of a box and spend the next year trying to follow it like some sort of role model."

"So that's why we used to build boxes for cards on Valentine's Day in grade school?" Helen asked.

Leis nodded. "We've more or less put the kibosh on

the whole saint emulation thing, but that's it in a nut-shell." She stopped and looked up at the building in front of them. "We're here."

Helen stopped beside her, looking up too. She knew the place well, even without its upper windows lit up red in the shape of a giant heart. Where else was one expected to go on Valentine's Day in New York City *but* the Empire State Building?

Security used *to be tight at all the landmark buildings right after 9/11*, Helen thought, *but so many years later? Not so much.* Not that Helen had been worrying about getting herself in, but she had already seen Leis' crossbow in action. Who knew what else lay inside the folds of her cloak? Helen needn't have worried. When the guard saw two cute twentysomething NYU students flash their IDs, he waved them toward the bank of elevators without a second glance. A rush of people crowded in after them, pushing them both up against the back wall of the tiny space.

Helen felt her stomach drop as the tremendous speed of the express elevator pulled at her.

"We going to see if Cary Grant and Deborah Kerr are up here?" Helen asked.

"I was thinking more of Tom Hanks and Meg Ryan," Leis said with a smile. Her face grew more and more grim the higher they went, and by the time the elevator slowed to a stop and the doors opened, Leis looked dark and focused. Her expression actually frightened Helen.

After the elevator emptied, Leis rushed out of the doors, leaving Helen to jump out before the elevator doors closed. "Hey!" Helen called. "What the hell do you want me to do?"

Leis spun around, her cloak twirling around her in a

perfect circle. Her alert eyes darted about as she replied, "Just act nonchalant. Enjoy the view or something."

Before Helen could respond, Leis whirled around again and ran out onto the observation deck just on the other side of the small, enclosed art deco lobby. Not sure of what to do, Helen walked off in the opposite direction and headed through the nearest set of doors.

The wind at the top of the Empire State Building made it significantly chillier here than on the street, making her wish she had worn a heavy cloak too. Couples were packed around the entire deck arm in arm, hand in hand, almost all of them staring lovingly off at the setting sun. Helen found an open spot along the high ornate fence surrounding the deck and stared out over the city, impressed as always with the wonder that was Manhattan.

After a few moments of drinking it all in, Helen turned and leaned back against the fence, taking in the crowd. Not everyone was a couple. A few hopeful romantics, both male and female, seemed to be here by themselves. Helen watched as Leis nearly bowled one of them over in a purposeful patrol around the deck's perimeter. The man swerved to avoid her, nearly crashing into Helen.

"Easy," Helen said, patting him on the shoulder. "Sorry about my friend."

The man smiled, revealing quiet confidence in what Helen discovered were a gorgeous set of deep blue eyes. "Your friend seems a little crazed there," he said, shoving his hands back into his coat pockets.

Something in his smile felt contagious, and Helen couldn't help but smile back at him. "Yeah, she can get a little excitable."

"So . . ." Helen started, "are you here with someone?"

She dreaded his answer, but was relieved when he shook his head.

"Actually, no. I thought I'd take my chances by chilling up here, taking in the view, see if anyone else had the same idea to come up here all alone ..."

"I'm Helen," she said, holding out her hand. "Helen Leda."

The man took her hand and Helen was surprised at how warm it was, how inviting. He raised it to his lips and kissed it. *Sure,* Helen thought, *it's a bit corny, but sweet nonetheless.*

"Enchanted," he said. "My name's Jason. Jason Eros."

At the mention of his name, Helen's face fell. "Oh ... shit ..."

Jason cocked his head at her, still holding her hand. "What? What's wrong?"

Leis was standing right behind him. A loop of ornate chain was stretched between her two hands and she threw it over Jason until it came down across his arms and she pulled it tight. "Gotcha!" she cried.

Jason's arm fell to his sides. Leis lashed her foot out behind one of his knees and dropped him to the observation deck tiles.

"Leis," Helen called, "don't! He's a nice guy."

Leis glanced up at her and shook her head, an amused look on her face. "Sure he is," Leis said. "Let me guess. Came off as rather sweet, rather charming, felt yourself warming to him quickly ... ?"

Helen nodded.

Leis pushed Jason over, planting him face first onto the observation deck before rolling him over on his back again. She bent over and looked him in the eye. "Not a sincere moment to all of it," she said. "Calling yourself

Jason Eros now, are you? Aren't you just a clever little creature of habit?"

The chain wrapped around the man couldn't have been thicker than a necklace, yet Jason seemed totally immobilized. "What the hell is that?" Helen asked.

"It's amazing what the university has in its archeological archives," Leis said. "This is made from the same material as the crossbow bolt tips. It's all Hephaestian steel."

"I know this one," Helen said. "Hephaestus. Mythical Roman blacksmith, right?"

"So close," Leis said. "Greek. Roman version of him is named Vulcan."

The observation deck crowd around them had all backed off considerably. Leis grabbed Jason's face and turned it toward Helen as well.

"I knew you'd take my bait," she said.

"Excuse me?" Helen asked. "I'm your *bait*?"

"Yep," Leis continued without any real reaction. "See, I knew I'd have trouble identifying him. Wasn't sure what form he'd be in, but he can be oh-so-predictable when it comes to a pretty lady."

Helen couldn't believe what she was hearing. "So you brought me along as bait?"

"Don't get your panties twisted," Leis said. "It worked, didn't it?"

Helen felt the rage rising in her. She hated being used. It was one thing when Leis drank the last of Helen's *clearly* marked orange juice in the fridge, but putting her in harm's way on purpose? It was beyond the beyond. Before she could stop herself, Helen stalked over to Leis, reached down with both hands, and shoved her hard. Leis stumbled backward, rising to her feet to keep her balance.

"Hey!" Leis shouted. "What the hell?"

"What are you going to do?" Helen asked. "Stake me through the heart with one of your Hephaestian bolts?"

"Keep pushing me around," Leis said, "and it just might be an option."

Leis' eyes flared with rage, but Helen didn't back down. She was too pissed at being dangled like a worm on a hook. Leis threw open her cloak, her arms shooting out to shove Helen. It stung, but Helen pushed back, grabbing Leis's cloak and trying to pull it closed in the hopes of containing her. The wind whipped against them as they struggled, the cloak enveloping them, blinding Helen as she held on to it for dear life.

When the wind dropped back to normal, Helen batted away the end of the cloak covering her face, but almost wished she hadn't. Leis had pulled her crossbow free and was aiming at her. Helen let go of the cloak, backing away as fast as she could and raising her arms in hopeless defense. Leis fired and Helen closed her eyes, bracing for the impact.

The crossbow's string twanged. The thrum of it firing hummed in the air, but although Helen waited for its impact, she didn't feel a thing. She opened her eyes and looked around. Jason stood behind her, the almost-removed chain draped across one of his shoulders. The crossbow bolt protruded from his shoulder, a look of pain spreading across his face.

Helen felt Leis push her out of the way, sending her stumbling. By the time she righted herself, Leis had the chain in one hand and pulled it tight, cinching it around Jason's neck and under his shoulder. With her free hand she grabbed the bolt and twisted.

Jason let out an inhuman scream, and Helen was

surprised to see that he no longer looked like Jason. His body had morphed. In seconds he was flipping from form to form, becoming a whole string of people Helen had seen Leis date over the past few years—the drummer who had stolen her Bose system, the lighting tech who'd squatted in the room for three months, then the barista from down the corner on West 3rd Street. Dozens of faces flashed by, but they were moving so fast Helen couldn't follow them all. Eventually, the scream turned into a far more feral sound, almost a howl of pain and as if to match it, Jason's form shifted to that of a man with a wolf's head. Its tongue lolled out of the side of its mouth through its sharp teeth, but with the chain of Hephaestus wrapped around him, he seemed powerless to do anything.

"Bad doggie," Leis said. She lashed out with her fist, hitting him in the gut and dropping him to his knees. "Lykaion couldn't resist coming out for Lupercalia now, could he?" Leis kicked him, catching him in the side this time and knocking him over. The creature growled weakly, but didn't move.

"Stop it," Helen said, despite being horrified by the creature before her. She was surprised at how hurt she felt watching him suffer. "You're killing him!"

"I'm not killing him," Leis said, rolling her eyes. She knelt next to the wolfman, grabbing his face and turning it to face her. "Something like him can't be killed, am I right?" She grabbed him by his snout and nodded his head for him. Leis voice turned mocking. "You can't kill love!"

"Jesus," Helen said, "if that's the case, then why did you come here?"

Leis looked up at her. "To put him on notice," she said, turning back to him. She pulled the arrow from his shoulder. The man wolf hissed in pain, then slowly turned back into the man Helen recognized as Jason, albeit a bloody version of him. "Look at you, all happy with this Valentine's action going on all around you."

"Not really my holiday . . ." he said, panting. "Covers some of my old ways, though. Just works out nice that way."

"Lovely," Leis said, pulling the chain tight around him to shut him up. "Point is, I'm done with you. I've had it."

"Don't be ridiculous," he said, laughing through his pain. Leis stood up and kicked him viciously in the face. Blood went everywhere, and again, Helen felt overwhelmed with feelings for the poor man. She knew it had to be a part of his power, but she couldn't help it.

"Shut *up*," Leis said. "I've had enough heartache. If I catch you cavorting about with an arrow in my presence, I'll do more than kick the stuffing out of you next time, got it? You think you want to tackle me? Just look at how quickly I found the instruments to bring you down. You come after me again and I'll be sure I *do* have the tools to end you. Now let's hope it doesn't come to that. For now, though, if you see me coming, you walk the other way. Got it?"

The bloody man on the ground hesitated, but then nodded without saying a word.

"Good," Leis said. She uncoiled the chain around him and tucked it under her cloak. She looked at Helen. "Let's get out of here."

Helen hesitated.

"Let's *go*," Leis said, impatient and still fueled by her victory.

Helen shook her head. "I don't think so," she said.

"What?"

"Just go," Helen said. She walked over to the curled-up figure on the ground. "I'm staying."

"Are you kidding?" Leis said, on the verge of bitter laughter. "You're not falling for this, are you? It's love. It's a sham."

Helen gave a weak smile. "Yeah, I know, but the way it's making me feel . . ."

"It will go away when this all turns to shit, believe me."

"But if this is the only way I can get it," Helen said, looking down with concern at the wounded crumple of a man that was Jason Eros, "then I'll accept that if the time comes."

"Ha!" Leis said, actually laughing out loud this time. "Not *if*. When. When the time comes, and it will, Helen."

Helen turned away from Leis and completely back to Jason, kneeling next to him, checking him over.

"Fine," Leis said, storming off toward the elevators, "but don't expect me to be back at the dorm when you get back. Go crazy, no, really. Maybe you'll have little wolf babies, or some of those creepy cherubim. If nothing else, maybe this will keep him off my back."

Realizing only the tourists and clichéd lovebirds were listening, she stormed off.

Helen didn't even notice Leis was gone and with every passing moment, it mattered less and less. She was too busy worrying over poor beaten and bruised Jason to care about much else.

Jason looked up at her with a tremulous smile. Helen's heart accelerated to an immediate flutter, not even minding the blood on his face that was already drying and flaking away. Why should she mind? Didn't that just make him look a little more rugged?

"Happy Valentine's Day," he said, that irresistible smile growing stronger.

"Are ... are you okay?" Helen asked, standing. She offered her hand to him. He took it and she felt an even stronger spark of connection pass between them. She knew it was just his power at work, that it was just the power to charm, but she didn't care. After all, she had never been sure if the love in her life previous to this moment had ever been real anyway. At least Jason's power gave her a thrill that certainly felt real enough. "Seriously, are you okay? Leis beat you pretty badly."

"Yeah," he said, standing and brushing off his clothing, the blood and debris fading away as he did so. "Don't worry about me. I'm used to it. It happens all the time."

MURDER, SHE WORKSHOPPED

Kristine Kathryn Rusch

Spending six weeks at a writers' workshop in the Midwest would drive an empath insane. Or maybe it would make the empath suicidal. Or homicidal, depending on the emotions swirling around the empath that day.

I think about such things because 1) I am trapped at just such a writers' workshop, and 2) I am in the process of divorcing said empath. He's at home, with all our belongings and our cats, while I'm here for week four, when my target finally arrives. Fortunately for me, said empath (who shall remain nameless) didn't get the bright idea to clear out our bank accounts until yesterday. I had that bright idea three hours before I started researching my lawyer months ago. All the money once labeled ours is now in several accounts now labeled mine, and no matter how hard said empath screams over the phone, he'll never be able to find them.

Empathy works two ways. He can feel all of my emotions when we talk and I can feel all of his. His are extremely powerful. Mine are generally muted, which explains the initial attraction.

It also explains why I do what I do.

I kill people. Well, not people per se. Evil magical creatures that misuse a human form. Lest you think I am insane myself and use this explanation to rationalize my murderous tendencies, let me simply tell you that I have few murderous tendencies. That's why I get the jobs I do. I'm a highly skilled, highly paid assassin who works only once every four to five years.

I also happen to have a 100% success rate.

Which might completely vanish on this particular job, distracted as I am by said empath and by the silly workshop itself.

Here's the problem: I'm thinking seriously of retiring and taking up writing as a new career. Secretly, I've always wanted to write.

But if you had asked me—oh, say, three weeks ago— which would be harder, becoming a writer or an assassin who specialized in magical creatures that misuse human form, I would have answered writer every time.

Then I met the first three of my so-called professional instructors. The best thing I've learned at this workshop is this: *if they can become professional writers, then anyone can do it.*

Sure wish I'd known that twenty years and five assassinations ago.

But I wouldn't have ended up here on the campus of a major state university at a program for serious unpublished writers taught by the professionals. Theoretically, I'm here to assassinate someone.

In reality, I'm taking these six weeks to learn how to write.

So I'm a busy little writer bee, handing in a story per week to each new instructor and letting my fellow students shred me in public. At first, I thought I'd get

assistance from the instructors, and while the first one
was helpful, the instructor for week two was more interested in fomenting discord—which was relatively easy
to do, considering most of the students have nothing to
do except read about two short stories per night.

The instructors come from different fiction genres
and are supposed to give us insights into their various disciplines. As I'm learning, the use of the word
"discipline" along with the word "writer" verges on
oxymoronic.

That oxymoron seems to apply more than usual to
week three's instructor, a has-been award-winning western writer who hasn't published a book in more than a
decade. She's subbing for a bigger name who got sick
and couldn't come. She's always the sub at this workshop because she needs the money. She doesn't have a
lot to teach except gloom and doom, and so after Discord from the week before, she's only making things
worse.

My handlers warned me this would happen. Apparently this workshop has a pattern. By the middle, the
inmates—I mean students—have forgotten everything
they knew about home and have now become convinced
that the workshop is the world.

Weeks Three and Four are when the big blowups happen. Students quit, affairs end, and fistfights occur. One
group stripped the least liked student naked, painted
her green, and carried her like an offering to the dean of
the English Department.

That was the year the workshop had to change university sponsors.

I was told to pay special attention starting in week
three, because my target would arrive in week four, and

she would make sure this workshop was one for the record books.

My target, Margarite Lawson, writes lurid bestselling novels based on actual crimes. Margarite picks a famous crime, changes the names, maybe even moves it to a new location, and gives it her personal spin. The weird thing about Margarite's books is that the more she published, the more likely she was to have a hand in solving the famous crime. In fact, in the latter five books or so, the famous crime became famous because Margarite was on-site when it happened.

It's become a joke that whenever Margarite shows up, someone is going to die. In fact, my workshop has been nervously kidding each other about this since our first night together. Everyone, that is, except me.

Because to me, Margarite's talent for finding the crime in a given community isn't coincidence. It's part of her unnatural charm.

Margarite arrives on Friday night of week three, so that she can confer with the western writer before the poor sap leaves on Sunday morning. If all goes according to script, someone on this university campus will die on Saturday.

Margarite will organize the police investigation, handle the media, and solve the case by the following Friday. About two years from now, she'll published a novel about the case.

She'll get wealthier while she's feeding the demon within.

My assignment is simple: I'm supposed to stop her once and for all. If possible, I take her out on Friday night, before anyone else gets hurt.

But after nearly three full weeks undercover in this rather unique circle of hell, I'm not sure I want to prevent anyone from getting hurt. I'm tired of the drama, the petty jealousies, the bickering, and the backbiting.

These people need something real to whine about.

And I figure Margarite Lawson is going to give that to them.

Nine AM Friday morning, the workshop meets as usual. We have full run of a graduate student dorm that opens into a private courtyard. At one end of that courtyard is the so-called lounge—really an oversized conference room filled with uncomfortable upholstered chairs, flimsy tables, and one extremely loud Coke machine. Laptop users have to make certain the batteries are charged before they arrive, or fight for a seat nearest one of two unused outlets on the only wall without a window. That wall is covered with whiteboards, because—apparently—in university circles, chalkboards have become passé.

My "student" laptop—a battered first generation iBook—is always charged. Whenever I'm out in public, I carry that thing.

My business laptop stays in my silly little graduate student suite, under lock and key. The laptop is unlike anything anyone around here has seen, except maybe in some of the secret R&D labs around campus. Maybe not even there.

Because this thing is high-powered—not just with tech, but with the occasional magical connection. And how to explain magic to the nonbelievers in my audience? It's simple, really.

Magic slips into the real world. Or the real world slips into the magical world, depending on your point of view.

Mine is the point of view of a person who uncomfortably straddles both worlds. I can see the magical, even though I have little magic myself.

I have little magic, but I have access to magic. Thanks to engineers with magic who also happen to design computers, I have at my fingertips the simplest of spells. I also have commonsense nonmagical remedies to magical potions, and other such things that occasionally come in handy when dealing with the other side of reality.

In truth, I've only used those things with said empath's friends. In my work, I've used the standard gun/knife/whatever's handy to complete the job.

Which is looming.

That's what I'm thinking as I approach my usual chair. It's a wingback with high arms that sits directly across the room from the instructor's chair.

I staked out this chair on day one of the workshop, and although one of my less observant compatriots tried to take it from me on day two, no one will ever try that again.

They say I'm touchy.

I'm just a little protective.

The problem is that I don't look touchy. If you were to walk into our little critique session on this Friday morning, I'm the one you'd ignore. I'm older than most of the class for one thing. I also have cultivated the don't-pay-attention-to-me vibe so essential in my job.

Maybe it's one of my little magics.

If you glanced at me, you'd see a once-pretty woman who allowed time and lack of attention to make her seem faded. But if you looked, really looked, you'd notice a few anomalies. I wear baggy clothes to give the impression of flab, when in truth I have none. I also have a hard time hiding the intelligence in my eyes, so I look through my eyelashes a lot like an unrepentant Southern belle.

My fellow students have yet to notice these things about me, but the instructor week two, Discord, noticed right away. He never picked on me, even though I was the one who had two (rather mediocre) stories in for critique that week. Instead, he avoided me as much as possible, making him rank just a bit higher in my mind than he normally would have.

Apparently, he became a bestselling thriller writer through observation, not through all that tough-talk he imparted to the other students.

But I digress.

I also arrive at my seat before everyone else, so I can watch them enter. I ignore most of them. They're the background for my two missions. But a handful of people are impossible to miss.

Like our teaching assistant, Raj O'Driscoll. He's a glorified gofer, and not bright enough to realize that should anything go wrong with this workshop, he will get the blame.

Then there is the faculty advisor, Lawrence B. Hallerhaven. Hallerhaven has taken on the job to schmooze with the famous writers. He's terrible at planning and even worse at following through. He leaves all of that to poor Raj, who is spending this morning preparing for Margarite Lawson.

Apparently, she made an unusual list of demands before she agreed to come. Raj is trying to meet those demands before her arrival tonight.

All of his running about makes me nervous, and I'm just sitting in my chair, typing random thoughts in my student laptop as the rest of the class arrive.

They're carrying a variety of things: the laptops, hard-copy manuscripts covered with their inept scrawls, and various poisons from lattes to regular coffees to donuts to apples to leftover pizza.

We don't have a lot to say to each other any more except *Shut up* or *Move your ass, I need some room here* or *Were we supposed to read Steve's story for today?*, so there's a lot of rustling without a lot of conversation.

That's okay. It gives me a chance to figure out, once and for all, who is going to die.

That person has to have no redeeming characteristics. This is the person we all love to hate. When that person dies, we're all going to be relieved he's dead. We'll just wonder why someone hasn't killed him sooner.

As the class wanders in, I contemplate the possible candidates.

The three likeliest victims arrive in a clump. These three are miserable and proud of it, because they believe (erroneously, in my opinion) that misery begets book contracts.

First through the door is Hamlet Thorshov who deserves the Most Miserable Person of the Workshop Award just because his horrible parents decided to name him Hamlet. He's an underdeveloped twenty-something of very obvious Russian lineage. His white-blond hair matches the color of his white-blond skin and fails to accent his pale blue eyes. He has somehow managed to find T-shirts that are too small for him, and he wears a watch half the size of his arm.

His watch is where the trouble begins, every single workshop. The damn thing can probably fly an airplane on its own. And he toys with it in the middle of the first critique, pressing buttons as if he were setting the stopwatch for his mid-morning run (if he ever exercised, which he most clearly does not).

No one tries to get him to stop any longer, although two days ago, Carlotta Sternke—one of the other three troublemakers—tried to cover the thing in bubble wrap, just to silence it.

That was probably the only time the workshop cheered for her. Carlotta Sternke was the workshop goat long before we decided to pick on Hamlet.

Carlotta is chubby and shows way too much skin through fishnet stockings, tops that deliberately leave her stomach bare, and leather skirts that are both too short and too tight. Her lips are always covered with black gloss and she outlines her eyes in late season raccoon.

Her hair is black with a white streak that might be deliberate, although with Carlotta, it's impossible to tell. She's as unpleasant as her clothing, with a high-pitched nervous giggle that makes me long for fingernails running along blackboards.

She feels like she needs to police everyone—hence the bubble wrap on Hamlet's giant watch. And the person she loves to police more than anyone else is the third in our nasty triumvirate.

Norman Zell makes a good first impression. He's tall, lanky, and reasonably good-looking. He's embarrassed by the name "Norman," so he insists that everyone he meet call him Zell, which, I have to admit, is an improvement.

The problem is that Zell has the attention span of a gnat and the energy level of a hummingbird. He's in constant motion—either one knee jiggles or an arm or every single finger (and not in unison). In the first week, he managed to sleep with or proposition every woman here (I said no with probably more enthusiasm than I needed to express), and made it clear by the end of the week that he considered every woman who tumbled into his bed to be a conquest.

A conquest that he had the right to write about in Margarite Lawson roman-a-clef style. Only he wasn't nearly as good at changing the names or the events. The instructor in week two actually made Zell stand in front of the group and apologize to everyone.

Zell burst into tears in the middle of his apology and yet somehow didn't command any sympathy. We all had had enough by then, and even though the tears were probably genuine, they wouldn't change his behavior. And sure enough, by week's end, Zell was sleeping his way through the cafeteria staff, and the first story he turned in this week is titled, "Love in A Time of Meatballs."

This morning, Hamlet, Carlotta, and Zell manage to sit equidistant from each other, forming a perfect equilateral triangle. They are getting out the first story for critique when the door opens again, and Margarite Lawson sweeps into the room.

She's taller than I imagined she would be, blonder, and prettier. Or maybe that's just how her human covering manifests itself in person. She wears a gauze lilac tunic over black pants, and manages to appear imposing and charming at the very same time.

I can see the magic flickering off her, sending sparks around the room. And inside that marvelous human form, I see the TrueSelf, spiny, scaly, and moss green—rather like an upright alligator with tusks.

She surveys the room and sees exactly what she should see: surprise, shock, and dismay. Surprise because she's hours early. Shock because no one picked her up at

the airport. And dismay because most of us were looking forward to our last few private hours with our sad
sack western writer.

"Well," Margarite says, "what a motley crew."

She actually licks her lips, but it doesn't look out of
place unless you can see those tusks like I can. Everyone else just stares at her, no one more than Raj. I don't
have to be an empath to know he's worried about losing
his job. Somehow he failed to escort the most important
guest writer of the workshop to her accommodation.
Never mind that no one told him she'd be early. Never
mind that she probably didn't tell *anyone* that she'd be
early.

Margarite doesn't seem upset by the reaction to her
appearance. If anything, she's probably pleased by it, although she doesn't show that pleasure. She doesn't dare.
It would ruin her entire plan.

How do I know her plan? Because if you chart the
appearances she's made before a murder, you can see
a pattern of twenty-two months between unfortunate
events.

The twenty-two months are the tip-off to the fact that
she's a chaos dragon. The first part of the name fits—she
does thrive (and I mean thrive, as in need it to live) on
chaos. The second name is a misnomer given by someone like me who can see the upright alligator in these
imposters and somehow mistook it for a dragon.

More accurately, you should probably call her a chaos
reptile or a chaos demon—but again, you find yourself
in linguistic hell. Since she doesn't have as many powers
as the average demon, and she has considerably more
than the average reptile.

Still, the bottom line is that every twenty-two months,
she needs to snack on the distress caused by the release

of a soul. That soul must die by murder most foul, and there must be some kind of investigation in which at least five people are suspects. If the chaos dragon doesn't get her negative emotions within a two-year window, she will waste away.

Unfortunately, for her, she can't overindulge either. The handful of chaos dragons who become police detectives or defense lawyers tend to explode—quite literally. These deaths are usually blamed on bombs or car accidents or, in one rather dramatic case, some weird kind of poison.

The disciplined chaos dragons feast every twenty to twenty-two months, which gives them two to four months leeway should the earlier feeding go wrong. And the disciplined chaos dragon also has a cover story for why she's near so many horrible homicides.

She needs the cover story because the real story is more sordid. The real story is that the actual homicide itself is triggered by the chaos dragon's presence.

In fact, she's probably triggering someone right now. I watch her work, see her make eye contact with half a dozen people in the room, including—not surprisingly— my triumvirate. She doesn't make eye contact with me, for which I am grateful.

Then Margarite smiles. She's seen what she wanted to see. I know this because the reptile within smiles as well. She says, in a voice I'm already beginning to hate, "I just wanted to say hello and envision all of you before I go to my hotel room for my beauty nap."

(She's the only instructor who insisted on a hotel room. Even the bestselling discord thriller writer, from week two, had no trouble staying in graduate student housing for the duration of his instructorly duties.)

Then Margarite waggles her fingers at us, says,

"Toodles," and goes out the door into the courtyard. We watch her walk away, except Raj, who scurries after her.

He catches her arm, which makes me wince, and then gestures as he talks to her, probably telling her he needs to come with her to check her into that hotel.

Poor guy. He's always been good and fair to me whenever I've had issues with the workshop (and I've had a few). I don't envy him that moment of contact, which probably sent a small shock through his already-overburdened system.

They disappear through the courtyard's main door. Our sad sack western writer, still nominally our instructor for the week, sighs, and somehow refrains from commenting. Instead, she holds up the three manuscripts we're to critique today and asks who wants to go first.

Class ends a half an hour late, what with book signings and hugs and heartfelt cries of *I thought you were the best instructor so far* (which the other instructors also heard on their Fridays). I go back to my room and make myself a bologna and cheese sandwich, then carry it to the kitchen table where I bring out my other laptop, so I can catch up on industry news while I eat.

I probably should be with the group, eating lunch and gossiping. They'd be surprised, though, because it's not my thing. I have to do my job—my real job—but I can't be obvious about it either.

I figure the murder won't take place until tonight. That gives me most of the afternoon to finish a story and probably the early evening to make sure my weaponry is in the proper state.

I bring a kit with me wherever I go. Different evil magical creatures must be killed by different real-world tools. But you already know that. You've seen it in a variety of stories.

The stories get various elements right, but not all of them. For example, the wooden stake that kills vampires must be made out of the no-longer existing cedar of Lebanon. The silver that kills werewolves must be old-fashioned European silver, not the purer, prettier stuff from the Americas.

Chaos dragons are a modern phenomenon, so they die in more modern ways. First, you have to touch the thing with an authentic bowie knife, preferably one from the nineteenth century. That makes the human form dissipate. Then you have render the thing immobile, which is a lot more difficult than it sounds because, at this point, you're fighting with a small alligator. It has alligator claws and alligator teeth and in addition, really big tusks.

I've only killed one chaos dragon, which is one more than my colleagues, and even though my handlers like to attribute that to skill, I know that the death was simply luck.

Because there's a third step: you have to remove the tusks or the thing will regenerate. The tusks are pretty simple to remove. You grab one and tug. The tusk comes out easily, like a fake fingernail comes off a hand. But you have to be able to get close enough to tug.

I learned my lesson the last time. I have reptile tranquilizer darts—the large kind used for crocodiles. I didn't use this the last time. Instead, I managed to knock the chaos dragon unconscious.

But, as I said, that time, I was lucky.

This time, I doubt luck will run my way. That's probably the other reason I'm finishing the story.

Because a part of me thinks it might be my last.

I'm finished with the bologna sandwich when someone knocks on my door. I sigh. I thought I'd discouraged knocking during the first week when I made it clear that I wasn't into socializing or making nice.

Still, the knock's pretty insistent. I peer through the window to the left of the door and see Raj standing there, fist up, looking frazzled. Poor guy. I actually feel sympathy for him. He probably spent the last hour with Margarite. I'll wager he returned to a variety of errands for Hallerhaven, and one of those errands includes me.

I pull open the door—

—and dodge the giant arch of a knife.

Raj pushes his way inside, kicks the door closed with his foot, and tries to knife me again. His eyes are glazed, and spittle runs off the side of his mouth.

How had I missed that?

I grab his knife hand and shove it behind his back. He starts kicking. Then he grabs my hair and pulls my head forward. Somehow he spins me, and gets the knife out of my hand. He jabs at my neck and succeeds in sinking the knife into the flesh above my right breast.

It's startlingly painful. I break out of his hair-hold and grab him by both sides of the face. Then I twist.

His neck breaks with an audible snap, and he crumples, clearly dead.

I'm breathing hard. I'm not bleeding much—the knife somehow managed to avoid important stuff like arteries and nerves. But I have a hunch that some muscle has been compromised.

Then I realize I'm thinking like a person in shock.

Maybe because I am a person in shock. I'm injured, but that's not what's causing the shock.

What's causing the shock is that jolt you get when your perception of yourself gets turned upside down.

The goat at the workshop, the person everyone wants to kill, the one who would generate the most suspects if he/she/it died isn't one of the triumvirate.

It's me.

I splash cold water on my face to force myself to think clearly. Then I put my magic laptop away and call the police. I try to sound like a damsel in distress, which isn't easy for me.

I say, "I let him in and he stabbed me."

I say, "I think he's dead."

I don't say that I used a technique I'd learned in my assassin training to snap his neck.

The campus police arrive almost immediately, look in my room, and confirm with someone on the other end of their radios that indeed I've been stabbed and there's a dead man in my room. They offer me an ambulance, which I accept as part of my damsel in distress disguise (hoping the whole hospital thing won't take long), and then the real police arrive.

They take one look and start asking questions.

Like, "How did a little thing like you break his neck?"

And "Where did you learn how to snap necks?"

And "You really snapped his neck?"

I blink a lot and make my eyes tear up, and say things like after watching many episodes of "Buffy the Vampire Slayer," I decided I needed a self-defense class, and there they taught us to grab someone by both sides of the face to distract him and then knee him in the groin.

I say he must have turned oddly when I kneed him, because I heard his neck snap.

I say I've never heard that before.

In other words, I lie.

Eventually, the EMTs arrive and haul me away to the university hospital where the emergency room doc X-rays me, pronounces me lucky that nothing much was hurt, and sews me up. Then he sends me out into the wild with a prescription for enough painkillers that I could sell them on the street and still have some left over for me.

I fill it, but take none of them. That's for later. Instead, I arrive back at my room to find crime scene splatter everywhere (fingerprint dust, Luminol, and a general mess). No one has discovered my magic laptop or my weapons kit. (Thank heavens.) The last of the photographs have been taken, the body has been removed, and the room is being returned to me, blood and all.

My classmates have shown up. They actually seem concerned, but more that Raj has gone off the deep end (and that concern manifests in a "who's next?" kinda way). They try to be solicitous, offering to feed me and comfort me and give me advice on how to take care of a knife wound (as if any of them has ever done that).

Hallerhaven shows up to let me know the university will take care of everything, including my tuition (in other words, *please don't sue us*) and promises me I'll be just fine.

I thank everyone for their kindness and plead exhaustion. Slowly, I get them out of my room and sigh with relief.

Then I wait until the little clump in the middle of the courtyard is gone. While I was being questioned and poked and prodded this afternoon, I got to thinking.

I have screwed up Margarite's plan. She isn't going to

get the chaos she wants. In fact, a straightforward stabbing/self defense probably doesn't even register as an energy spike.

I have a few precious hours before she tries to rile up someone else to kill me.

I'm going to have to take care of her now.

And if I do it right, no one will ever blame me for her death.

Of course, doing it right means I can't use the tried and true chaos-demon killing techniques. Doing it right means I do something no one has ever done before.

I don't even know if it'll work.

But I'm going to have to try.

The fanciest hotel in town isn't all that fancy. It's basically a mid-level hotel with a Four Seasons attitude and a Holiday Inn budget.

I slip in the front doors, and walk purposefully to the house phone near some potted plants. The nice thing about me, remember, is I'm one of those beige middle-aged women, formerly pretty, that most people see but don't really see.

Of course, the security cameras see me, but most hotels put them in the same locations—facing the registration desk (because of the money), the offices (again, the money), and the entrances and exits. Elevators and stairwells have them too.

No one cares about the house phone, however. I use it to verify that Margarite is here (she is) and what room she's in. I do that by asking for her direct dial phone number. Hotels always put a nine in front of the hotel room number as the direct dial, and they're usually happy to give that out to other guests—or the person who booked the room, namely one Raj O'Driscoll acting on the part of the university.

Apparently, the hotel operator has no idea that Raj is a male name.

Which works to my advantage of course. Margarite's room is on the top floor (as I expected) and is probably one of the few suites in the hotel.

I take the stairs, because it's easier (and more logical) to keep your head down in a stairwell than in an elevator. I'm carrying a purse instead of my weapons kit, having already prepared my tools.

I have my standard equipment inside the purse—a pistol and a couple of knives as well as the bowie knife in its sheath. I also have the tranquilizer ready to go. Fortunately, I learned that the best way to tranquilize an alligator is to use the same tranquilizer needle that vets use on elephants. So I have a few in stock.

I'm as ready as I'll ever be.

Except for the aching knife wound and the slowly growing exhaustion. I might be at more of a disadvantage here than I thought.

I make it to the eighth floor, find the room, and get confirmation that yes, she's in a suite. If I had more time, I'd finesse the room next door or find a maid's cart or something, but I don't.

So I go the old-fashioned route.

I knock.

It only takes a moment for the door to sweep open. Margarite is standing there in a lovely pink negligee, complete with matching pink mules.

I of course see both her and the tusked alligator within, and I have to admit the pink looks a lot better with scaly green than the purple ever did.

She looks surprised to see me.

"We have a problem," I say and walk inside as if I've been invited.

She has no choice except to follow me.

Here's the moment of truth. With one quick movement, I grab the tranquilizer and shove it—not in her neck, like you'd do with most humans—but in that poochy belly of hers.

If she were a real human, that just might kill her, but she's not. And my aim has to be perfect, because I'm trying to drill through the fake human skin into the soft spot where the alligator's jaw meets its neck.

If I miss and survive, I have to go to plan B, where I try to get rid of the human form (which'll be tough because now she's prepared) and then go for the alligator soft spot.

She looks at me in stunned surprise, and then growls. Or roars. Or whatever it is alligators do. I feel the damn tusks clamp down on my wrist—something I hadn't thought of at all. What if she disables my good hand? I'll be damaged on both sides.

I push the plunger and hold it down, praying this stuff works. She starts wailing and wreathing. Her human face changes from pasty white to gold to a sickly green and back again.

Bone snaps and it's not hers. It's mine. My right hand is useless. The syringe falls away.

She keeps digging those tusks into my skin.

I'm not sure plan B is even possible. I'm not sure escape is possible. I'm not sure how anyone is going to explain this one to the cops.

Then her eyes roll into the back of her head (both sets of eyes in both heads) and she topples over backward.

Her tusky grip on my wrist, however, gets stronger.

I probably only have a few minutes. I'm trapped by those damn tusks, but I still have one hand free. That it's the hand with the damaged arm is less important than it would have been, say, half an hour ago.

I grab a regular knife, the closest thing I have to the knife Raj used on me, and proceed to use it to slit the alligator within from gullet to gizzard. Then I pull out the tusks.

They still don't come off my wrist. It's like they've adhered on.

But the alligator within has curled up and turned black, and because I've seen it before, I know that means only one thing.

She's dead.

I was going to slip out the balcony and rappel down the side of the building, just like they taught us in assassin school, but with one arm disabled and one useless wrist, I'm not going anywhere—at least by rope.

I have to let myself out of the hotel room and slither unrecognizably down the hall.

Not for the first time do I wish assassins of the magical are given their own powerful magic. I have to keep my head down and my movements inconspicuous like any other hired killer.

And I can't think about the searing pain in my wrist.

I get to the stairwell and stagger down, careful to always look away from the cameras.

All the way, I'm reevaluating my thinking. Maybe I should have killed her the prescribed way. Of course, how do you explain to university and hotel personnel that a famous writer has gone missing and in her hotel room is a dead alligator? It was hard enough to explain that the first time when the chaos demon wasn't famous.

It'd be even tougher now.

No. I used poor Raj to my own advantage. He'll get blamed for Margarite's death (that's why I used the same kind of knife) and the cops'll decide that after killing her, he came after me. Maybe, they'll say, he was going to kill everyone connected to the workshop.

Poor guy. If I could rehabilitate him, I would. But right now, I need a crazy version of Raj, not a brain-washed version. And I have to get back to my room before anyone sees me.

It's not as hard as it seems. As long as I keep my tusked wrist tucked inside my purse, no one looks at me. I walk as best I can back to campus and back to my room.

Once there, I use an all-purpose pair of pliers in my nondominant hand to try to remove the tusks. It's so hard to do, I almost have to get help. (The question of who is what stops me.) Finally I manage to get the things off, but not before I hear my stitches rip.

The bone is broken, but I can't do anything about that now. Tomorrow I'll go to the hospital, say they over-looked the wrist, and I didn't notice until morning. By then the scrapes will have bruised up nicely, and they'll look more like something you'd get in a fight with a human than, say, a tusked alligator.

I clean the new wound, bandage it as best I can one-handed, then take as many painkillers as I can without killing myself and fall into bed.

When I wake up, it's twenty-four hours later, and Carlotta Sternke is sitting on the edge of my bed.

"I was afraid you were dead," she says in a tone that implies she wasn't afraid at all but was, in fact, looking forward to it. "We cleaned up your floor."

We, it turns out, was Hamlet Thorshov and Norman Zell. Turns out I had misjudged them. What I took for alienation was actually friendship among the most anti-social of writers.

They want to take care of me. I let them discover the wrist and insist on another hospital visit.

Where I get a splint, more stitches in the other side, and another prescription for painkillers.

Which I need, since it turns out that the triumvirate was being nice to me only because I woke up while they were stealing my pain pills. Or maybe they were being nice to me because they felt guilty about stealing my pain pills.

It doesn't matter either way. I'm not going to report them. I want this workshop to continue.

It looked shaky for a few days, but the school psychiatrists said we'd all be better off if we finished our workshop than if we left now. We agreed. Hallerhaven found someone to take over Margarite's week, and we tried to get back to normal.

Or at least I did.

Because I'm getting out of the assassination racket. In fact, I can't work assassinating even if I wanted to. I'm short-term recognizable. I've been interviewed by all the major networks, asking me why Raj came after me and Margarite. (*I don't know!* I claimed in my best damsel in distress voice.)

Then I got an idea.

The western writer called her agent because she wants to write the true crime version of what happened.

I can't write the true crime version because it would be too true and too unbelievable.

But I can write the fictionalized version.

If I play this right, I can become the new Margarite Lawson. I know of enough mysterious and unsolved crime scenes (not all of them my own) to keep me in novels for decades. I don't have to go around magicking graduate assistants into forced homicides.

So even with the damaged breastbone and the broken wrist, I'm pecking away at the keyboard. I'm going to learn as much as possible these remaining three weeks.

And then I'm taking the publishing world by storm.

HEART OF ASH

Jim C. Hines

Lena Greenwood poked the vampire with the broken remains of her white ash staff. "She's dead. Deader, I guess. Help me drag the body upstairs. Come sunrise, she should be nothing but a smear on the library roof."

Janice didn't move. "She's been so strange ever since Thanksgiving break. I thought she was sick. Like mono or something." She stared at the creature who had been her roommate, then turned to Lena. "You're hurt!"

Lena grimaced and checked her side. "I'll be fine so long as I don't inhale too deeply. A night in my tree and those ribs will be good as new."

Janice clenched her hands together, clearly trying to stop them from trembling. "I thought dryads were supposed to be flighty and weak. You know, the sex fantasies of Greek mythology."

Lena smiled and ran her fingers through Janice's short hair. "I'm a nymph. I'm whatever you want me to be."

Nine years later, Lena twirled a wooden baseball bat in one hand as she strode through Red Rock Park in Tucson. The night air was dry and hot, though for Arizona in May, this was positively mild. Swing set chains clinked in the distance. The park was empty save for a single group gathered at a picnic table.

Three months she had been tracking them. Three months, and eight victims left scattered through the city, brains rotted to mush. She was getting slow.

She smiled as they noticed her. Most were no more human than she was, but they were still men. Their stares warmed her skin, taking in the heavy boots and tight jeans, moving up to the "Plays well with others" T-shirt and the blood-red leather jacket Janice had bought her last year, the one with Animal from *The Muppet Show* on the back. Wisps of brown hair teased the smooth skin of her face.

Seven men, only two of them mortals. A pair of jaguars circled the picnic table, one black and the other spotted like a leopard. Neither one leashed or restrained in any way.

Lena reached into her jacket and pulled out a baggie of what looked like ash. She tossed it onto the table. "Humans will do a lot for pleasure. Gods know I've seen almost everything. Heck, I've participated in most of it. But snorting powdered zombie brains? Really?"

The two humans took off running. Lena ignored them. She wanted the dealers.

They were younger than she had expected. None looked old enough to drive, though they were bulkier than most teens. Their movement was graceful, almost fluid as they spread out to surround her.

"Who the hell do you think you are?" asked one with short-cut hair and a valiant attempt at a moustache. Dressed in jeans and sleeveless flannel rather than the more pretentious threads she usually saw from drug dealers, he could have passed for a migrant worker. His teeth gleamed white in the moonlight.

Lena tapped her bat against one boot, keeping most of her attention on the jaguars. Switching to Spanish, she said, "You're outmatched, boys. I've killed far worse than a pack of prepubescent weres. Tell me how you're bringing this stuff over the border, and I'll let you live."

"Maybe if you ask us nicely," said another, earning laughter from several of his friends.

The first cuffed him into silence. "You think your little stick is going to protect you, bitch?"

Lena smiled. Faster than any human could act, she reached into her jacket and pulled out a Ruger Redhawk revolver. Silver-plated bullets punched through the skulls of both jaguars before the others could react.

They had guts, Lena would give them that much. Three charged, bodies shifting into their jaguar forms even as she fired. She dropped two more, then struck the third with her bat. In her hands, the wood was hard as steel. The jaguar whimpered and drew back, holding his broken foreleg close to his chest.

By now the remaining two had drawn guns of their own. Lena jumped aside as the leader fired. The bullet grazed her ribs. She rolled and leaped again. Another bullet hit the ground beside her, spitting dust into the air. Before she could recover, the wounded jaguar crashed onto her back.

Claws dug into her shoulders. She slammed her head back, striking the great cat in the nose. Butcher shop breath puffed against her neck as his teeth caught her hair and skin.

Lena ripped free and rolled onto her back, grabbing the jaguar's broken leg in one hand and squeezing. Now it was the cat's turn to try to break free. Lena used his

movement to pull herself upright, then grabbed the
back of his neck. The jaguar had to weigh a hundred and
fifty pounds. Lena grunted as she hurled him through
the air.

What was wrong with her? She should have been
stronger than this.

"Drop the stick." The remaining two had spread out,
guns leveled at Lena's chest. Even at her best, she wasn't
fast enough to escape, and this was far from her best. She
had once thrown a vampire through a church wall, but
tonight she could barely hold her own against children?

She tossed the bat to the ground.

"Who else knows you're here?" asked the leader.

Lena relaxed, opening herself up until she could
hear the man's heart pounding in his chest. Her own
pulse sped to match his. She could smell the musk of his
sweat, dripping down his neck and back. His body was
still human, and it responded to Lena's call. He shifted
uncomfortably as his lust built.

"Nobody." She stretched her arms overhead, wincing
as pain tore down her back. Nine years ago their claws
would have found her flesh as solid as aged hardwood.
Sweat and blood made her shirt cling to her body. Just
the sort of macabre wet T-shirt show a creature like this
should appreciate. "It's just you and me."

He stepped closer, but wasn't foolish enough to lower
his gun. Sirens screamed in the distance. He stooped to
pick up the bat. "What *are* you?"

"What would you like me to be?" She glanced at the
bat. "Pointing that thing seems a little Freudian, don't
you think?" Lowering her gaze, she said, "A girl might
almost think you're compensating for something."

As she had hoped, he snarled and swung. The bat
struck her head and splintered, showering them both

with shards of wood. Lena had made that bat from the wood of her own ash tree back in Michigan. Attacking her with it was like trying to drown a fish. She struck the gun from his hand and ran, trying to keep him between herself and the remaining werejaguar.

Lena swore as a bullet punched through her side. She glanced over her shoulder to see the second was tossing his empty gun aside. He shifted into his jaguar form, even as his friend shouted for him to stop.

Lena ducked past the slide and vaulted over the merry-go-round, heading for the park office. The parking lot was empty. She would never make it to the main road.

Instead, she ran for the landscaped garden in front of the office, where prickly pear surrounded a pair of saguaro cacti. Her feet crunched on decorative gravel as she turned around, her back brushing the spines of the saguaro. She waited for the jaguar to close the distance.

Lena's lips tightened into a grim smile. As the beast slammed into her body, she allowed herself to fall backward, dragging the cat into the cactus with her.

"It's been a week and I can't stop thinking about that fight. If I had been stronger, none of this—"

"Only God is omnipotent." Father Castelo shook his head sadly. "Powerful as you are, Lena, even you have your limits."

A car horn blared outside the church. Lena jumped to her feet.

"Try to calm down. You're safe here."

Lena relaxed, knowing he was right. Built in an old Spanish mission, Grace Fellowship Community Church was probably the safest place in all of Tucson. Castelo had sheltered her here more than once. The adobe walls

appeared old, but the spirits inhabiting them were power-
ful enough to turn away most threats. For two hundred
years they had served the master of the church.

That was how Lena had first met the middle-aged
priest, shortly after Janice's studies brought them to Tuc-
son. Lena and Castelo found themselves working together
to defeat the church's former leader, a man corrupted by
power and dark magic who had been using the ghosts to
punish those he found unworthy.

If the werejaguars found her here today, they would
have worse to worry about than just Lena.

"I'm glad you've come. I've been worried." Father
Castelo was handsome enough for a priest, with thinning
black hair and oversized silver-rimmed glasses. "I'm so
sorry, Lena."

The last thing she wanted was sympathy. "I've looked
everywhere." Lena twisted in the pew, running her fin-
gers over the back. Buds sprang from the wood at her
touch. "You don't understand, Father. I should have been
stronger."

"No one can fight the world's evil alone. What hap-
pened isn't your fault."

"I never said the fault was mine. I am what I am. Like
Popeye," she added with a wan smile. "Whatever Janice
wanted, that's who I was. In the beginning, she wanted
her lover to be a hero. Beautiful, sexy, smart, and strong.
She was so young, my little geek princess in her first year
at college, dorm room overflowing with comic books and
anime. Lately though, her tastes have changed."

Lena waited until she was certain the remaining two
werejaguars had left. Only then did she stagger out,
leaving her attacker trapped in the saguaro.

She hated cacti. Somehow they always left her feeling

both dry-skinned and bloated. Her hair caught in the spines, and she pulled free as gently as she could, not wanting to damage the plant.

"Damn," she whispered as she examined herself. Fresh scabs covered the holes in her side where the bullet had ripped through. The wounds cracked and oozed as she moved. At least the cactus had healed her enough to reach her truck without bleeding to death. She was sweating by the time she climbed into the old Chevy pickup.

It was a toss-up which was in worse shape, Lena or her truck. With Janice's grad school loans and Lena working a part-time job at the university bookstore, they were lucky to cover rent, let alone keep the truck running. The windshield was cracked and the vents blew only hot air, but the engine revved to life on the second try.

She and Janice lived in an apartment complex off Interstate 10, a short distance from the U of A campus. Not the most glamorous place in the world, but it was cheap, and more importantly, it supported a healthy scattering of palm trees around the parking lot in back. Lena liked the city for the most part, but it was like the gods had run out of green before making the place.

Lena felt the pull of her grove even before she left the truck, but she forced herself to go inside.

She found Janice sitting in the old recliner, chewing the cap of her pink highlighter as she pored over her books. Despite her pain, Lena warmed at the sight of her.

"Did you find them?" Janice caught her breath as she saw Lena. She slammed the book shut. "What happened?"

"I'm all right." Lena caught Janice, holding her back. "Don't. I'm still bloody. You don't want—"

"I don't care about that." Janice bit her lip as she took in Lena's injuries. "You're bleeding."

"Only a little." Lena winced as she stripped off her jacket. "I found the Z dealers."

"You said you could handle them," said Janice.

"No, *you* said that." Lena sighed. Now that she was here, she wanted to forget the whole thing. Let someone else handle the remaining monsters for once while she snuggled up with Janice to watch *The Daily Show*. Or not watch, depending on how things went. "It's all right, Janice. You want a real life. A real partner."

"I want you," Janice said. "I always have. Even before you saved me back in Michigan."

"I know." Lena smiled and kissed her hands. "But you don't want a superhero. You want something stable. A woman to grow old with. You think it's coincidence I've been so domestic lately? Cooking meals that don't come in a box, cleaning—"

"I never asked you to—"

"That doesn't matter." She shrugged. "I enjoy cooking, actually. Despite the lasagna disaster."

"But this world needs you." Janice pulled away. "Look at how much you've done, how many people you've saved. Just because some selfish part of me wants something different, that doesn't mean you should change what you are."

"That selfish part is the only one that matters," Lena said. She could feel Janice's conflict reflected within herself, the part of her that longed for peace warring with the need to fight the darkness most people couldn't even see.

"What do *you* want?" Janice asked softly.

It was a question with no answer. Lena kissed her, loosening her normally tight control until she felt

Janice respond. She slid a hand up Janice's back, beneath her shirt, nails sliding over skin. Janice's arms tightened around her.

Pain exploded in her side, and Lena pulled away, gasping.

"I'm sorry," said Janice. "I didn't mean—"

"Not your fault." Lena drew a deep breath. "Looks like my body isn't ready for what I want. But give me a night to rest, and I'll give you a wake-up call you'll never forget."

"I love you." Janice kissed her with nymphlike passion, almost enough to make Lena forget about the night's defeat.

"I love you too," said Lena. "First and always."

"Good." Janice spun her gently toward the door. "Now get out there and get your sleep. I'll be waiting for you."

Lena glanced around as she crossed the small open area behind the building. Barbeque pits sat to one side of the parking lot. Beyond stood a row of young palms and a burnt-out street light. Maintenance had long since given up on that particular light. No matter how many times they worked on it, the roots kept destroying the wiring.

Lena smiled as she crossed into the darkness, glancing back at the windows to make sure nobody was watching. She saw only Janice, staring down from their window.

Lena blew her a kiss, knowing she was just a shadow to Janice. She turned and touched her hand to the largest of the palm trees, pressing the scalloped bark until her fingers penetrated the wood.

Moments later, she was gone.

"Change is normal," Father Castelo said, taking Lena's hand in his. "I've seen it with many couples. People grow

*and change. Over time they discover their partner is no
longer the same person they married."*

"I like who I've been." Lena bowed her head. "I remember my former lives. Before Janice, I was a prepubescent Chinese girl who couldn't speak English. Before that, an improbably endowed blonde with an I.Q. of seventy. But with Janice, everything was different. I was stronger. I could protect myself, protect her. I always knew what to do. But now . . ."

"Nothing lasts forever, Lena."

"The monsters do." Lena dug her fingers into her arms. "I do."

"You can't keep torturing yourself," Father Castelo said.

Lena shrugged. "I'd torture the werejaguars, but I can't find them. This city is too damn big. I've questioned every junkie I could find. The only lead I've got came from Animal Control. They said jaguars are solitary creatures. The exception is when they're young, when they stay with their mother."

"You think these were children?" Castelo asked.

"Maybe. I don't know. It's still not enough to find them." She bowed her head. "There was a time no evil could hide from me. Now . . . I can't do it, Father. Janice was my strength."

Lena knew something was wrong the moment she emerged from her tree. She closed her eyes, reaching inward. For nine years, she had carried the memory of her first time with Janice. Crying out together in Janice's dorm room as Lena uncovered Janice's fantasies, her unspoken desires, fulfilling not all of them—there was only so much time in the night—but enough to bind Lena to her.

This morning, that memory was a distant thing, the intensity gone.

"Oh please gods, no." Lena ran for the back door. Inside, she took the steps three at a time. She spotted the police the instant she reached the second floor. Her apartment door had been ripped from its frame. One officer stood questioning the couple from across the hall. He glanced up, spotting Lena.

"Ms. Greenwood?"

Lena ran past him. How could she have been so stupid? "Janice!"

"You don't want to go in there, ma'am." The officer grabbed her arm. "You don't need to see that."

Even from the doorway, Lena could see enough. The door splintered on the ground, furniture overturned, blood everywhere. Two other uniformed officers moved through her apartment. One carried a chair leg with blood and fur in the broken end. Janice had given them a fight before she died.

"What happened to you, Lena?" The officer's grip tightened every so slightly. "I know this is a shock. Would you mind coming with me to answer some questions?"

Lena glanced down at herself. Her shirt was still a bloody mess. No wonder he sounded suspicious. "I don't have time."

"Where were you last night?"

"With a friend," she said numbly. "Father Castelo." Castelo would cover for her if they called. Not that it mattered. Janice was dead, which meant very soon, Lena Greenwood would follow.

She had been through it so many times before, but never like this. Never when it was her own fault.

Within a day, the grief would lose its edge. Two days, and she would begin to flirt with random strangers. A week, and her body would start to change, adapting to the desires of the people around her. Her mind would do the same, and she would float along until someone else claimed her.

"Do you have any idea what might have done this?"

Lena looked at his hand on her arm. "Yes."

Janice was dead, but Lena wasn't gone yet. She broke his hold with ease, tossing him through the doorway like a doll. The other officers did their best to break his fall.

Lena glanced at her neighbors. "I always liked you," she said to the girl. "I wanted you to know he's been cheating on you. I can smell it."

By the time anyone recovered, Lena was gone.

"You've done the best you could," said Father Castelo.

Lena bowed her head, hiding behind hair both longer and lighter than it had been a week before. Everything had been so clear, but lately she was having a harder time concentrating. She had put this off as long as she could. Another day, and she would be gone. "Even if I found them, I'm not strong enough to fight."

"What will happen to you?" He fidgeted uncomfortably, tugging at his collar. "Forgive me. I'm used to counseling the sick and the dying, but this—"

"I know. It's all right." She still couldn't look at him. "I don't plan to die."

Overhead, the stained glass in the arched windows brightened as the ghosts emerged, sensing her intentions. But they wouldn't interfere, not unless she directly threatened Father Castelo or if he commanded them to help.

Castelo rose, brow wrinkling as he watched the dead circle the church like blue smoke. "The werejaguars—"

"It's not them." Lena took his hand. "I need your help."

"I'm only a priest." Castelo chuckled softly, still not understanding. "Even in my younger days, I was never much of a fighter."

"I don't need a fighter." Lena pulled him around until they stood face to face. She stepped closer, her body brushing against his. "You're a good man. For years you've helped me. You're as passionate as Janice used to be about protecting the innocent from the darkness."

"I'm sorry, Lena." He shook his head and pulled away. "I understand you're grieving, but—"

"I'm no mourning widow seeking comfort, Eduardo." Lena smiled, refusing to release his hands.

"Is this why you came here tonight? To seduce me in my own church?"

"I came here to try to save myself," Lena snapped. "Because you loved Lena Greenwood. Because by giving myself to you, I might be able to hold on to some small piece of who I was."

She pulled away, moving toward the altar. "I've never had this chance before. I've drifted from one lover to the next, never caring about past or future. But Janice gave me more. Now, with her gone, I have the chance to choose."

"What about my choice?" Castelo asked angrily. "You would have me take you as a slave, or else turn you away and condemn you to God only knows what fate?"

She managed a smile. "You're welcome to take your complaints up with God. He's never listened to me, but you might have better luck."

"I can't help you." He chewed his lip, the only outward sign of conflict. "I can't be a part of your continued en-slavement. I don't want—"

"Don't lie! Not here." Rarely in Lena's existence had she ever known anger. This moment was one last gift from Janice. "You think you can hide your desire from *me? You've controlled it better than most mortals, but don't lie to yourself.*

"You want this. You want me. A strong woman to fight the darkness, protect the helpless, and look damn good in the process. One who loves and fights with the same passion. Powerful, but also vulnerable. One who needs you. I need you, Eduardo. I need the strength you can give me."

He flushed, but kept his distance. *"What kind of monster would enslave you like that? What is strength worth if it must be given by another?"*

"Strength is strength." She raised her chin, allowing her own lust to seep forth and touch him. *"Do you think Janice was a monster?"*

"Of course not," he protested.

"I could force you. I can break through the walls you've . . . erected. I could give you pleasure few mortals have ever known."

"But you won't," he said, his voice unsteady.

"No," she agreed. *"Because some of what Janice made me still lingers."* She hugged herself. *"I understand your conflict, but you didn't create me. You're not responsible for my nature. And if not you, who knows what I'll become."*

She could feel his resolve weakening. *"If I'm to be cursed to such servitude, let me find a higher purpose in it."*

Elena Madera made her way along the Santa Cruz River toward the Interstate. She spotted the were-jaguars immediately, watching her from the darkness beneath the bridge. Gold eyes shone in the beam of her flashlight.

A familiar figure jumped into the water and waded

toward her. From a distance, he could have passed for just another vagabond living at the edge of the city, if not for the easy, predatory confidence in his movements. "Go away."

"Territorial, aren't you?" Elena smiled. She counted two others in the darkness. "Most cats hate water, but not jaguars. No wonder you love it here."

He sniffed the air. "I know you."

"Thank you." Her scent had changed over the past month, along with the rest of her. But if he still recognized her, it meant something of Lena Greenwood had survived. Her hair was longer now, tied back in twin black braids. Her skin was soft and brown. She wore a long white coat which would be murder to keep clean, but did a nice job of hiding the three feet of Toledo steel sheathed on the back of her belt.

"I've been volunteering at the homeless shelters lately," Elena said. "Strange how many of them talk about monsters, especially here at the river. Creatures chasing them away, hunting them in the night."

All three werejaguars were approaching now. The mother and her young. Apparently, the family that ran drugs together, stayed together. The mother's features shifted, fur covering her body, though she remained humanoid. Combining the best of both forms. Her sons simply drew their guns.

This time, Elena was faster. Her coat flew out behind her as she leapt, drawing a chrome-plated .45 and killing the first werejaguar before he could react. She put a bullet into the arm of the second, and his weapon dropped into the water. Undeterred, he charged, slamming into her with his full weight.

Elena rolled back, planted her feet in his gut, and flung him away. By the time he attacked again, she was ready. Her sword hissed through the air, and he fell into the river.

She spun, hurling the sword to catch the mother in the stomach even as she leapt.

"What are you?" the last werejaguar asked, sharp teeth distorting her words.

Elena walked toward her. "Bow down to him, for he avenges the blood of his children and takes vengeance on his adversaries. He repays those who hate him and cleanses his people's land. Deuteronomy, chapter thirty-two."

She grabbed the hilt of her sword and planted a foot on the werejaguar's chest. "Answer my questions, and I'll be merciful." Eduardo would like that. Much as he hated the darkness, he also hated suffering of any kind. She would do her best to make this quick.

JIANG SHI

Elizabeth A. Vaughan

My doorway was filled with a small army of angry bikers, dressed in leathers and tattoos. The one in front snarled at me, his fist still tight from pounding on my front door. "Lady, your van was found with our stolen hogs alongside I-75. WHAT THE HELL HAPPENED?"

Uh-oh.

Itty and Bitty, my two white Westies, stopped barking and smelled the biker's boots, their little tails wagging like mad.

Now, normally, my pre-menopausal middle-aged response would have been to curse and slam the door in the biker's faces, but it had been a rough couple of days, what with attacks by evil possums and ninja rats, trips to the ER, mysterious doctors who threw lightning, and one ancient Chinese sword-wielding mouse with a magical artifact who still hadn't explained much of anything. So what the hell . . .

I shushed the dogs, opened the front door wide, gave the group a weary smile, and lied through my teeth. "I have no idea. Would you like some coffee?"

They all just looked at me, and the anger bled from their faces. One of the bigger ones, the bald one with the nose ring, said, "That would be real nice, ma'am."

Ma'am. Swell. "Please," I said. "Call me Kate."

It took two pots of my special stash of Michigan Cherry coffee before they really calmed down. I just kept listening to their outrage, nodding, pouring fresh cups, and repeating my lie. "I have no idea what happened. Sugar?"

They'd thank me and tell me again how their hogs had been stolen from outside the honky tonk where they'd been hanging out. They'd found their bikes gone, and gotten the runaround from the cops and the impound lot where all the vehicles had been taken.

I think they'd have forgiven the thefts, but the bikes had taken the worst of it when the rats had attacked my minivan as I was driving home from the hospital. Bud, the one with the nose-ring, was especially upset, since his ride had been found in the ditch. "Some sumofabitch side-swiped it." He mumbled into his coffee.

I made sympathetic noises and topped off his mug. In point of fact, I'd rammed the bike from behind with my van. The sparks had been very impressive as it slid across the expressway.

Not the time to offer that detail.

Tiny, who was not, leaned back and made my dining room chair creak in alarming ways. "The world is going to hell, ma'am. Plain and simple, just going to hell . . ."

There was a stirring under my collar at that statement. Wan, short for Wan Su Yi, the aforementioned ancient Chinese mouse, had been riding on my shoulder when they'd knocked. He'd taken cover just before I opened the door. He'd been carrying his sword at the time, and the point was digging into my neck as he squirmed.

"You don't mean that literally, Tiny." I said, knowing that Wan would take it as such.

"Well, no, ma'am, but just the same." Tiny dropped the chair back to the floor with a thud and slapped the table with his palm. "What kind of dirty, thieving lowlife scum would be stealing our rides?"

Well, in point of fact, it had been a possum and his ninja rats, but damned if I was going to tell them that. I just shook my head, kept my mouth shut, and ground the beans for another pot. As the riders all agreed with Tiny, I took a quick survey of the kitchen and the great room.

The damages in the house from the epic battle between us and the ninja rats weren't really obvious. The broken glass had been swept away, the blood mopped up. I'd put the toilet brush back into its holder in the bathroom. But I still didn't have a clue as to what the hell was going on, and Wan, who may or may not be the "Lord of Ten Thousand Years," had better provide some answers and soon.

But first, I had to get rid of the bikers.

It took the rest of my precious stash of coffee to get them on their way. I told them where I bought the coffee at a place up in Dundee. They gave me the name and phone number of the impounded lot where my van was. Tiny winked at me, and slipped me his cell number as he walked out the door.

Oh yeah. That was happening.

I closed the door firmly and leaned my forehead against it, listening to the rumble of their hogs as they pulled away.

"We must talk, Kate." Wan wiggled out from under my collar to stand on my shoulder. He stood upright, his tail whipping back and forth. His sword was on his back, the bright red tassel hanging from the pommel. "There is much you need to know."

"Oh sure," I snapped, as I turned back toward the kitchen. "Now you want to talk. Now, after we've fought off possums and ninja rats and wrecked my van, damn it." I started to gather up the coffee mugs and load them into the dishwasher.

"The Honorable Doctor McDougall—"

"Do we know he is honorable?" I growled.

"—has warded this house," Wan said, easily balancing as I moved back and forth. "We cannot be complacent and assume that those forces allied against us will—"

"And what forces might those be, Wan?" I stopped abruptly.

"Kate," Wan's voice was soft. I could see him out of the corner of my eye, and for a moment I could swear that he was looking at me with pity in those small black eyes. "Perhaps we should sit, Honorable Lady."

I sighed. "All right." I dumped soap into the machine and got it started. The familiar sound of water was comforting in an odd way.

I went to the living room and plopped down on the sofa. Itty and Bitty ran for their usual spots, each on one side of me. They jumped up, circled around, and then settled down for a nap.

Wan leapt for the coffee table, standing on a pile of magazines next to the remote.

"Okay," I said, sagging into the cushions. "Explain."

"Let me begin by asking you—what do you know of the history of the Middle Kingdom?" Wan asked.

"China?" I tilted my head back and closed my eyes. "Well, let's see. There's the Ming Dynasty and the Han Dynasty. The last empress, the Opium Wars. Lao Tzu, Confucius, Mao Zedung, and Ho Chi Minh ... no, wait,

I think he is Vietnamese." I opened my eyes. "That's about it."

Wan was frozen in horror, his mouth gaping open.

"Er . . ." I thought about it a minute. "General Tso's? Dim sum? Moo shu? There was that Disney movie . . . what was the girl's name?"

Wan put a paw over his eyes. "The level of your ignorance is appalling."

"Oh, excuse me," I said.

"What of its religion?" Wan asked, keeping his paw over his eyes.

"Mythology?" I asked.

Wan dropped his paw and glared at me. "Shall we offer comparisons with Christian mythology?"

Eeep. "Point taken," I felt guilty. "Wan, I'm sorry, but—"

"What happened when you touched the talisman?" Wan was staring at me intently. "Tell me, Kate."

My mouth opened, but the words wouldn't come. How could I explain?

I was floating, suspended between earth and the heavens, moving freely as if underwater, clouds all around me.

I gasped at the change, then gasped again when cool air rushed into my lungs, with a taste of rain and spring on the air. I breathed again, filling my body with energy and light, lost in the sensation.

The clouds eddied around me, heavy with mist, white and intangible. I started to try to tread the air, to see if I could turn, but my hands passed through the clouds, collecting the heavy drops within. I couldn't move.

Something else could, though. I caught the movement out of the corner of my eye. There was a rumble, like far-distant thunder on a sunny day. I saw a huge form mov-

*ing in and out of the clouds, flowing like a snake. I had
a quick glimpse of scales that glittered all colors of the
spectrum, then a huge head reared up before me.*

*I'd seen enough to know a dragon. No wings, just a
fierce, lovely face and huge teeth and claws. A museum
print come to life, the only source of color in the white
billowing clouds.*

My throat closed at the memory, lovely and fearful at
the same time. "I saw—"

"A dragon," Wan said.

"Yes," I licked my lips. "Wan, what ... who ..."

"Kate," Wan placed his palms together and bowed
his head to me. "You are the Wise One, Bearer of the
Scale, chosen of the Emperor Dragon, Lord of the
Dragon Kings, Ruler of the Weather, and the Waters of
the World."

I stared at the small talking mouse on my coffee table
for one solemn moment, and then reality came crashing
in. "Bullshit."

Wan jerked his head up. "Wha—"

"That is the biggest load of crap I've ever heard,"
I started to struggle up out of the sofa cushions. The
dogs opened their eyes for a moment, then returned
to their naps. "Of all the stupid—" I glared at him as I
fought free of the cushions. "How stupid do you think
I am?"

"Kate," Wan looked up as I towered over him. "Kate,
please—"

"Bullshit," I snarled. "Tell me again how the Emperor
Dragon has chosen a fat, middle-aged woman from Toledo, Ohio. Go ahead, I dare you."

"Our enemies have sought me over the centuries to
gain control of the jade necklace that bears the talisman
of the Wise One," Wan replied. "But once you touched

the talisman, you became the target. They will now wish to kill you, Kate. I have placed you in grave jeopardy. Doctor McDougall knows this. He will return, hopefully bringing his colleagues wise in the ways of magic, to protect you."

It had been a mistake. The doctor had demanded to know why they were attacking us, and Wan showed us the necklace concealed in the hilt of his sword. It had been so tiny, and so lovely. Heavy pieces of jade, with an odd-looking circular medallion that had looked like mother-of-pearl, with all the colors reflecting in the light . . . I had reached out, just barely brushing it with my fingertips. . . .

I closed my eyes, and for a moment I could feel the jade on my skin, heavy and cool on my shoulder-blades . . .

I shook myself from the vision and opened my eyes. Wan was staring up at me, a satisfied look on his face. "It calls to you, does it not?"

"Wan, that is ridiculous." I rolled my eyes and threw my hands in the air. "That's as crazy as—"

"Talking to a mouse," he snapped.

I glared at him, and ran my fingers through my hair. "I need to pee."

Wan crossed his arms over his chest. I could feel his tiny glare on my back as I walked away.

I sat for a bit after my business and stared at the floor of my Green Bay Packer themed bathroom without really seeing the yellow and green of the bathmat. Magical necklaces . . . ninja rats.

And what about McDougall? He'd stitched up my hand in ER and then rescued us, throwing lightning around, his stethoscope still around his neck. Those sharp grey eyes, warning me from leaving the protection of his wards. Where did he fit in all this?

This was nuts. Well and truly unbelievable. Wise One, chosen by the Elemental Forces. It was just crazy.

But then again, so was the idea of a talking mouse.

I rolled my eyes, sighed, and went to wash my hands. I needed to know more. I needed to listen to the talking mouse. To Wan. Without throwing up my hands and exclaiming my disbelief. It was far too late for that. I'd passed the intersection of Crazy and Sane a long time ago, and I'd turned down Crazy Street the minute I had rescued Wan from my koi pond. There was no turning back now.

I looked up at the mirror and sighed. Why did "wise" always seem to really mean old and wrinkled? I thought adventures happened to the young, the lovely, the pure of heart?

But in that instant, when the dragon had looked at me—at me, as is, as I was—

It saw me. Not just me, it saw through me somehow, right down to my soul and I shook as I hung there, pierced by its gaze. Then it threw its head back, and shook its mane, and laughed.

The heavens resounded, and the earth trembled with the sound, as if all of creation shared the joy of this being. For it did not mock, nor was it threatening. It was a joyful sound, and my heart shared in its delight.

That joy . . . that happiness. I hadn't felt anything like that in years.

I took a deep breath, straightened my shoulders, and threw open the bathroom door.

"There is much you will need to learn," Wan said as he paced back and forth on the dining room table. "But we will start with the very beginning."

"A very good place to start," I warbled, back on the sofa with the two dogs at my side.

Wan gave me a puzzled look.

Heh. Score one for popular culture. "The necklace?" I prompted.

"No, Kate." Wan shook his head. "The very beginning. Of the world."

"Oh. Of course." I tried to keep an interested look on my face, but inside I groaned. The whole thing? He was going to tell me the whole thing?

"To begin, I will provide you with an overview of the major dynasties." Wan started pacing, and his voice took on the same droning tone of some of my old professors at UT. "Now, in your modern time scale, the Hsia Dynasty was formed in 2000 BCE—"

Crap. My brain twisted in my skull. Four thousand years? He was going back four thousand years?

"Arising along the banks of the Yellow River. Founded by Yu the Great, who—"

If this were a marital arts film, there'd be an attack about now. I glanced over at the sliding door to see if, by chance, there were any ninja rats in the backyard.

No such luck.

"Yu was a feared and cruel Emperor, who bound the petty warring states—" Wan was pacing, his tail in his paws as he moved, intent on his words.

I ever-so-casually moved my hand and poked Itty's butt. With any luck, my little dog would wake up and need to go outside.

Itty yawned, and rolled on her side to show her tummy. She never even opened her eyes.

I scratched her belly, and slumped into the cushions. Doomed . . . I was doomed. My eyes started to roll back into my head. Doomed . . .

"The next dynasty arose in 1523 BCE. Scholars differ

as to whether it should be known as the Shang or Yin Dynasty. My studies have led me to theorize that—"

I stifled a yawn, and looked out the sliding glass door again. Maybe McDougall would appear again to rescue me from this horrible fate. He was damned good looking, with those sharp grey eyes. Those grey eyes that—

"Kate!"

I jerked my eyes open.

Wan was glaring at me, his little paws on his narrow hips.

"Wan, I—" Desperation born of pure boredom forced me to speak. "I might have some books in the attic."

The attic stairs creaked as I pulled the chain, lowering gently to the floor. Wan was on my shoulder as I set my foot on the first step.

I'd always loved fantasy from the moment I learned to read. Magic, swords, dragons . . . I read every book I could get my hands on, and when that wasn't enough, I made up stories in my head. I discovered gaming in college . . . role-playing games that let me be the characters I'd dreamed of. I never looked back. Computers, LARPS, MUUDS, SCA . . . my life and friends revolved around those wonderful imaginary worlds.

Then I tried to write my stories to share with the world. And all my wide-eyed innocent hopes had been shredded, one after the other. Until the 53rd rejection letter, when I'd woken up to reality. Seen the truth in all its sweaty, hopeless, ugliness.

So I'd walked away from old friends, and quit all my gaming groups. I'd left SCA and closed my online accounts. I'd cleaned out my bookshelves and donated everything fantastical to the library. I'd wiped my hard drive, expunging my folly with the press of a key, reformatting my life and goals with a stroke. I'd taken my rejections, my manuscripts, my characters, my worlds, and stuffed them in a few boxes in the attic.

I didn't want to climb those stairs, didn't want to open those boxes. Too much damn pain, too much failure contained within. I didn't want to do this.

But I didn't want to listen to the entire history of China, either.

The attic was unfinished, so I'd have to watch my step. I pulled the chain on the light and looked around. The beams made it hard to stand upright, and I reached for one to balance myself. The wood felt rough and dry under my fingers. I breathed in dust and disuse and tried to remember the last time I'd been up here.

"Which boxes, Kate?" Wan asked, his nose twitching.

"Over there," I said, moving carefully on the plywood. "In that corner."

They were piled in one corner, isolated from the boxes of Christmas ornaments and college memories. Sealed with duct tape, with my shaky handwriting on the sides in black permanent marker. The lettering was hard to read, but then I'd been crying at the time. Sobbing my eyes out, to be exact.

I reminded myself to breathe and kept moving.

Wan bounded down from my shoulder, his sword slung over his shoulder, red tassel dancing from the pommel. "What is in this one?" He asked, scrambling through the opening that served as a handhold.

"Hell if I know," I grumbled, my stomach knotting. Probably from drinking too damn much coffee. I started moving the boxes, looking at the sides. "There should be one that says 'gamemaster' on the side."

I could hear him rummaging around, talking as he did

so. "There are gemstones in here, Kate. With numbers on them." His voice was muffled, but I could hear his excitement.

"Those are dice," I said absently. I'd found the box I was looking for.

I had to work at the duct tape, and then gave up, tearing the cardboard off the top, just enough so I could look inside. Just as I expected, it was filled to the brim with ... worlds.

Adventures, campaigns, epic quests, and short side distractions designed to strip a character of gold, money and magic. My throat closed at the sight of three-ring binders, folders, and plastic envelopes.

I reached in and dug past those things to find my source books. I knew full well that I had kept some of those, unable to bear the idea that someone else would use them.

"Kate, what is this?"

Wan was peering at me from the handhold, his paws extended into the light. He was holding a small metal figurine.

My breath caught in my throat at the sight.

Her plate was still as shiny silver as the day I had painted her. Her long blonde hair trailed out behind her, a few strands covering her face. Those had been a bitch to paint. Her eyes were wide, her mouth turned up in an open-faced smile as she lifted her halberd to strike. Pole-arms were highly underrated as weapons. Useful from the second rank, giving me an extended reach over the meatshields in front. "No helmet, Katling," Gerald used to tease, his blue eyes—

I swallowed hard, then forced the words out. "Put it back, Wan."

His paws pulled the figurine back into the box. "Very

well," he said, his voice muffled as he turned away. "But there are many more, and they are well painted. This other one has lost its sword, but still—"

"Wan," was all I could get out.

His face appeared from the depths of the box, his gaze steady as he considered my face. "My apologies, Kate."

"I found it," I blinked quickly as I pulled the book from the box.

Wan crawled out of the box. I reached out a hand absently and he crawled up my arm to my shoulder. He peered over at the book in my hands. *"Legends and Lore?"* he asked doubtfully. "Gaming materials?"

"Sure," I opened the book and rifled the pages. "Here we go, 'Chinese Mythology.' "

Wan stiffened.

"Er . . ." I quickly turned the pages. "Look, here is a summary of the history and an explanation of a some new spells . . ." This wasn't going the way I had planned. Especially when the next few pages listed stats and hit dice for the various avatars.

Wan crossed his paws over his chest and gave me a flat look. "And where are the combat statistics for Holy Mary, Mother of God?"

I closed the book, and shoved it back into the box. "Okay, bad idea."

"Perhaps instead we could use original source materials," Wan said firmly. "I have many scrolls and—"

I stood up and reached for one of the beams as I headed to the stairs. "Hey, Wan. Remember what I told you about Wikipedia?"

I'd forgotten that we hadn't cleaned up the office.

Wan's small library, which sat on the top of my computer hutch, was a mess. His tiny white scrolls, tied with red ribbons were scattered about the teak floor. Wan jumped from my shoulder to the hutch, placed his sword on its rack, and started to pick them up, using paws and tail. The whole prehensile thing still freaked me out, but in comparison to evil possums, it didn't rate a second glance.

I sighed and looked at my computer. I'd used my ergonomic keyboard to whack at the rats and it cracked right in half. I might have an old one in the closet, but my wrists would let me know fast if I used it for any length of time. Lovely. I'd have to order a new one. I dug out the info as Wan was muttering curses to himself. I snorted as I dialed, resigning myself to dealing with New Delhi and an hour on hold.

I got American English. I almost dropped the phone.

"Oh no, ma'am." The clear voice chirped. "Your keyboard is covered completely by the warranty. I'll have a new one overnighted to you immediately."

"What's that cost?"

"No cost, ma'am. Part of the service on your account. Has your address changed?"

"No–no . . ."

"You will receive it by early morning delivery tomorrow. Anything else I can help you with, ma'am?"

I stared at the dial tone coming out of the handset.

There was a soft cough, and I looked up to see Wan facing me, a scroll in his hands.

"Wan, the strangest thing . . ."

"What is needed will be provided, Wise One." Wan's eyes were gleaming with excitement.

"Really?" I thought about that for a moment. "Because I really need to lose weight."

Wan sighed. "What is needed, Kate. There is a difference between needs and desires." Wan held up the scroll, letting it unroll to dangle before me. "As K'ung Fu-tzu says—"

I squinted at the scroll. "That's Lao Tzu, not Confucius."

Wan smiled. "You are certain?"

"Wan," I growled. "It's the Tao Te Ching, Chapter 1. 'The way that can be spoken of is not the constant way.'" I rolled my eyes. "Which is not particularly helpful, if you ask me."

Wan rolled up the scroll looking rather smug.

"Wait," I considered my self-satisfied little scholarly friend. "I didn't think you wrote in English."

"I do not," Wan said, turning to replace the scroll. "It would appear that you can now read the original source materials."

Oh, hell. His miniature library was stuffed to the gills with those tiny scrolls. "Wan, I am not reading—"

"Oh, but you are." Wan said over his shoulder. "The more you read and learn, the less your adversary will know."

Crap.

Itty came into the room, yawning and stretching. Bitty was right behind her, making the familiar whining sound. I reached down to pet them both. "Need to go out, my babies?"

They both barked, and raced for the living room.

"Wait for me, Kate." Wan picked up his sword and slung it over his shoulder, then leapt for mine.

"The doctor warded the backyard, Wan." But I waited until he was on my shoulder until I headed for the great room.

"Still, we should have a care," Wan said. "Once the foe knows that you have taken on the role of Wise One, their anger will be a thousandfold."

I slid open the glass door and the dogs raced out ahead of us. The day had been a nice one, but the clouds had gathered now, dark and heavy, and the breeze was picking up. I grabbed up the koi food, and moved to the side of the pond to feed them. "They still want the necklace."

"Their goals will have changed." Wan was scanning the sky. "Now they will want to—"

The dogs howled.

I jerked my head around to see them at the fence, pawing and clawing, trying to get at a possum sitting on the post. Not any old possum, either. This one was sitting there, holding its walking stick, glaring at them. Old Ugly-Stinky, who had tried to kill me in my own kitchen.

It raised its head and stared at me.

It knew.

I don't know how it knew. I don't know how I knew it knew, since the possum's face didn't really change all that much. His teeth were already bared and he was hissing like a cobra. Except now, the hatred in its eyes was palpable. I took a step back, but didn't let my gaze drop.

The possum's nose wrinkled up even more, and it reached out with its staff. There was a flash, and he pulled it back, its tip charred and smoldering.

"The wards," Wan said. "Still . . . call the dogs, Kate. We need to get back into the house."

"Itty, Bitty," I called out, shivering as the wind picked up. I called again sharply, but both my babies were two intent on their target to pay much attention. I whistled. Itty turned and ran a few steps toward me, but when Bitty didn't follow, Itty tore back for her fair share of the barking.

"Fool dogs," I muttered, starting toward them.

"No, Kate." Wan pulled his sword from its sheath. "Go no closer."

Now, Wan is an impressive fighter, but the whole two-inch-high-defender thing made it just a little embarrassing. "The wards will hold."

The possum lifted its stick, and started chanting in a voice like fingernails on a chalkboard. The dogs whined and backed off, looking at me, then up at the animal in confusion.

"Itty. Bitty. Right here, right now," I commanded, and they came tearing over to me. They whined at my feet for a moment, circling around, begging to be petted.

"Come on, my babies." I bent to pet them.

Wan grabbed at my shirt collar. He was eyeing the possum, who was starting to get louder and shriller, if that was possible. "Inside, Kate. Hurry."

"Okay," I stood, taking a last look at the sky. The clouds were getting thicker and darker fast. The wind was picking up and . . .

The possum cried out in its horrible shrill voice and thunder boomed through my bones. The dogs yelped and ran for the house. I cringed, then looked up. There'd been no lightning, what was—

He was floating over the fence, his arms outstretched as if poised for flight.

His long blond hair floated around his head like a cloud. His armor was black and gold. His face was angled and mysterious, with a scar that ran over one eye and down his cheek, and his eyes . . . his dark eyes burned like fire over my skin.

Pure desire lanced through me, the warmth flooding between my legs and surging up into my chest. My knees wobbled, and went weak. I couldn't breathe, couldn't hear anything but the pounding of my heart.

One corner of his mouth quirked up, and he reached out his hand. I watched as those warm supple lips started to form my name. He wanted me, desired me, and my skin rippled, anticipating his touch. My nipples tightened, as if his fingers were already—

Pain—something cut into my ear. Something yammering in my ear, making frantic noises. I reached up and brushed it away. It didn't matter, nothing mattered except lying skin to skin with my lover. I took a step, and then another, reaching up to unzip my sweatshirt, tear off my clothes and—

Something sliced into my ankle.

I stumbled, looking down to see blood pouring from a cut. Wan was standing next to my foot, his sword in one hand, its pommel hanging open. He had something in his other hand, and when his gaze caught mine, he screamed against the rising wind, and threw it at me.

It arched up . . . something small, that grew larger as it rose up higher, something white . . . no . . . mother-of-pearl. I reached out and caught the medallion, letting the necklace warp around my wrist.

It felt like a bucket of ice water had been thrown in my face.

The man was now a corpse, floating in midair, grinning at me with horrible teeth, holding out its decaying hand, gesturing.

Desire went to revulsion in two seconds flat. I fell to the ground and heaved up everything in my stomach. Let me tell you . . . Michigan Cherry's not so good the second time around.

"Up, Kate. Up, and in the house." Wan was in the grass, keeping well back from the splatter. "Hurry."

"Wan," I gasped, trying to clear my mouth. "What is that thing?"

"Now you want lessons?" Wan asked. His sword was in his hand, the pommel closed. "Move! I will hold them off!"

The back yard exploded with light. That thing . . . it was pounding on the wards, trying to break through them. Light and smoke flared again and again. The possum, still perched on its fencepost, cried out in its shrill nasty voice. "Aid us!"

All around, ninja rats climbed up the posts and started to beat on the wards as well.

The dogs were frantic now, racing back to defend me as I scrabbled to my feet, the necklace still wrapped around my hand. They ran just passed me, and took a stance, barking and farting for all they were worth.

I staggered up, trying to look everywhere at once. Dr. McDougall had planned the wards for ninja rats, not corpses. I didn't think—

The possum shrieked something and gestured with its free hand. The ninja rats all started to glow . . . and became man-sized.

Time to go.

I started moving back, unwilling to turn my back. The dogs ran behind me, then in front, barking madly.

Wan retreated as well, focused on the corpse, waving his tiny sword back and forth as if in challenge.

The corpse paused for a moment, as the others continued their assault. Its dead eyes raked over me and it smiled. *"Kaaaaaate."*

My stomach heaved. I retched a bit, but kept moving back toward the house. I wanted walls between me and that thing.

The corpse laughed, as if it knew my fear. From nowhere it pulled an odd hooked sword with a flourish. The blade glowed green. That couldn't be good.

The corpse gripped the blade with both hands and brought it down with a scream. The edge sheared through the golden glow. The ward popped like a bubble.

The ninja rats flowed up and over the fence like a tide.

The dogs yelped and ran for the house again.

"Kate," Wan screamed over his shoulder. "Put it on. PUT THE NECKLACE ON."

I looked at my hand.

The necklace was full size now, no longer hidden from the world in the pommel of Wan's sword. The large pieces of cut jade were linked with golden strands, and the medallion hung down, glimmering softly in the light. I lifted it with both hands, and slipped it over my head. Somewhere, someone or something shrieked in anger as it settled on my skin.

Time seemed to stop. The ninja rats were still coming, but slowly, all *Matrix-y*. Sort of a *Flying Mouse, Hidden Possum* kinda thing.

But even as I watched time slow, I was focused on the necklace. I'd been right. The jade pieces felt cool against my skin, but they warmed quickly, taking heat from my body. The medallion fell right between my breasts, as if designed to lie there and cover my beating heart.

"What do you need?" It wasn't a voice, it was just a question that formed in my being, a feeling of support, of strength. "What do you need?"

I lifted my eyes to the oncoming rats and the corpse was floating over the fence toward me. "Help," was my only thought. "Help us."

The movie effects ended. The first of the rats reached Wan, swinging its sword straight down at my little friend.

Wan raised his sword—

Another interposed.

A girl stood there, dressed in traditional flowing robes the color of a daffodil in spring. She had two sharp daggers in each hand. As she parried the blow with one, she drove the other into the rat's heart.

It collapsed.

Suddenly there were a dozen girls, each in a spring color, fighting the rats. I froze, watching as they took out their opponents with graceful, flowing movements more dance than battle.

The possum was still on the fence post, gesturing with its walking stick, cursing. I reached down to the rim of the koi pond, grabbed up a rock, and hurled it with all my might.

It hit old Ugly-Stinky right between the eyes, rocking him back.

Hah! I reached for another rock.

"Kaaaate . . ."

I'd forgotten the corpse.

It had floated down behind me and grabbed my uplifted hand, pulling me off balance. The stench was eye-watering and I gasped in an effort to breathe.

The corpse reached for the necklace.

"KATE!" Wan screamed, but he was too far away and too small to do much of anything.

Two of the girls darted toward me, their blades out.

I turned, grabbing at the thing's hair, trying to yank its head back and away from me. But the monster chuckled and jerked me around, forcing my arm up into my back. I cried out, my nerveless hand dropping the rock. Now it had my hair, pulling my head back, exposing my neck. I could feel its thick black nails on my skin.

"So sweet," it hissed into my ear. "You will taste so sweet. I will lick your blood from the jade and—"

Three girls ran up dressed in colors of peach, green, and daffodil. Their faces were lovely, but their eyes were like steel. "Release the Wise One," Peach chirped.

"Or face our blades, vampire." Wan said, standing on Daffodil's shoulder.

Vampire? Oh, fu—

Shards of lightning lanced the air around us, making my skin tingle. The thing holding me screamed in rage and pain. Suddenly I was free, and to my complete mortification, I slid to the ground like a limp sock.

I barely managed to stiffen my arms, and lifted my head to find myself surrounded by pastel colors. The girls had surrounded me, protecting me from that thing.

Lightning was still flashing, and I could hear someone—hopefully the vampire—screaming in pain.

The girls swirled about me, a living moving shield, but I could see glimpses. The Doctor was driving that thing off, back toward the fence, using lightning like a scalpel. Further and further, until it finally screamed defiance and vanished up into the clouds.

The possum was still on the fence post waving its walking stick, but I couldn't have cared less. My vision was going with my strength, and I let it. They could handle the possum without me. I sagged down into the grass and let the darkness take me.

The poor doctor ended up hauling me into the house. I woke to find myself in his arms, being settled on the sofa. He knelt next to me, taking my pulse. "Coffee?" he asked as my eyes opened.

Bleh. Not for a while. "Jack Daniels," I said, trying to clear my throat. "Bookcase."

"A woman after my own heart," he said as he moved off.

I struggled to sit up, only to find myself facing two rows of girls kneeling before me.

"Wise one," they bowed, and then knocked their foreheads to the floor three times in quick succession.

"What the hell—"

"They kowtow in respect. Befits your position as elder." Wan was perched by my head, wiping his blade with part of a paper napkin.

Elder. Hell. I put my head back against the cushion. The necklace was a warm comforting weight on my shoulders. The jade was warm and—

There was a tinkle of ice, and the doctor thrust a glass in my hand, filled with Jack. "Here. I think you are going to need this."

I closed my fingers on the cold wet wonderful glass, and took a huge gulp. "What was that thing?"

"Jiang Shi." Wan said. "A vampire."

"That wasn't a vampire," I said. "Vampires are—"

"A Chinese vampire," Wan corrected. "From our folklore. They are created when a person's soul refuses to leave their body."

"Powerful," Doc said with a grimace.

"Yes," Wan said. "This one is very old and very powerful. It could move its arms freely, and it was dressed in the armor of the Qin Dynasty."

"You beat it off." I looked over at the doctor.

He shrugged. "I took it by surprise. Not sure what would happen if it caught me that way."

"Lovely," I took another gulp and realized that all the girls were staring at me. I dropped my voice to a whisper, and hid my lips behind the glass. "Er . . . Wan . . . where did the girls come from?"

Wan sheathed his sword, and gave me a wide-eyed innocent look. "Ah. Perhaps I neglected to mention your guardianship over the Twelve Sacred Warrior-Virgins."

The doctor spit out his Jack.

Oh, hell no!

NO MATTER WHERE YOU GO

Tanya Huff

"I overheard a couple of uniforms talking today."

Her head pillowed on Mike's shoulder, palm of her right hand resting over his heart, Vicki made a non-committal *hmm*.

"There's been some vandalism in Mount Pleasant Cemetery the last couple of nights."

She tapped her fingers on sweat-damp skin to the rhythm of the rain against the window, wrapping it around the steady bass of his heartbeat. "You don't say."

Mike closed his hand around hers, stopping the movement. "Someone dug a small firepit on a grave and cremated a mouse. The officers responding found wax residue on the gravestone, chalk marks on the grass, and evidence from at least four people."

"Uh huh." Vicki rose up on her left elbow so that she could see Mike's expression. He seemed to be completely serious. Although the pale spill of streetlight around the edges of the blind provided insufficient illumination for him to see her in turn, his eyes were locked on her face, waiting for her to draw her own conclusions.

"You think some idiot's trying to call up a demon."

"I think it's possible."

"And you think I should . . . ?"

He shrugged, a minimum movement of one shoulder. "I think *we* should check it out."

"We?"

His fingers tightened, thumb moving down to stroke the scar on her wrist. "I don't want you there alone."

She had a matching scar on the other wrist, a pair of thin white lines against pale skin, a reminder written in flesh of a demon nearly unleashed on the city by her blood. But that had been years ago, when Vicki Nelson, ex-police detective, not particularly successful private investigator, had only just discovered that creatures out of nightmare were real.

"Things have changed." Turning her hand in his, she stroked in turn the puncture wound on his wrist, already healing even though it had been less than an hour since she'd fed. "I'm pretty sure vampire trumps wannabe sorcerer." When he didn't answer, merely continued to look up at her, brown eyes serious, she sighed. "Fine. A vampire and an exceedingly macho police detective *definitely* trumps wannabe sorcerer. Worst case scenario, it won't be much of a demon if all they're sacrificing is a mouse. We'll check it out tomorrow night."

Dark brows rose. "Why tomorrow? It's barely midnight."

"And it's pouring rain. They won't be able to keep their fire lit."

"So tonight . . ."

Vicki grinned, tugged her hand free, and moved it lower on his body. "Well, if you're so set on not sleeping, I'm sure we'll think of something to do."

*   *   *

Mike Celluci had spent most of his career in Violent Crimes. One night, back before the change, when alcohol had still been able to breach the barriers Vicki kept around her more philosophical side, she'd called the men and women who worked homicide the last advocates of the dead—bringing justice if not peace. Over the last few years Mike had learned that, on occasion, the dead were quite capable of advocating for themselves. That knowledge had added a whole new dimension to walking in graveyards at night.

By day, Mount Pleasant Cemetery was a green oasis in the center of Toronto, the dead sharing their real estate with a steady stream of people looking for a respite from the press of the city. At night, when shadows pooled in the hollows and under the trees and clustered around the hundreds of headstones, the dead seemed less willing to share.

"Isn't this romantic." Vicki tucked her hand in the crook of Mike's elbow and leaned toward him with exaggerated enthusiasm. "You, me, midnight, a graveyard. Too bad we don't have a picnic." She grinned up at him, fingers tightening over his pulse. "Oh, wait . . ."

Mike snorted and shook his head but he understood her mood. It had been too long since they'd worked a case together. And okay, a cremated mouse and some wax residue wasn't exactly a case, but it was more than they'd had for a while.

He tugged her off the path, following the landmarks from the original police report. "It was this way."

As they moved farther from the lines of asphalt and the circles of light that barely touched the grass, Vicki took the lead.

"Do you know where you're going?" he asked. With

no moonlight, no starlight, and, more importantly, his flashlight off so as not to give away their position, he stayed close.

"I can smell the wet ash from their fire. The candle wax." She frowned. "Smells like gardenia."

And then she froze.

Mike froze with her. "Vicki?"

"Burning blood. This way."

He knew she was holding back so he could match her pace, his hand wrapped around her elbow as he ran full out, trusting her to steer him around any obstacle. They headed into the older part of the cemetery where ornate mausoleums housed the elite of the early 1900s. Clutching at her outstretched arm as she suddenly stopped, he nearly fell but found his balance at the last minute. They were close enough together, he could see her turning in place, head cocked.

"There." A mausoleum set off a little from the rest. "I hear four heartbeats."

Not for the first time, he wished she could return to the force. They had a canine unit, they had a mounted unit, they had a mountain bike unit for Christ's sake— why not a bloodsucking undead unit? Her abilities were wasted within the narrow focus of her PI's license.

He could see a flicker of light through the grill in the mausoleum's door as they moved closer.

Teenagers. Peering carefully through the ornate ironwork, Mike could see four—three watching the fourth as she chanted over the smoking contents of a stainless steel mixing bowl set between the four white candles burning on the marble crypt in the center of the mausoleum. A triple circle about six feet in diameter had been drawn in what looked like sidewalk chalk on the back wall—a blue ring, then a red ring, then a white ring. In the center of the innermost circle was a complex scrawl of loops and angles.

Mike knew better than to equate youth with an absence of threat but nothing about the kids looked dangerous. Two of them—a thin white female and a tall East Indian male—were all but bouncing out of their black hightops. One of them—white male, shortest of the four—stood with his shoulders hunched and hands shoved into his hoodie's pockets, looking a little scared. The body language of the girl doing the chanting suggested she wasn't going to accept failure as an option.

He glanced down at Vicki and mouthed, "Demon?"

She shrugged and lifted her head to murmur, "I have no idea," against his ear.

Whatever it was they were doing, they hadn't done it it yet. Teenagers, he could handle. Demons . . .

He could, but he'd rather not.

Pushing his coat back to expose the badge on his belt, he pushed open the door. "Tell me," he snapped in his best voice-of-authority, "that you're not raising the dead, because that never turns out well."

The scared boy made a sound Mike was pretty sure he'd deny later. The other two froze in place, mouths open. The chanting girl stopped chanting and turned—white female, pierced eyebrow, pierced lower lip. She had what looked like a silver fish knife in one hand and an impressive scowl for someone her age. This close, he doubted any of them were over fifteen.

"Ren!" Scared Boy took a step toward her. "It's the cops."

"I can see that." She shoved a fall of black and white striped hair back off her face. "It doesn't matter. It's done!"

"What's done?" Vicki asked.

Mike hadn't seen Vicki move so he was damned sure Ren hadn't. In all fairness, he had to admire her nerve— if he hadn't been watching her, he wouldn't have seen the flinch as she turned to find Vicki smiling at her from about ten centimeters away.

"The ritual."

"I don't see a demon." Vicki peered into the bowl. "Unless it's a very small demon. Another mouse," she added, glancing over at Mike.

"Demons." The bouncing boy rolled his eyes. "As if."

"That's so last millennium," the girl beside him snorted.

Ren's gaze skittered off Vicki's face but, with the Hunter so close to the surface, Mike gave her points for the attempt. "If you must know," she said as pride won out over a preference to keep the adults in the dark, "I've opened a portal."

"A portal?" Mike repeated, glancing around the mausoleum.

"Might be a very small portal," Vicki offered.

All four teenagers looked over at the circles chalked on the rear wall.

"It takes time!" Ren said defensively. She set the knife down forcefully enough that the metal rang against the stone, then moved around the crypt so that nothing stood between her and the wall.

Given that Vicki made no move to stop her, Mike figured the odds of the portal opening were small.

"Come on." Ren beckoned to the others. "We need to be ready."

"But Ren, they're cops!" the scared boy protested, hanging back as the other two joined her.

"Their laws have no relevance here."

Mike sighed. The last things he wanted to do was spend the night arguing with teenagers. "Okay, guys, I get that you're bored and looking for some excitement, but at the very least this is trespassing, so let's just pack things up, promise to take up hobbies that don't involve graveyards, and we'll see you get home."

Ren ignored him. Spearing the scared boy with an imperious gaze, she snapped, "Cameron!"

Cameron ran to join the others. Just then, the center of the chalked circle flared white, then black, then cleared to show a dark sky filled with stars too orange to be familiar. Mike thought he saw the dark silhouettes of buildings and was certain he could smell rotting meat.

"We are so out of here," Ren sneered as she stepped back through the circle, pulling Cameron with her. An instant later, Vicki stood holding the black and silver hoodie of the unnamed girl as the other two followed.

Almost immediately, someone began to scream.

Cameron.

The circle started to close. The first fifteen centimeters in from the white chalk line had already returned to grubby stone and flaking mortar.

Mike knew what Vicki was going to do before she did it. As he charged around the crypt—to stop her, to join her, he had no idea—she shot him a look that said half a dozen things he didn't want to consider too closely, and dove through a hole no more than a meter across. Then half a meter. He couldn't follow.

All four kids were screaming now.

Vicki was stronger, faster, and damned hard to kill, but in another world she might be no more of a threat than Cameron was.

Barely a handspan of portal remained. Mike snapped his extra clip off his belt, threw it and his weapon as hard as he could into the dark, then stood staring at a blank stone wall.   .

The silence was so complete he could hear the candles flickering on the crypt behind him.

Vicki had no idea what the hell she was facing. It looked a bit like the Swamp Thing, but was a phosphorescing gray with three large yellowing fangs about ten centimeters long—two on the top, one on the bottom, across a wobbling lip from a jagged stub. It was big— three, three and a half meters high although it was hard to tell for certain, given that it rested its weight on the knuckles of one clawed hand as it stuffed bits of Cameron into its mouth. The other three teenagers crouched among the rubble at the base of a crumbling wall and screamed.

Moonlight and starlight reflected off the pale stone of the ruins, denying them the merciful buffer of full darkness. It was light enough to see their friend die.

The scent of Cameron's blood pulled the Hunger up and, although Vicki drew her lips back off her teeth and shifted her weight onto the balls of her feet, she held her position. She could do nothing for Cameron.

If the creature was willing to move on, she'd let it.

It wasn't.

The kids realized that the same time she did.

On the bright side, as it lurched toward them, ramped up terror stopped the screaming.

It roared and swatted at her as she raced up the closest pile of rubble, too slow to connect. When the rubble ended, she launched herself onto its shoulders, wrapping both hands around its head.

Her fingers sank deep into rubbery flesh, but got a grip on the bone beneath as she twisted. Back home, bipedal meant a spine and a spinal column, but she wasn't in Kansas any more. Nothing cracked.

It wrapped a hand around her leg.

Snarling, she wrapped her hand in turn around one of the upper fangs, snapping it off at the base and jabbing it deep into the creature's neck as it yanked her off its shoulders. The flesh parted like tofu wrapped in rubber. It essentially cut its own throat.

Just before she hit the ground, Vicki realized that the orange fluid spilling from the gash was not what she knew as blood.

One problem at a time! She rolled with the impact and bounced up onto her feet ready for round two.

Rising up to its full height, throat gaping, it staggered back a step. Cameron's leg fell from lax fingers. It wobbled in place for a moment, then it collapsed with an entirely unsatisfactory squelch.

Under normal circumstances, Vicki'd make sure it was dead, but nothing about this even approached normal so she turned instead to check on the kids. Heads down, huddled close and weeping, all three still cowered at the base of the wall. Stepping toward them, she kicked something that skittered across the uneven pavement.

The 19-round magazine for a Glock 17.

Mike's scent clung to it.

A heartbeat later she had the Glock in her hand. He hadn't been able to follow her through the contracting portal so he'd . . .

Which was when it hit her.

Even through the nearly overpowering scent of Cameron's blood, Vicki knew exactly where she'd first touched the ground in this new world. There was no sign of the portal.

No way to get . . .

The air currents against her cheek changed. She threw herself down and to the side as an enormous flock of black, featherless birds dropped out of the sky—those that could landing on the fallen creature, the rest circling, waiting for their chance to feed.

With curved raptor beaks, they ripped off chunks of flesh, fighting challengers for their place on the corpse with the bone spurs on the tips of their pterodactyl-like wings. About a dozen fought over the pieces of Cameron.

They weren't particularly large, but there was one hell of a lot of them.

A shriek of pain brought her back up onto her feet and racing toward the kids. Denied their place at the feast, a few of the birds were making a try for fresher meat, wheeling and diving and easily avoiding Ren's flailing arms. Vicki could smell fresh blood. One of the kids had taken a hit.

Twisting her head just far enough to avoid a bone spur ghosting past her cheek, she grabbed the attacking bird out of the air, crushed it, tossed it aside. And then another. And then she was standing over the kids, with blood that wasn't blood dripping from her hands, teeth bared, killing anything that came close enough.

After a few moments, nothing did.

Recognizing a predator, those scavengers not feeding pulled back to circle over the corpse.

Ren screamed when Vicki turned toward her.

"Be quiet!" Vicki snapped, giving thanks for the whole *Prince of Darkness* thing when Ren gave one last terrified hiccup and fell silent. Considering the welcome they'd already had, the odds were very good screaming would not attract bunnies and unicorns. "Now do whatever it is you have to do to get us the hell out of here."

The girl's eyes widened. "What?"

"Open the portal that'll take us home." Vicki gave her points for looking in the right direction but, given Ren's rising panic, didn't wait for a response. "You can't, can you?" She kept her tone matter-of-fact, used it to smack the panic back down, didn't let her own need to scream out denial show. "Not from this side."

"We weren't going to go back." Ren waved a trembling hand at the corpse and the scavengers and the sky of red stars. "It wasn't supposed to be like this!"

"Yeah, well, surprise." A scavenger with more appetite than survival instinct tried to take a piece out of the top of her head; Vicki crushed it almost absently, wiping her hand on her jeans as she watched the circling birds. Some of them were flying fairly high. They'd be visible as silhouettes against the night to anyone—or anything—with halfway decent vision. It reminded her of lying on the sofa with Mike, soaking up his warmth, and watching television.

"They're going to draw other scavengers. The way vultures do. Maybe other predators. We have to find cover."

"How do you know that?"

"'Animal Planet.'"

"But you're a . . ." Even though she was clearly fine with poking holes into other realities, Ren couldn't seem to say it.

This was neither the time nor the place for denial.

"Vampire. Nightwalker. Member of the bloodsucking undead." Vicki frowned, trying to remember the rest and coming up blank. Three would have to do. "I have cable. And I'm your best bet if you want to survive this little adventure." Hand on the girl's shoulder, Vicki could feel her trembling, but whether it was from Cameron's grisly death or the proximity to one of humanity's ancient terrors, there was no way to be sure. Unfortunately, Vicki had no time for kindness that didn't involve keeping these three kids alive.

No time to give into fear of her own.

She studied the area, for the first time able to look beyond the immediate need to kill. This wasn't the night she knew. The portal had opened on a broad street that looked a bit like University Avenue by way of a hell dimension, the paving cracked and buckled. The closest stone buildings were ruins, but some offered more shelter than others. The solidest of the lot was on the other side of the corpse—not worth the risk—but about two hundred meters away, where the road began a long sweeping arc to the left, was a structure that still had a second and third floor even though the actual roof was long gone. Better still, it looked as though the colonnaded entrance had partially collapsed, leaving an opening too small to admit Cameron's killer—or more specifically, under the circumstances, its friends and family.

"There." She pointed with her free hand, giving Ren a little shake to focus her. "We need to get those two up and moving and into that building. What are their names?"

"I don't . . ."

"What? You don't know?"

"Of course I know!" A hint of the girl who'd faced them in the tomb emerged in response to Vicki's mocking tone. Vicki gave herself a mental high five; anger wouldn't hobble the way fear would. "Their names are Gavin and Star."

"Star? Seriously?"

"What's wrong with Star?" Ren demanded, jerking

her shoulder out from under Vicki's hand. "It's her name and it's better than the dumbass name her mother gave her!"

Vicki didn't care who gave her the name, as long as she answered to it.

Gavin had a long, oozing cut along the top of his forehead; Vicki let the scent of fresh blood block the stink coming from the creature's corpse as unfamiliar internal organs were exposed. The kid's eyes were squeezed shut and he had both arms wrapped around Star. Star's eyes were open, her pupils so dilated the blue was no more than a pale halo around the black. Calling their names had little effect.

Vicki could feel terror rising off them like smoke.

Given what a joy this place had been so far, if she could feel it, so could other things.

She could work with terror if she had to. When she snarled, Star blinked and focused on her face. Gavin opened his eyes. As she pulled her lips back off her teeth, she could hear their hearts begin to pound faster and faster as adrenaline flooded their system. *She* was a terror they understood. Hauling them onto their feet, she pointed them the right way and growled, "Run."

Hindbrains took over.

Stumbling and crying, they ran.

Ren shot her a look that promised retribution, and raced to catch up.

"So a teenage girl opened a portal to another reality on the wall of a mausoleum, went through with her friends, Vicki followed them, and then the portal closed—is that it?"

"That's it."

"Are you bullshitting me?"

"Why the fuck would I joke about something like that?" Mike growled into his phone.

Thousands of kilometers away in Vancouver, Tony Foster sighed. "Yeah. Good point. Okay, it's eleven now; if I can get on the first plane out in the morning, I won't be there until around three in the afternoon, given the time difference, so . . ."

"Too long." Over the years, Mike had heard more screaming than he was happy admitting to. The kid on the other side of the portal had been screaming in pain, not fear. Not under threat; under attack. And Vicki had landed right into the middle of it. "You need to reopen that thing now."

"Over the phone?"

"Now," Mike repeated. Years ago, Tony Foster had been Vicki's best set of eyes and ears on the street. Then Henry fucking Fitzroy had gotten his bloodsucking undead self wrapped up in the kid's life, and Tony'd headed out west with them while Henry taught Vicki how to handle the *change*. After Vicki'd come home, Tony'd stayed with Henry. Next thing Mike knew, Tony'd actually had the balls to walk away and make a life for himself—a life that included a job, a relationship, and magic. Real magic. Not rabbits out of a hat magic, that much Mike knew, but not much more. In all honesty, he hadn't asked too many questions. Vicki was about all the *it's a weird new wonderful world* he could cope with.

Tonight, his ability to cope with the fact Tony had gone all Harry Potter was moot. He needed to get Vicki and the kids back. Tony was the only one he knew who might be able to do it.

Who *could* do it.

"All right." On the other end of the phone, Tony took

a deep breath. "Was one of them a sixty-year-old Asian dude?"

"No, I told you . . ."

"I know what you told me but I had to check. That means the girl who opened the portal wasn't actually a wizard; she just found a spell and had enough willpower and need to make it work. So all you have to do is repeat exactly what she did."

Mike glanced around the mausoleum at the bowl and the candles and the chalked circles. "*All* I have to do?"

"Send me pictures of everything she used. As much detail as you can. Doesn't matter how small or insignificant. I'll run it through my database and see if I can identify the verbal portion."

"You have a database for this sort of shit?"

"Yeah, well, I like my shit organized."

"She burned a dead mouse."

"She probably killed it first. Send me the pictures, then go looking for a mouse of your own."

A mouse of his own? "Tony, where the fuck am I going to find a live mouse in Toronto at one in the morning?"

"No idea. You may have to use your badge and go all fake official business on a pet store owner."

"I can't . . ." He rubbed at his temples and sighed. "Yeah. Maybe. Pictures are on their way . . ."

The ruins were dry and didn't smell too bad, and if something skittered away while Vicki checked the first floor, well, it was skittering *away*. Good enough. She let Ren maneuver her friends through the partially blocked entrance while she kept watch, then slipped in behind them.

The gaping windows threw patches of gray against the marble floor. Ren tucked the other two at the angle where the gray met a pile of fallen masonry. Hands clasped, knees drawn up to their chests, they stared out into the darkness and shuddered at every sound.

As Vicki moved past her, Ren grabbed her arm and snarled, "Leave them alone!"

The scent of blood was still too strong for Vicki to push the Hunger completely back, but she damped it down as far as she could before she turned. Not quite far enough if Ren's reaction was any indication but, in spite of a surge of fear so intense Vicki could all but taste it, the girl maintained her grip and repeated, "Leave them alone!"

"I'm not going to hurt them."

Ren snorted. "Yeah, right." She tipped her head to one side, exposing her throat. "Come on then. If you're going to do it, do me."

Tempting.

"Let's table that offer until I have to feed," Vicki sighed. If she hadn't fed before meeting Mike at the cemetery, she doubted she'd have been able to tear her gaze away from the pulse throbbing hummingbird fast under the pale—and slightly grubby—skin. As it was, she glanced down at the fingers still clutching her arm and said, "Let go; I'm only going to put them to sleep. Give them a bit of a break from this place."

"Why should I trust you?"

"Because I'm asking you to, when I could be telling you to."

"Oh. Right."

When Ren released her, Vicki ignored the way the girl's fingers trembled, nodded once, and moved to deal with the other two. A command to *"Sleep. Dream of pleasant things"* wasn't the way she'd been trained to deal with shock but hey, whatever worked. Star's hoodie was back in the mausoleum, so she shrugged out of her jacket and spread it over them before straightening and returning to Ren's side.

"So how was it supposed to be?" she asked from just behind the girl's left shoulder.

Ren flinched but kept her gaze locked on the road outside the entrance to their shelter. "How was *what* supposed to be?"

"This. You told me that this wasn't how it was supposed to be. So . . . ?"

"It was supposed to be . . ." She swiped at her cheek with the palm of her left hand. "I thought it said, it was the home we always wanted."

Vicki waited.

"My grandma died," Ren continued after a moment. "I hadn't seen her since we moved to Toronto, like four years ago, but she wanted me to have her Bible. My mom, she checked to make sure there wasn't any money in it but totally missed this piece of stuff like leather that had writing on it. Probably because it was in Greek and my mom never learned to read Greek. My grandma taught me when I was little." She paused to swallow a sob and rub her nose against her sleeve before repeating, "I thought it said this was the home we always wanted."

"What was wrong with the homes you had?" The look Ren shot her suggested she not be an idiot as clearly as if the girl had said the words out loud. "So no one cared that you were sneaking out at night?" None of the kids looked like they'd been starved or beaten but Vicki knew that didn't have to mean anything as far as indicators of abuse went. "And no one's going to care if you never make it back?"

Ren snorted. "You really don't get it, do you?"

"Actually ..." Vicki didn't bother finishing and Ren clearly didn't need her to.

"This is my fault. I told them about this. I convinced them to come."

"You didn't force them to come here."

"I didn't tell them we were coming *here*."

"True."

"You're not very comforting."

"Not my ..."

The skittering returned.

Pulling Mike's Glock from where she'd tucked it up against the small of her back, Vicki whirled and blew the head off something that looked like a cross between a rat and a rottweiler seconds before it took a bite out of Star's leg.

"... job," she finished, ignoring Ren's scream in favor of grabbing the rat thing by the tail, carrying it outside, and whipping it about forty meters back toward the flock of scavengers. On her way back inside, she scooped up a double handful of gray sand from where the building met the road.

She could feel Ren watching her as she scattered the sand over the blood and brain spatter on the floor.

"You have a gun. What kind of vampire carries a gun?"

"One that'd like to keep us all alive until morning," Vicki told her, rejoining her at the door. With any luck the bang had scared off the rat things and hadn't attracted anything else. "The gun's Detective Celluci's. He must've tossed it through as the portal was closing."

They turned together to face back down the road where the arc of ribs stripped clean of flesh gleamed in the spaces between the black birds.

Vicki could hear Ren's heartbeat and breathing speed up. "We're never going back, are we?"

"Please." Given the light levels, Vicki made sure the eyeroll could be heard in her tone as she stretched the truth a bit. "This isn't our first portal; Mike'll work it out."

"The cop?"

"He's got resources." He'd probably been on the phone to Tony before Vicki'd hit the ground on the other side and Tony'd know how to fix this. Tony had to know how to fix this.

"But he's a real cop?"

"He is."

"And you're a real vampire?"

"I am."

"Oh man, that's totally like a bad romance novel!" And this time, Vicki could hear the eyeroll in Ren's voice.

She grinned, thinking of Henry. "Kid, you don't know the half of it."

Something skittered in the background but didn't come close enough to shoot. Ren's shoulder pressed up against hers, although Vicki doubted the girl had consciously sought out the contact. "You're a vampire, right? And given the whole nonsparkling, lack of emo thing, I'm guessing you're like a traditional vampire?"

Vicki frowned, decided not to bother translating the teenspeak, and shrugged. "Traditional enough, I guess. Why?"

"If there's like even a sun here, what happens to you when it rises?"

"All right, I've got the mouse." It was in a little green plastic carrying cage and Mike felt like shit every time he looked in at it. He'd had to drive out to the Super Wal-Mart at Eglinton and Warden to get it and that went on the growing list of experiences he never wanted to repeat.

"What color is it?"

"What fucking difference does the color make?"

"It's probably safest if we keep as close to the original ritual as possible."

Setting the cage on the crypt, Mike took a deep breath and reminded himself that he—and more importantly, Vicki—needed Tony. "Probably?"

"Well, magic is mostly a matter of will so you should be able to bull through any minor variations but . . ."

There was a whole wealth of things Tony clearly didn't want to say in that *but*. And that was fine because Mike didn't want to hear them. He shone his flashlight down into the bowl and scowled. "I can't tell what color it was—too burned. She must have used an accelerant."

"That was the spell working. Is there dirt in the bowl? Toss it out and get fresh," Tony instructed when Mike grunted an affirmative. "I've sent you the symbol you have to draw in the middle of the circles."

"That's not what was there before." Mike squinted down at his screen. "It's, I don't know, backward."

"It's supposed to be. This thing's a cut-rate gate; one way only. This is the inbound symbol."

He found a broken piece of sidewalk chalk, no doubt tossed aside by the idiot teenager who'd gotten them all into this mess. "I'll call you back when I'm finished."

"Don't take too long, remember . . ."

"You don't have to fucking remind me about the time," Mike snapped and hung up. Sunrise hadn't been his friend for some years now.

*   *   *

Returning from disposing of another rat thing's body, Vicki glanced up at the sky where the stars were definitely a little dimmer. Clearly it had been too much to hope that this shithole would be a shithole without a dawn. Sitting down next to Ren, she sighed. "Okay, I didn't want to do this, but can you shoot?"

"A gun? Eww, no. Guns are stupid."

"Guns are dangerous. People are stupid. And we don't have time for that lecture right now." Vicki pulled out Mike's weapon and held it resting across her palms. "If I shut off at dawn, you're going to have to keep us all alive until sunset."

Ren shook her head. "I can't."

"Kid, you opened a portal between worlds. In my book, that says there's not a lot you can't do if it comes down to it. Hopefully, it won't come down to it, but if it does . . ."

"I don't even like first-person shooter games!"

Vicki ignored the protest and held up the Glock. "How much can you see?"

"What?"

"I can see in the dark. How much can *you* see?"

Frowning, Ren leaned away from the gun. "It's not as dark as it was."

Not an answer but it would have to do. "Okay, these are the sights—ramped front sight and a notched rear sight with white contrast. You aim with them but I'll use some wreckage to build a shelter with a limited access so all you'll have to do is point and shoot. Now the Glock has a triple safety system to prevent accidental discharge, but once you've released the external safety, here, the two internal safeties automatically disengage when the trigger is pulled."

"Forget it!" Ren shoved at Vicki's arm. "I'm not going to shoot anything!"

"Would you rather be eaten by a giant rat?"

"No, but . . ."

"Then pay attention."

"It's arunda-*ay*!"

"It's nonsense!" Mike protested. "It doesn't mean shit!"

On the other end of the phone, Tony sighed. "It means we get Vicki back," he said quietly. "Try it again from the top."

One hand gripping the edge of the crypt, Mike glanced over at the square of sky he could see through the grill, took a deep breath, and started again.

And then again.

One more time before Tony muttered, "Close enough."

"Close enough?"

"Look, like I said before, it's mostly a matter of will. The rest is just a way to focus power."

"I don't have that kind of power."

"How badly do you want Vicki back?" The phone casing cracked in Mike's grip and although he couldn't have heard it, Tony snorted. "That's plenty of power, trust me. Light the candles and get the mouse."

The mouse seemed oblivious to its fate. Mike thanked heaven for small mercies. He couldn't have coped with a terrified animal. "Why . . . ?"

"Its death symbolizes the journey from one world to another. I don't like this either, but I don't think you can skip it. Put it in the bowl and cut its throat then set it on fire and start the chant. When you finish, the gate should open."

"And if it doesn't?"

"I'll be on the first plane to Toronto. Don't hang up, just set the phone down. I'll chant with you."

"Will that help?"

"It can't hurt."

The silver knife was surprisingly sharp. The mouse's head came right off. It helped, a little, that it didn't have time to suffer. Its fur had just started to smolder when Mike began the chant.

The rat things were getting bolder. She'd killed two more and had just given thanks that they didn't hunt in packs when she saw a large shadow moving through the building across the road. Back home, a lot of predators hunted at dusk and dawn. It figured, Vicki noted silently, that would hold true here as well.

No, not *moving* through the building. *Slithering.*

All things considered, she supposed she shouldn't be surprised by giant snakes. "And no fucking sign of Samuel Jackson when I could really use him," she muttered rubbing the back of her neck. She could feel the dawn approaching. The shelter she'd built would give Ren and the kids a chance against the rat things, but giant snakes were a whole different ballgame.

"What are you looking at?"

Vicki glanced down the road to where the portal wasn't, and shook her head. "Nothing."

The portal wasn't opening.

The stone under the symbol remained solid.

He should have known this magic shit wouldn't have a hope in hell of working. Charging around the crypt, Mike smacked the wall with both palms. "God damn it! Open up!" And again. And then with his fists. "Open the fuck up!"

There was a whoosh behind him.

He turned to see the mixing bowl melting in the heat of the flames.

Turned again to see the center of the circle flare white, then gray under a smear of blood.

"All right, you're going to have to . . ." The flash of light she caught in the corner of her eye had probably been nothing more than an indicator that dawn was closer than she thought, but Vicki turned toward it anyway.

"Is that?" Ren's fingers closed around her arm hard enough to hurt.

"It is."

"But what if it doesn't lead home!"

Vicki took another look across the road. She couldn't see the snake. Probably not a good thing. "Trust me, we'll still be trading up." It was hard to find the Hunter this close to sunrise but somehow she managed it. "Gavin! Star! Wake up and come here. Quickly!"

Still wrapped in her imperative, they did as they were told.

Vicki shoved Ren out into the road and the other two out behind her. "Get them through the portal," she growled. "Get them home."

"What will you be doing?"

"I'll be right behind you." She could *hear* the slithering now. "Run!"

To her credit, Ren grabbed her friend's hands before she started to move.

They'd made maybe twenty meters when the rush of wind at her back had Vicki spin around and squeeze off five quick shots.

Giant snake.

With arms, of a sort.

And no visible eyes.

The bullets dug gouges in the charcoal gray scales. It paused, head and arms weaving about three meters off the ground, but seemed more puzzled than injured.

"Vicki!"

"Keep running!" Next time she ended up on another world with teenagers, she'd add *don't look behind you*.

On the bright side, the giant snake thing had to be keeping the rat things under cover.

Fifty meters further and hunger apparently won over annoyance. Vicki felt air currents shift as the snake lunged. She dropped, rolled, came up, and grabbed the nearest limb above the . . . well, fingers, given their position, snapping it at the elbow.

Leaping clear of the flailing, she raced down the street and hauled Gavin back up onto his feet. He'd torn his jeans and his palm was bleeding and desperate times . . .

She dragged her tongue across the torn flesh and shoved him toward Ren adding what should have been a redundant, "RUN!"

Pain did not seem to make the creatures of this world cautious. If forced to guess, Vicki'd say the snake thing was pissed.

Diving under its charge to the far side of the road, she got a grip on its other arm, braced herself against a piece of broken pavement, and hauled it sideways. There was a wet crack at the point where the arm met the body.

And more flailing.

Ren had shoved Star through the portal and was working on Gavin by the time the snake got moving forward again.

Another time, Vicki might have admired that kind of single-minded determination. But not right now. She grabbed the polished leg bone of the creature she'd killed when they arrived, made it between the snake and the portal just in time, and slammed it as hard as she could on the nose.

"Vicki, come on!"

A glance over her shoulder. The kids were through.

And the portal was about twice as big around as the snake.

The snake didn't seem to know the meaning of the word *quit*.

She hit it again.

"Vicki! It's closing!"

Mike.

The portal was still bigger than the snake.

And the sun was rising.

She threw the bone. It skittered off the scales. When the snake lunged, she stood her ground and emptied the Glock into its open mouth. Changed magazines, kept firing. Ignored the pain as a fang sliced into her upper arm.

Stumbling back, she could smell burning blood.

A hand grabbed her shirt, then she was on her back, on the floor of the mausoleum, still firing into the snake's open mouth.

The portal closed.

The snake head dropped onto her legs.

"Vicki!"

She felt Mike pull the weapon from her hand. Grabbed his hand in turn, and sank her teeth into his wrist. Mike swore, she hadn't been particularly careful, but he didn't pull away. One swallow, two, and she had strength enough to tie up a couple of loose ends. "Star, Gavin, forget this night ever happened!"

"I don't . . ." Ren began.

Vicki cut her off. "Your choice."

"I want to remember. Well, I don't really want to remember but . . ."

A raised hand cut her off and Vicki managed to growl, "Sunrise."

"Got it covered."

She was heavier than she had been but Mike lifted her and dropped her into the open crypt. The open, occupied crypt.

And then the day claimed her.

"Okay, I'm impressed with your quick thinking . . ." Vicki shimmied into the clean jeans Mike had brought her, "but waking up next to a decomposed body was quite possibly the grossest thing that's ever happened to me."

"At least the body didn't wake up," Mike pointed out, handing her a shirt. "Given our lives of late, that's not something you can rule out."

"True." She shrugged into the shirt and moved into his arms, head dropping to rest on his shoulder.

"You need to feed."

The wound in her arm had healed over but was still an ugly red.

"Later." She needed more than he could give and right now, she needed him. "The kids?"

"They're all home. The two you told to forget are . . ." She felt him shrug. "I don't know . . . teenagers. The other girl, Ren, she's something. You're going to have to talk to her."

"I know. Cameron?"

The arms around her tightened. "Teenagers run away all the time."

She could tell he hated saying it. "I was too late to save him."

"Yeah, Ren told me." He sighed, breath parting her hair, warm against her scalp. "There isn't enough crap in this world; they had to go looking for another."

Vicki shifted just far enough to press the palm of her right hand over his heart. "There isn't enough love in this world; they had to go looking for another."

SIGNED IN BLOOD

P.R. Frost

A lovely onyx fountain pen landed with a small thud on my desk, bouncing slightly on a pitifully thin manuscript printed for editing. The latest Tess Noncoiré fantasy novel was taking its own sweet time getting written. I picked up the pen. The nib was gold, broader than I liked, and the body fatter than my hand wanted to fit around. I ran my thumb over the smooth stone, absorbing the slight coolness. It nestled more comfortably in my grip, conforming to my hand. I'd held one like it before. I knew that. My memory refused to jog the image loose.

Layers of color spiraled around the pen's heavy body, ranging from dark red to light cream, like the desert spires that filled the Valley of Fire outside of Las Vegas. A place of mystical beauty and terrible danger. Did the pen share the danger or just the beauty?

I knew words would flow easily from this pen. Beautiful words that melded together into a story.

Something tickled the back of my mind. An idea? A sentence, then a paragraph filled my head. I touched the nib to the pristine page of a new notebook. Ten words. Two dozen.

Then nothing. My mind pulled back to reality. Where the hell had the pen come from? I pondered the mystery as I wiped the blue ink off the pen with a tissue.

I looked up at the ceiling. Lacking a large glowing hole in the ceiling, the pen clearly had dropped out of thin air. That left one option.

"Scrap?" I demanded of the ether.

A low hum skirted the back of my mind, lodging at the top of my spine.

I jabbed with the pen into the air. "Scrap, where did this pen come from?"

Dahling, I found it, Scrap replied from elsewhere. Scrap was an imp. He could transform himself into my Celestial Blade when danger demanded it. He could slip between dimensions and times. Today he chose demure and invisible.

"Spit it out, buddy," I searched my cluttered office for a glimpse of his translucent gray-green body. I detected motion. A hint of a barbed tail twitched between an American English dictionary and a French lexicon on the top shelf of my book case.

I crept away from my station at the computer and latched onto that tail, winding it around two fingers in a special grip that kept him from popping out into another dimension.

Ah, Tess, you didn't have to do that, he cajoled, trying to yank his tail out of my grasp. I held firm.

"Tell me about the pen. Where'd it come from?"

I told you, I found it.

"Where?"

I tightened my grip as Scrap tried to slither up my arm to my shoulder.

"Cuddling won't persuade me to relent," I told him firmly.

Finally he crossed his arms and pouted at me from the edge of the bookcase. I could almost see the book covers through his half-present body. The blue and black leather bindings faded and brightened with Scrap's attempts to disappear.

Nowhere you'd want to look.

"If *you* found it, then it's more than a fancy pen." I looked down in my opposite hand. It still held the pen. Hadn't I put it down? "Who dumped it and what was it used for?" I looked beyond the graceful lines of the onyx and the tiny slit that revealed the empty ink reservoir. I'd drained it writing my feeble paragraph.

Tiny flecks of rusty brown stained the gold nib. I'd wiped it clean. I knew I had.

Ugh, great. Dried blood. Someone had used the pen to sign in blood. I'd done that once. Blood contracts were irrevocable.

The details of signing the contract poured back into my mind. The pen. This pen. I had used it.

Someone, or something had buried that memory pretty deep so it wouldn't surface easily or often. Probably me.

My blood on the nib.

Well, you see, the Powers That Be don't like to use a pen more than once. In case the blood mixes between two clients and there's crossover in their contracts, Scrap explained in a gush of words. Straight words, no drawled "dahlings" or endearing "babes," not even a flick of his hot pink feather boa—which was missing from around his neck.

"So they discard the pens after each use. Go through a lot of them, do they?"

Not as many as you'd think. People and demons alike kinda avoid dealing with the Powers That Be. You're the

*only one stupid—I mean desperate—enough to actually
seek them out and negotiate terms in, like, centuries.*

"So why did this one get dumped instead of smashed
or burned or whatever?"

Scrap shrugged, trying unsuccessfully to look clueless
and innocent.

I tugged on his tail.

*Okay, so I grabbed it out of the furnace fired by a
full sized J'appell dragon. Would you let go of my tail,
already!*

"Why? Why'd you grab it?"

*You are going to need it, Tess Noncoiré, Warrior of the
Celestial Blade. Trust me.*

"For what? I'm not about to sign any other blood
contracts."

It will do other things.

"Like?"

*Your blood stains the nib. It will never come com-
pletely clean. So if you mix another being's blood with
yours in the pen and then write its name, it is bound to do
your bidding, just like you are bound to the bidding of the
Powers That Be in the terms of your contract.*

"Interesting idea. But first I'd have to draw blood
from someone I really didn't like. I wouldn't do something like that to a friend. Or even a casual enemy."

*Well, um, well, the nib is pretty sharp. I bet if you
stabbed someone with it you'd draw blood.*

"I might with a human. I doubt that itty bitty nib
would penetrate demon hide. Bullets shot from an AK-
47 won't penetrate demon hide. If I'm close enough to
a demon to stab it with a pen, I'd rather just use you in
blade form to take them out. We've killed a fair number
of demons in our day."

That might not always be possible.

"Explain? Why would I need to stab someone with a pen when you aren't around? You are always only a thought away." Most of the time, anyway. There were a few instances . . .

Because I might not always be here.

The lump in my throat sank to form a solid mass in my gut.

It's not so bad, babe. Really. I'll be back before you know it.

"Back from where?"

I can't tell you exactly where or why. Imp law.

I didn't like the sound of that.

"Do you have to report to some authority?"

He nodded again. His skin turned more gray than green and paled.

"And what happens if the authority finds you lacking?"

They won't. I promise.

"Sure about that?"

Very sure. Well, almost sure. You never can tell with imps.

I let go his tail, confident that he'd tell me what he could before popping out.

In response he crawled up my arm to my shoulder and rubbed his face along my cheek. A mere whisper of a tingle on my skin reassured me of our bond.

"Promise to come back as soon as you can?"

The pen will turn out to be more useful than you think.

Three hours later I'd written eight pages of a short story about a pen capable of killing a demon. Words flowed out of the pen almost faster than I could think.

The phone interrupted the next thought and made

it flit into the autumnal humidity rising from the Willamette River below my third-story condo.

"Hey, girlfriend, what're you doing tonight?" my friend, Holly Shannon, asked.

"Hadn't planned anything more than popcorn and a schmaltzy romantic comedy on the classic movie station," I replied.

"Such a deal I have for you," she proclaimed on a forced, brittle laugh.

The hair on my nape stood straight up and my Warrior scar pulsed from my right temple to jaw.

"Should I pack my bags and run the other way?" I quipped, fishing for more information.

"No. Just come sing with me tonight." She sounded serious.

"Sure." Normally I'd jump at the chance of blending my soprano to her sultry contralto. Her Celtic harp added its own lustrous voice to our blend. "Why such short notice?"

"My backup cancelled. I need you. Please, I know I could wing this gig by myself, but it's more fun bouncing off someone else."

"Where should I meet you and when?"

"Kelly's on the riverfront about seven. I go on at eight."

"My favorite. Do they still have Riverdance pale ale?"

"Of course. It was so popular they moved it from seasonal fare to the regular menu. Since we're performing, the first two rounds are on the house."

"See you at seven."

"With bells on."

"Oh, it's that kind of evening!"

We rang off and I tried to return to that short story. But the idea had fled. So I tucked the pen into the spiral of a notebook and set them inside my purse. Then I spent the next hour and a half deciding what to wear.

Seven o'clock came and went. I circled Kelly's five times, expanding my search for parking by an additional block with each circuit. Saturday night at Kelly's with Holly singing, I should expect something else? Wherever Holly sang her unique blend of traditional Celtic music, her own compositions, and upon occasion, parodies of science fiction/fantasy themes known as filk, she drew a capacity crowd.

I finally settled into a ten-level parking structure and forked over an exorbitant price for it. Then I had to trek through a less than savory part of town.

"Can you spare a buck for a cup of coffee," a scruffy man whispered from a darkened doorway.

I hurried my steps past him and the sour wine and vomit odors of eau de neglect that permeated the neighborhood.

"Dear Scrap, wish you were here," I composed a virtual postcard. I'm a Warrior of the Celestial Blade, trained in a variety of weapons. If I found myself weaponless and couldn't defend myself, I knew how to flee danger.

Yeah, right. When had I ever been prudent and fled?

I was on my own without a weapon. I had only the dubious pen and notebook in my purse, and my wits. Subtly I shifted the pen to my skirt pocket. Despite the cool of the evening it felt warm in my hand. An idea slithered around my brain. I scribbled it into the notebook as I walked.

The bouncer at the front door recognized me and passed me into the standing-room-only bar and grill. I was still scribbling when I spotted Holly discussing arcane equipment and settings with the sound engineer.

"Tess, you're a lifesaver!" Holly Shannon said as she threw her arms around me. Tendrils of her bright red mane tickled my nose and threatened to curl into my mouth.

That edge of nervous laughter still clung to her voice. Her substantial body felt stiff and fragile in my arms. She clung a little too long for casual friendship, her fingers tight with anxiety.

"The crowd is really jumping tonight," I said, looking around at the laughing patrons who raised glasses of beer and ate the excellent sandwiches, hamburgers, or corned beef platters. A series of loud guffaws drowned out the piped-in overly romanticized Irish ballads.

"That's what I'm afraid of," Holly said quietly into my ear. Not something to share with others.

I beckoned her to a tiny backroom. Cement walls muffled the noise to a dull roar.

"What's wrong?" I asked, rounding on her as soon as I was sure of some privacy.

"Um." Holly looked around warily.

"Spill it, Holly. We're friends."

A frisson of alarm climbed my spine and set my scar to throbbing. I don't believe in coincidences. I land in situations like this for a reason.

And it had to happen on the one night in four years that Scrap had taken off for elsewhere.

"It's been happening a lot around town. A musician gathers a larger than usual crowd. They start off pumped." She hung her head, letting that fabulous hair swing forward, masking her face. (I'd give my eyeteeth for hair like that. Or hair that behaved. My short, dirty blonde, wire-tight curls never did what I wanted.) She forgot that at five-seven, she topped me by a good five inches. Dropping her face brought her closer to eye contact.

"What's been happening? You should be thrilled with a crowd like this."

"By the end of the show the crowd is listless, silent, dragging their feet, almost too tired to walk back to their cars."

"Not good."

"Last week a young man fell asleep at the wheel on the way home from my concert. He's still in critical condition," she wailed.

"Oh, my God!"

"The entire audience acted as if a vampire had fed on them. All of them!"

"There's no such thing as a vampire," I insisted, as much to reassure myself as her. "No one gets to come back from the dead."

"Not a blood vampire," she whispered. "A psychic vampire."

I didn't laugh. I hung out at the science fiction/fantasy conventions. Psychics got invited frequently. Where psychics gathered, so did those who needed to feed on their energy to fill a lack in their own personality or mental health.

This sounded like something more drastic.

Holly shook her head. A tear bubbled up at the corner of her eye. "If it happens again, I won't sing any more. Not in this town anyway. But this is my home. My fanbase is here. This is the heart of my music. What am I going to do, Tess?"

I gulped. What could I do other than keep my eyes and ears open? Without Scrap's nose for magic and otherworldly critters I was psychically blind.

"I won't sing tonight, Tess. Not if that thing is out there." She shook her head, the hair swishing back and forth reminded me of a horse flicking flies away.

That triggered a different memory that came and fled before I could latch on and reel it in for examination.

"You can sing, and you will, Holly."

"But . . . but."

"Let me be your eyes and ears. Let me prowl the crowd for the first set. If I see something, or it starts happening, I'll tell you on break. If not, I'll come on stage and watch from behind you. I can bang a tambourine and sing on the chorus while I watch for something unusual. Once I've identified the culprit I can get that hunky bouncer at the door to deal with it. Just don't sing the battle song. That builds more energy than most humans can absorb."

Or maybe I'd try something with the pen. I had to know the creature's true name to make it work though.

From the main floor came a rhythmic thumping of feet followed by a chant of "Hol—ly, Hol—ly, Hol–ly."

Holly checked her locket watch—nothing on her wrists to interfere with the harp. "Show time. Wish me luck."

"Break a leg." Superstitious? Me?

You bet your life I am.

Holly opened her set with some low-key ballads and love songs. A little melancholy, like her mood. The crowd stirred a little but didn't become involved. A few sang the sweet choruses with her, eyes closed, imaginations running.

I circled the room three times, weaving a maze among the tables. I waved at an acquaintance here, nodded to a half-familiar face there. No one stood out as more avid than anyone else. My eyes slid over costumes, fairy wings, and elf ears, vaguely Renaissance and medieval garb. In Portland on a Saturday night, people embraced the weird. Nothing unusual.

The next time I came near the stage I nodded to Holly. She ramped up the tempo about three notches. Her fingers flew over the harp in a happy jig.

Someone pounded on a table, adding a drum beat to the dance music. Three couples stood up and began prancing along the aisles until they reached the open pit—the area just in front of the low stage. I'd seen all three couples do much the same thing at other of Holly's performances.

A reel followed the jig, and then another lively dance tune. Four single women and a couple of men joined the dancing. I noted more gelatin elf ears and semi-costumes, knickers and vests, peasant skirts and flowing blouses. Part of the Keep Portland Weird movement. They showed up everywhere.

Holly signaled for me to join her. I skipped up the two steps to the stage and took my post to her right and slightly behind her. Then she handed me a mike and introduced me. At least I got a round of applause from the patrons who recognized my name.

I hummed as Holly played the opening chords to "Blowing In The Wind." We leaned our heads together and crooned, "Where are all the aliens? Gone to Roswell every one."

We got some laughs. I scanned the crowd. A young man with long black hair and white skin the color of my pearls almost rolled on the floor with paroxysms of laughter.

It wasn't that funny.

I kept my eye on him as Holly launched a new round of bawdy sea shanties and drinking songs. Mr. Black Hair got up to dance this time. He reared his head so that his thick tresses flew back like a mane. His hands came up, elbows bent in imitation of a four legged critter standing on his hind legs, not knowing what to do with the front ones. I couldn't see his feet, but he stomped and made a lot of noise as if he wore heavy boots.

The image of a horse rearing and prancing in glorious celebration of freedom on the open range flicked across my memory. This was the image I'd almost lost when Holly threw back her red tresses.

I banged a tambourine with a St. Brigid's Cross painted on the front in vivid colors.

One by one, the other dancers returned to their tables, guzzling their tall glasses of beer and ale, then plunking down in their chairs to recuperate.

The prancing young man slowed but didn't falter.

I flicked my fingers at Holly. Her gaze shifted to the dance floor. She nodded slightly, then changed the tuning on her harp and returned to the slow songs, a lament straight out of the Scottish Highlands.

The dancer with the black hair looked up bewildered.

"Pookah!" Holly mouthed.

Of course. That was the name of the creature we faced. Obvious now that I knew.

I shuddered. Sighting a black Pookah in horse form portended death. I had no idea what a Pookah in human form signified.

But one music lover fought death in the hospital after being around this Pookah.

I faded off stage into the shadows, tambourine held tight against my thigh so it wouldn't jingle.

"Now if you'll take your seats again, I have a new song to try out on you," Holly said, a little breathlessly. She sipped greedily at her water bottle, then deliberately replaced it at her feet.

While her gaze was directed away from the audience, the few remaining on their feet either found places to sit or retreated to the perimeter and held up the walls. Including the young man doing a great imitation of a horse.

I snagged his elbow the moment he merged with the crowd.

He resisted.

"I'm a Warrior of the Celestial Blade," I whispered into his ear. I had to stand on tiptoe and stretch high to reach that ear. It flicked back and front in acknowledgement.

"It's not killing me you'll be wanting," he protested in a thick Irish accent.

"Not here I won't. Your survival depends upon co-operation." I tugged harder on his arm. He didn't need to know my imp had gone walkabout. Without my imp I had no weapon. The St Brigid's Cross on the tambourine might act as a ward.

I fingered the pen in my skirt pocket. I had a chance.

Light drizzle caressed my face and hair out in the alley. Drops glistened in the light of a lamp a block away.

"What's your name?" I asked. Keep it casual. Just making conversation.

"I'm not supposed to tell," he replied sheepishly.

Damn. A smart one who knew the rules.

"I can't help you if I don't know your name." I fluttered my eyelashes in mock innocence.

"And how would you be knowing I need a wee bit o' help?"

"You are out of your element."

He hung his head and pawed at the ground with his foot. A hoofed foot, not boots. He blended perfectly with the Keep Portland Weird crowd.

I held the tambourine in front of me, cross facing out.

"Please, 'tis not be killing me, would you. It's not hurting anyone I meant." He crossed his arms in front of his face, palms out, fingers twisted in his own ward.

"You are feeding off the audience's energy. Draining them."

"Aye. But it's just tired they are and recover they do after a good meal and night's sleep," he protested. His eyes gleamed with strong emotion that I couldn't read. Not enough light back here.

"One man fell asleep while driving home from a concert. He won't recover completely. He might not live."

"Oh." The Pookah seemed to collapse within himself. "I didn't mean to do that. But the music is so grand, so much like me home, I couldn't help myself. When Holly sings, I'm feeling like I can go home."

"Why can't you go home?"

He dashed a tear out of his eye and looked longingly down the alley toward the Willamette River and the wide expanse of grass beside it.

I led him in that direction. We'd both be more comfortable with soft earth beneath our feet and away from the smells of discards and disuse that collected in most every alley.

Did I want him comfortable? I jingled the tambourine a bit to remind him all was not well between us.

He dug at the damp grass with his hooves at first touch. Then he lay down and rolled, wriggling his back and pawing the air. A huge sigh that stirred the fronds of a nearby Douglas fir escaped his lungs. "And don't I hate cities?"

"Then why did you come here?" I resisted the urge to get down on the ground and roll with him. He had horse hide beneath his velvet knickers and jacket. He wouldn't chill in the November mist. I would.

" 'Tis a mission I had," he replied and wriggled some

more before bounding to his feet and tossing his mane again.

"You appear to a person to let them know that death stalks them. A warning so they can prepare their estate and their soul," I recited the phrases from a legend read long ago.

"Yes!"

"Who were you supposed to appear to?"

He turned his back on me and studied the grass as if choosing the right morsel to graze upon.

"Who?" I had to know. "Is it me?"

"No, no, not your lovely self, Warrior of the Celestial Blade." He looked ashamed that I had misinterpreted his mission.

I set the tambourine on a park bench.

"Holly?" I barely dared breathe. If Holly died, a huge gaping hole would be left behind, in my life, in the lives of her fans, in the world of music. I had to get back and warn her.

"Not Holly. I be wishing her long life and much music. 'Tis a gift to humanity she is."

"Then who?" I thought back to news headlines of the past few weeks. Had someone significant died recently?

"I was supposed to appear to a peace activist and grand writer of the philosophical in Ireland." He grew quiet again. "He has been instrumental in bringing an end to the violence. He deserved a warning."

"You were *supposed* to appear to him?"

"I got lost. He still lives. The assassin's bullet went astray, harming no one. I'm right glad he still lives. Ireland needs him."

"How does a Pookah get lost?"

Even in the dim light I could tell he blushed.

"You are a Warrior; you know of the Chat Room?"

"I call it Purgatory, but yes, I've made incursions into the great white nothingness between dimensions."

"Then you know how many of the doorways be looking alike. You know how easy it is the wrong one to be choosing, or to misjudge the time when you step through."

"I usually have an imp who takes care of that."

He looked up hopefully. "Your imp could take me home. Or set me on the right course."

"Scrap isn't here right now. What were you thinking about when you stepped through the portal to Earth?"

"Twas a jig I was humming."

"One of Holly's jigs."

"Aye. And the portal took me right to her. I was so hungry I began drinking in the music and the laughter, and the next thing I knew I be dancing and enjoying me freedom from my mission. I'd forgotten how to celebrate life until I found Holly. And doesn't too much of me life revolve around Death?"

"I know the feeling."

We stared in silence at the river for a time.

"I can't go home or complete my mission."

"But you have! You were sent to warn a person that death stalked them. Death does stalk the young man in the hospital."

"But I was sent to the peace man."

"A man who needs to live."

"I hope the young man in hospital lives."

"Sometimes people outsmart death."

"Yes! You have, many times."

"How do you know that?"

He smiled knowingly and dipped his head, letting his mane fall forward. "Death and me be linked like old drinking mates, half loving and half hating each other."

"I think I know how to help you. You need to go home to be available for your next mission. How do you know where to go and when to go?"

He shrugged and tossed his head in that horsey way of his. "I walk beneath the moonlight and the knowledge comes to me like a mist filling the holes in me feeble brain. At dawn, 'twixt day and night, when neither sun nor moon rules the sky, I step between worlds through the mists of time and place. 'Tis a mercy I be giving, so that Death does not take people all unawares, so they have time to prepare."

"Or figure out a way to cheat Death." We both grinned. "You need to go home. I need to know your name to send you there."

"Isn't there some other way?"

"Not unless we wait for Scrap to return, and I don't know how long that will be. Please. Just tell me your name. I won't tell anyone. I promise. I'm Tess by the way." I held out my hand to him.

He stared at it as if unsure how to respond to our custom of handshakes.

"Thank you for honoring me with the gift of your name. I promise that when your time approaches, 'tis gently I'll be coming to you."

"That's more than I'd hoped for. What's your name?"

"Can you call me Liam?"

"Only if that's your real name. Short for William?"

He shook his head. Again his hair flew about in wild abandon.

"Spill it or I'll have to kill you to keep you from hurting anyone else." I didn't know how I was going to do that without Scrap. But I'd find a way.

"Doyle Dubhcoill is what me dam calls me."

"Dark Stranger of the Black Wood."

He nodded.

I pulled out the pen and stared at it. My memory of sign-•
ing a contract in blood nearly overwhelmed me. "There
has to be a bargain. We need to trade something."

"And don't I just have a prophecy for you? Will you
send me home in return for a prophecy?"

"I think I can do that. Though if it's bad news I'd just
as soon not know."

"Not totally bad news." His eyes rolled up and his
face went blank. "By the light of the moon trailing a
silver path along the river you shall find an end and a
beginning."

"What the hell is that supposed to mean?" I looked
out over the river. Too deep a cloud cover tonight to
allow the full moon to peek through.

" 'Tis not for me to be knowing."

"Never mind. I'll figure it out eventually."

"Can you send me home now?"

"I need a drop of your blood, Doyle of the Black
Wood. I'm afraid this will bind us together for all time.
But it's the only way I can send you home. I just hope
it works."

"And aren't you a Warrior of the Celestial Blade?
Honor adorns your actions. If we be bound together, I
can slip messages to you. And won't that be a help to
you now and then? Won't I be wanting to mind your
children in your absence?"

"I won't have any children." I gulped. The Powers
That Be had guaranteed that. "Okay, Doyle. This might
hurt a bit. Hold back your hair, please."

He grabbed a handful of long black tresses and bared
his neck. Then he leaned forward so I could more read-
ily reach the throbbing vein.

Abruptly I stabbed his neck with the gold nib of the onyx pen.

Doyle howled in pain and jerked away from me, prancing and kicking back his heels. He slapped a hand over the wound. His skin closed almost immediately. Three drops of crimson stained his white lace-edged ascot.

I had five more drops of blood on the pen. Enough.

Before I could think about the consequences of binding him to me irrevocably, or the blood dried, I scribbled his name on the back of my wrist. The writing glowed with unearthly red highlights, standing out clearly for any to see.

I burned slightly as it etched permanently into my skin like an invisible tattoo.

"Doyle Dubhcoill, I command you to go home now, without hesitation or delay," I said precisely and firmly. "And never come to this place again without a clear mission in mind or in deep friendship."

His pale skin and dark hair blended, lost definition. His long jaw looked like a digital picture pixilating.

A mist drifted up from the river. It flowed between us, obscuring him. He faded, becoming no more substantial than the suspended droplets of moisture.

"Thank you, Lady Tess," he whispered as the mist returned to the river. "Celebrate life. Sing well and die gently. I shall return to you when you need me." His words fell into the cadence of a lovely tune.

And then he was gone.

Not lost any longer. "Oh, Scrap, come home soon. Don't get lost like Doyle Dubhcoill. I'm lost without you. So don't stray between two worlds like that homeless man . . ."

I dug in my pocket and found an emergency five-dollar bill. Two blocks away, a neon sign announced a late night convenience store. I dashed in and bought a couple sandwiches and their biggest cup of coffee.

The homeless man was still slumped in his doorway, still lost and alone. I handed him the food and drink, along with the tubs of cream and packets of sugar.

"Thanks, lady. God bless you."

Maybe he wasn't quite as lost as I thought. And neither was I.

I returned to Holly's rollicking concert beating time with the tambourine and humming the music of the Pookah.

BROCH DE SHLANG

Mickey Zucker Reichert

A moist breeze cut through the usual heat of an Iowa June afternoon, teasing long brown hairs loose from Melinda Carson's sweaty neck. With the help of her younger daughter, six-year-old Kaylee, she plucked weeds from between the crooked rows of vegetables. Her 10-year-old, Paige, lolled in her wheelchair at the edge of the garden, bubbles crusting at the corners of her mouth.

Kaylee looked up. "Mommy, is this a weed or a veggable?" She pointed to a scraggly sprig of green poking through soil still damp from the morning rain.

Melinda studied the indicated plantlet. "Vegetable," she said, correcting the mispronunciation and answering the question simultaneously. "That's a baby cucumber plant."

"I like cucumbers." Kaylee picked a grass seedling beside it, tossing it toward her sister's wheels. Earlier somersaults in the grass left wet, green patches staining her jeans and blonde curls. The summer sun had brought out a spray of freckles across her cheeks and nose, and the dark lashes over her blue eyes betrayed the future color of her hair.

Paige looked on silently, uncomprehendingly. Strapped into her chair, an umbrella shading her from the sun, she made broad, rhythmical movements. At times, she shouted out piercing noises; but today she remained mostly quiet. Short, sandy hair lay pixishly around her tiny head, and broken areas in her irises made her dark eyes appear more hazel. Scarred lips, twisted leftward, revealed the cleft repair she had undergone in infancy. She had seven fingers on her right hand, six on the left, and her toes fused together like paddles. She had so little tone in her limbs that, without the straps, she would flow from her chair like liquid.

Melinda reached for another weed, smiling at both of her daughters. Just as she plucked one from the dirt, twittering sounds filled her ears. A small bird fluttered around her, so close she could hear its wing beats and worried it might get tangled in her hair. Instinctively, Melinda ducked, and the bird flew away, still tweeting wildly.

Kaylee pointed after it. "That bird just flied right in your face."

"I know." Melinda watched it disappear around the shed, toward the entrance on the far side. "It must think we're too close to its nest." She had seen songbirds attack humans before, as well as cats, dogs, and other birds. This one had seemed less aggressive and more frantic.

Before Melinda could return to work, the bird zipped from the shed again. This time, she could see it clearly, a slender bird, iridescent blue with a reddish chest and a long, forked tail. *Swallow!* She loved those special birds; they feasted on mosquitoes, blackflies, and other nuisance insects. It flew right for her, circling closely, letting out a series of squeaky twitters, then headed back to the shed.

Kaylee stood up. "Mommy, he wants you to follow him."

It seemed unlikely; yet, even as Melinda rose, the bird returned and repeated its bizarre behavior.

"Kaylee, watch your sister." Melinda trotted after the bird, around the corner, and into the shed. Pallets covered most of the floor, bits of rotting hay clinging to them. Bridles and halters dangled from hooks on the wall, and tools lay scattered across the concrete floor. The bird flew to a cross beam near the ceiling, perching upon an elongated nest composed of mud and twigs. It continued chirping wildly.

Three tiny heads poked out of the nest, beaks wide open, begging food; but the adult bird did not attempt to feed them. Instead, it flew toward one of the support beams, then practically into Melinda's face, then back to the nest. As her gaze followed its erratic flight, Melinda finally saw the problem. Crawling slowly and laboriously up the column was a large bull snake. Soon, it would reach the swallow's nest.

The snake had already climbed a good three feet over Melinda's head. She cast about for a tool long enough to dislodge it. Snatching up a rake, she poked it toward the snake, but the tines fell half a foot short, overbalanced in her hands. Seemingly oblivious, the snake continued its determined climb.

A second adult swallow appeared. Both perched on the side of the nest, shrieking hysterically. One made another excited flight around Melinda.

"Stay here," she told it, feeling immediately foolish. The bird could not possibly understand her. She knew the facts of life. The snake needed to eat, and it helped keep the rodent population low, just as the swallows handled the bugs. But, currently, the farm was teeming with bull snakes, while she knew of only one set of nesting swallows.

Melinda ran through the screened porch, into the house, and upstairs to the bedroom she now shared only with Paige. Three years had passed since Mike had left them, unable to cope any longer with Paige's condition. Melinda knew the shotgun still sat in its lockbox on his side of the bed. It took a moment to remember where he had left the key. She dug it loose, fitted it into the lock, and drew out the bolt action Mossberg 12-gauge with care. She knew he had left it for her, loaded, worried for rabid raccoons or skunks, for someone breaking in to harm her and the girls in his absence. They lived on an acreage inherited from Mike's uncle, their nearest neighbor nearly half a mile away.

Melinda had never opened the box before, had never fired anything stronger than a BB rifle. Now, she hauled it out gingerly, watching every step, walking swiftly but afraid to run for fear of tripping and firing it accidentally. A myriad of warnings ran through her mind: statistics about accidental shootings, about a gun in a house more likely to kill an occupant than a criminal, about never keeping a loaded firearm in a house with children.

The bird's frantic flight ran through Melinda's mind. It had come to her for a reason, had placed its trust and the life of its own little family into her hands. Melinda burst out the door, down the porch steps, and headed for the shed.

"What's wrong?" Kaylee called.

"Nothing that could harm us. Stay there." Melinda glanced over to make certain both girls remained safely near the garden. "You may hear a shot, but it's OK. I'll be right back."

Then Melinda rushed into the shed.

The snake had crawled further, nearly within striking distance of the helpless fledglings. The parent swallows swooped raucously through the barn.

Melinda pointed the barrel at the snake and pulled the trigger. Nothing happened.

Melinda swore. *Safety catch?* she wondered. She felt around for anything that felt lever-like, discovered a side latch, and shifted it. Only then, she realized she probably had to do something with the bolt on top as well. She wrenched it backward and forward. A shell shot out, though whether fresh or spent she did not know, as another one rammed forward into the chamber.

The snake reared its head. Both adult birds flew all around Melinda, seeming everywhere at once. She aimed and pulled the trigger.

A roar filled her ears. The stock bucked hard against her shoulder. The snake tumbled to the floor, bloody, torn nearly in half. An instant later, three fledglings toppled from the nest.

Guilt assailed Melinda. *I killed a living thing.* A second realization only added to the mass of discomfort taking shape in her brain. *Did I kill the birds, too?* She looked at the infant swallows on the floor, so like their parents, only smaller. They sat, dazed, for a moment. Then, one parent swooped down, herding them toward the back of the shed. The three hopped ahead, apparently unharmed. Then, the other parent swooped in, and the babies squealed, mouths open. The second bird shoved beakfuls of regurgitated insects down their open gullets.

Melinda finally managed a smile. At least, she had saved the babies; and the parents clearly had every intention of continuing to raise them on the floor. Finally, she looked up to the nest. Daylight trickled through a spray of holes in the shed roof. *Great.* She had not considered the possibility of roof repairs when she had made her decision to fire. As she passed the still corpse of the snake, she winced. "Sorry." She understood the cycle of nature, but this time she had to side with the birds.

Three days later, the Carson girls lounged on a front lawn in desperate need of mowing, enjoying the tickle of grasses. Paige sprawled on her belly, emitting occasional excited squeals, while Kaylee combed through the greenery seeking four-leafed clovers.

At length, Kaylee sat up, catching the eye of her mother. "Mommy, why is Paige so . . . different?"

Melinda opened her mouth to field the question in her usual manner, but Kaylee forestalled her.

"I mean, I know God makes people special in all sorts of ways. But why is Paige so . . . so . . . totally different."

Melinda considered. The parenting books said to answer even the most uncomfortable questions honestly and directly, at a level the child could understand. Clearly, Kaylee had reached a new phase of curiosity and need. Melinda's mind floated back to that painful day, more than ten years earlier; and, though she would address Kaylee more simply, memory could not help filling the gaps.

Melinda lay in a hospital bed, exhausted but infused with the excitement of becoming a mother, of having miraculously brought a new and precious life into the world. Her mind crammed with images of the perfect little girl she and Mike had created, of forever hugs and kisses, of laughter and tears, of a life eternally changed for the better. She could imagine them each clutching a toddler hand between them, nature-walking with a tiny blonde aghast at the beauty and wonder of the universe.

She saw walls painted pink, daisy chains, a refrigerator covered in crayoned pictures of rainbows. Sticky bouquets of dandelions, violets, and black-eyed Susans in grand vases on the dinner table.

But Mike's expression was uncharacteristically grim. "Melinda, there's something wrong with the baby."

The future was too strong, too real in Melinda's mind for that to be true.

"I tried to hold her, but she slipped right through my fingers. She's limp, like she doesn't have any muscles or bones."

Melinda laughed. "She's just born. All new fathers worry about dropping the baby."

Mike took Melinda's hand, squeezing reassuringly. "There's more, sweetheart. A lot more." He caught her gaze with his stunning blue-green eyes, willing her to listen. "She has a hole from her nose to her lip. Her eyes . . ." He shrugged, unable to find the words. "Not right. She has more than ten fingers and less than ten toes. Melinda, there's something wrong with our baby."

"Fingers and toes?" Melinda found it difficult to focus. The image of her ideal child refused to leave her mind. "So she has some flaws. We'll deal with them."

Mike nodded. "Of course, we will." But he did not sound as confident as Melinda. "As we can. But I think we need to realize that our child . . ."

"Paige." Melinda interrupted. Mike had chosen the name, his favorite, and she had come to love it too as the tiny life had formed inside her.

"That Paige may have many more problems. Inside, where we can't see them."

"We'll fix those, too," Melinda murmured, drifting into sleep.

The diagnosis, confirmed two weeks later, was devastating. Trisomy 13, the doctor called it. Paige had an extra chromosome in every cell in her body that caused her to have these abnormal features. Most died within days of birth, and ninety percent never reached their first birthdays. Mike and Melinda had prepared for the worst, even as they took the best care they could of their severely mentally and physically disabled daughter. They vowed not to have another child until they had fully mourned the death of the first.

But, as the years went by, and Paige clung to life, Mike needed more. Four years later, Kaylee came, all full of the normalcy and life that Paige could never have. To Melinda, it often seemed cruel to revel in Kaylee's achievements when Paige's were so few, so miniscule; yet Mike doted on his younger daughter, enjoying every moment that Melinda could not. Soon, Melinda found herself alone in caring for the daughter who so desperately needed her, every moment of every day, while Mike slowly ceased to acknowledge Paige's existence, so caught up in the bright and beautiful reality of their second, healthy child.

Then the fighting had started. The social workers had warned them about the stress of dealing with children like Paige, that the divorce rate for such families approached 100%. But as Paige bucked sensational odds, surviving not only her first year but several more, they felt certain their marriage would do so as well.

Except that it didn't.

Melinda resented feeling like a single mother, dealing with Paige's inordinate problems alone. Mike dared to suggest placing Paige in residential care or at least respite care so that they could do some things together, like a regular family, without having to worry about Paige's many special needs, her startling and inappropriate screams, the stares and glares of strangers. He demanded at least one Paige-less day per month to spend at an amusement park, where they could all go on the rides together. A day at the beach where they could all swim. A long walk in a wooded park. They argued constantly about what was best for Paige, for Kaylee, for their family. Ultimately, Melinda had insisted that Paige participate in all things, that she be treated as much like a regular girl as possible, that she have every opportunity that Kaylee did. And Mike had left them.

Though only three years old at the time of the separation and subsequent divorce, Kaylee knew her father well. He still spent every free moment with her, though he never asked for visitation with Paige, nor did Melinda offer it. The few times she had allowed Paige out of her sight for hours at a time, crises had developed, and Melinda trusted no one with her precious, fragile daughter, not even her father anymore.

Melinda refused to let any bitterness color her tone as she explained to Kaylee, "Paige was born with something called Trisomy 13 or Patau's Syndrome. When she was growing inside Mommy, something went wrong that caused her to have all these problems. God gave her to us because he knew we would take good care of her."

Kaylee nodded. That answer seemed to satisfy her, the right amount of information for a six-year-old. She went back to looking for clovers for a moment, then suddenly shouted, "Mommy, look!" Stepping up beside Paige, she lunged, then triumphantly held up her prize. She clutched a snake behind the head, the way her father had taught her to catch them. It writhed wildly, dangling from her hand.

Most of the snakes Melinda had seen on their acreage were harmless racers and hognose snakes. She liked the latter ones best, as they put on a grand display before playing dead. She worried more about the bull snakes. Though nonvenomous, they did tend to bite when disturbed.

The snake thrashing in Kaylee's grip did not appear to be any of those. It had light brown markings against dark brown, with a broad, triangular head. At first, Melinda assumed it was a hognose, but it lacked the telltale upturn of the nose. The body looked fat, the scales keeled. Sudden alarm seized Melinda. She had never heard of rattlesnakes in Iowa, but her attention leaped to the tail, where she saw exactly what she dreaded. It ended bluntly, with a series of oblong, bead-like rattles.

Stay calm. Stay calm. Melinda reminded herself. If Kaylee panicked, she might get bitten or hurl the snake wildly onto someone else. "Hold onto it," Melinda said, trying to sound as if nothing unusual were happening. "I'll get something to put it in."

If any fear seeped from Melinda's tone, Kaylee did not seem to notice. "OK." She continued to hold the struggling snake.

Melinda ran into the house, dumped the contents of a plastic cereal container, and dashed outside with it. Carefully, she guided the snake's body into it, then helped Kaylee release the head so that it dropped inside with the rest of the snake. Melinda quickly affixed the lid.

"Let me see." Kaylee tried to take the container from her mother's hands, but Melinda held on to it protectively. The girl contented herself with studying the snake through the clear plastic. "Shouldn't we cut some air holes?"

At the moment, Melinda's least worry was the comfort of the snake.

"Can I keep it? Please?"

"No, honey." Melinda took out her cell phone, punched in 4-1-1 and asked for the Department of Natural Resources. "This is a poisonous snake. Its bite can make people very sick. See the tail?" She made a mental note to tell Mike to teach their daughter to examine snakes before grabbing them.

Kaylee pressed her face to the plastic. "Are those rattles, Mommy? Is this a rattlesnake?"

"DNR," said a voice on the other end of the line.

"I found a rattlesnake in my yard."

"A rattlesnake?" A note of interest entered the man's voice. "Can you describe it?"

Melinda did so.

"Ma'am, do you happen to live near a swamp?"

Melinda had never thought of her neighbor's property as a swamp. That brought to mind images of quicksand-like muck and algae hidden deep in uncivilized pockets of Louisiana. "There's a peat bog across the gravel road. A working business."

"Yup." Melinda could almost hear the man nodding knowingly on the other end of the line. "What you have is a Masagua rattler. It's an endangered species."

Melinda glanced at Kaylee, still staring into the container. A shiver traversed her at the realization of what might have happened if Kaylee had moved a bit slower or the snake a bit faster. "Do you want to pick it up? Or should I bring it to you?"

The man chuckled. "Ma'am, it's an endangered species. That means you have to leave it exactly where you found it." He added quickly, "You haven't disturbed it, have you?"

"No," Melinda lied, not wanting any trouble from

the DNR. "But it's in my front yard. With my young daughters."

The man went silent for a moment, then said matter-of-factly, "You might want to get your daughters inside."

You think? Melinda found herself speechless. She cleared her throat. "Well, thank you for your help." She hoped she managed to keep sarcasm from her voice. There was no way in heaven or hell that she was going to loose a live rattlesnake back onto her front lawn. She set the container in the grass.

"Kaylee, don't touch that." She pointed at the captured snake.

Kaylee nodded. True to her word, she did not touch it, but she did stare at the creature moving around inside it.

It took Melinda thirty minutes to hoist Paige back into her wheelchair. Paige grew heavier by the day, it seemed, even as her mother aged. The lack of tone in her limbs made it a race to fasten the straps before she slipped out and had to be lifted again. Finally, sweating and tired, Melinda got Paige secured and wheeled her toward the house. "Leave the snake; I'll take care of it. Time to go inside."

Reluctantly, Kaylee followed. Melinda knew her younger daughter would have liked to play outside for hours, but she had grown so used to Paige's schedule that she did not bother to complain. It often took hours to feed the older girl; she drooled, swallowed slowly, and choked often, even on baby food. It took many jars to satisfy the appetite of a ten-year-old girl. Six hour-long meals a day cut deeply into their schedule.

Melinda wheeled Paige to the table and instructed

Kaylee to sit in her chair as well. Then, she rushed upstairs and unlocked the gun case. In the days since she
had shot the bull snake, she had handled the Mossberg
12-gauge enough to understand loading and unloading,
the safety, and the bolt action. She had found the shells
her husband had left and loaded three into the magazine. Shifting one into the chamber, she took it downstairs and outside to the container, where the snake
hammered its nose against the plastic in obvious frustration and anger.

You have to leave it exactly where you found it, the
man had said. Melinda intended to do so. But he had not
said what had to happen afterward. Cautiously, Melinda
pulled off the lid. Holding it as far away from herself as
possible, she dumped the snake onto the imprint left by
Paige's body in the grass. *Exactly where we found you.*
She expected the snake to race away in the opposite direction. But, to her surprise, it whipped around toward
her and coiled. She raised the gun and thumbed the
safety, believing the movement alone would send it skittering. Instead, it hurtled toward her.

She pulled the trigger.

As Melinda described it later to her ex-husband and
father, the snake died of "high-speed lead poisoning."
She expected them to chuckle, to praise her ability to
handle a crisis without upsetting the girls or anyone
coming to harm. Instead, they both expressed dismay
and discomfort, each in his own way. Mike volunteered
to search the entire property and to place a low fence to
deter snakes from crossing the road, which she politely
declined. Her father's reaction surprised her more. He
insisted on coming over, a two-hour drive, despite her
protests; and he brought her mother's Great Aunt Ruth

with him. Melinda could not recall the last time she had seen her great-great aunt; the woman had to be in her nineties.

For a time, father and aunt reacquainted with Melinda and the girls, speaking of school, the past, and weather. But, when the girls went down for the night, the conversation changed abruptly. The adults retired to the living room, the television off, shoving aside Legos and a host of developmental toys and therapy objects. Melinda sat on one couch, her father and aunt on the other.

Her father sighed deeply, clearly intending to raise a matter of great import. "Melinda, honey, I had hoped to spare you this information." He glanced at Aunt Ruth, who said nothing. She was short and deeply wrinkled, her hair thin and white. Her mouth pursed, her eyes recessed into folds, her expression gave away nothing. "Your mother's family carries . . . a curse."

Melinda turned her father a twisted expression of scorn. A molecular biologist, he believed in nothing supernatural. Or so she had always thought. "A curse," she repeated dubiously. Her brows rose in increments. "A curse?"

Her father chewed his lower lip. "I know it sounds insane. I didn't believe it until . . . until your mother . . ."

Mother. Now, he had Melinda's full attention. She had barely known the woman, who had died of a heart attack when Melinda was a child. As it clearly pained her father to talk about her mother, Melinda had learned to remain silent on the matter. ". . . died?" she inserted.

Her father nodded. "She was so . . . so young."

"Thirty-one." Melinda knew that much. Now that she had passed the same age, it seemed like an impossibility.

How does a healthy woman of barely three decades de-velop heart disease so severe. She had seen pictures of her mother: smiling, slender, full of life.

Father seemed to read Melinda's mind. "She knew the stories of her bloodline, had lived in dread of them since childhood. When the snake appeared—"

Melinda interrupted. "What snake?" It was the first time a snake had ever entered the story.

"A simple garter snake." Her father buried his face in his hands. "Completely harmless, yet she knew what had to come. And her heart could not take it." He peeked at Melinda through his fingers. "Melinda, honey, your mother died of stark and horrible terror. Nothing more. I tried rescue breathing. I tried to bring her back, but I . . . just . . . couldn't."

Melinda had never blamed him. Now, she felt nothing but confusion. "What? She died because she saw a . . . a garter snake?"

Her father only nodded. Aunt Ruth's head bobbed as well, rhythmically and silently.

"Why?"

Father spoke through poorly suppressed tears. "She had seen the curse take her own mother and knew what was coming."

Dread crawled through Melinda, but she said nothing.

"I thought it best not to tell you," he sobbed. "I wor-ried you might live a life in fear, that you might react the way she did. The curse often skips generations. At times, it seems to disappear. Your mother hoped it was a legend, tried to believe it did not exist, that neither she nor you would have to deal with it."

Melinda did not know whether to laugh or cry. If he

believed the curse a hoax, why bother her with it now? If he believed it true, why wait until she had daughters of her own to infect as well? "Dad, this is insane."

"Not insane!" Ruth spat out in heavily accented English.

Melinda felt a spark of guilt that she could not identify the accent. She knew her mother's family originated in an area that had frequently changed hands: Austria, Hungary, or, perhaps, Poland at the time.

"The curse is real, and it will kill you all if you don't take heed."

The old woman's tone sent a shiver through Melinda. She could almost imagine Ruth placing the curse upon her, if it did not already exist.

"It is called the *broch de shlang,* the serpent's curse, and it has plagued our family for so long that no one knows the insult that brought it down upon us." Ruth raised her arms, as if beseeching God. "Sometimes, it goes from mother to daughter, other times, it skips a generation or two, three, just long enough to nearly get forgotten. But it always returns."

Melinda glanced at her father, who shrank into his seat. He gave her a pleading look, willing her to listen. Clearly, he had gone from doubter to absolute believer. For the moment, she played along. "How does this brock . . . this curse . . . present?"

"The *broch de shlang* always begins with a snake."

"Snake," Melinda repeated, not yet convinced. "I've seen about a hundred snakes. At the zoo, loose, on Girl Scout hikes. I've even played with them a bit." She thought of the entertaining antics of the hognoses.

Ruth leaned forward. Her shriveled little body seemed to expand. "Ah, but the *broch de shlang* is different. It may start out innocent, but it never remains so. The interactions with snakes grow more intense and less normal until . . ."

Melinda waited for her great-great aunt to finish, but she did not. She sat back as if she had not yet spoken, a shrunken figure lost in the cushions of the couch.

"Until?" Melinda looked from her father to Ruth and back. "Until what?"

"Until," Ruth whispered so low that Melinda had to lean toward her to hear. "Until it kills its host."

Melinda's heart skipped a beat, and with it came a suffocating feeling of imminent death.

Her father explained. "Nearby innocents, usually female relatives, may also lose their lives to it. It becomes larger, more powerful and deadly, until it kills . . ."

". . . its host," Melinda finished. A picture formed in her mind of the Masagua rattlesnake on the lawn. She had shaken it from the container, expecting it to flee. Every previous experience with snakes, everything she had heard or read, suggested that, so long as it was not cornered, a frightened snake would choose escape over attack. But this one had coiled and struck, as if in vengeance for its capture. She shook her head to clear it. "This is madness!"

Neither father nor aunt replied.

"I killed both of the snakes I encountered. Shouldn't that end the curse, assuming it even exists?"

"The curse is real!" Aunt Ruth did not speak loudly, but her voice carried an intense authority. "To mock it is to succumb to it."

Melinda's father stayed the elderly woman with a touch to her shoulder. "As I understand it, the first encounters serve as a test. Each new one becomes more directed and dangerous until . . ."

Until. Melinda already knew how that sentence ended. She forced herself not to consider. To contemplate her own demise proved terrifying enough. She scarcely dared to consider what would happen to her daughters. By law, Kaylee would go to Mike, who loved and adored her; but Paige would surely wind up institutionalized. Melinda refused to allow images of that fate to enter her consciousness. "Isn't there any way to defeat the curse?"

Now, a smile wreathed Ruth's face. "I was hoping you would ask that, child. Because you seem, at last, the one strong enough to do it."

"How?" Though still uncertain whether her aunt was wise or crazy, Melinda had to know. "What do I have to do?"

"It is said," Ruth intoned clearly. "That the curse will lift when the *broch de shlang* is killed at the same moment as its host."

Melinda remained in place, leaning forward on the couch, waiting for the words to sink in. "So, either way, I die."

Ruth shrugged.

"Surely, there's a way to kill it and . . . not . . . also . . . die."

Ruth dismissed Melinda with a wave. "Feh. Weak as water, like the rest." She turned away. "And I thought you might be the one to end it."

Melinda considered aloud. "If the snake dies first, it returns, stronger. If the host dies first, the curse . . . continues. So, it has to be . . . the same moment . . ." She shook her head. "How does a person kill herself at the exact same moment as a snake?"

Aunt Ruth said nothing.

Melinda's father shifted nervously. "Melinda, I don't

know what to make of all this. But no one, *no one,* wants you to die."

Melinda glanced toward the oldest of her relatives. *Aunt Ruth does.* She did not speak the words aloud. "Except, apparently, this *broch de shlang.*"

As if reading Melinda's thoughts, Ruth spoke into the air in front of her, her back still to her great great niece. "It is not what I want, but it is the only way." With that, she rose and headed for the door.

With obvious reluctance, Melinda's father followed the elderly woman. "Melinda, do you want me to come back after I drop off Ruth? Do you want me to take the girls with me tonight?"

"Thanks, but no." Melinda shook her head, barely dislodging the swirl of thought that left her dazed and wondering. "I need some time to think, a chance to do some research."

"They all say that," Ruth intoned from the door. "They all think that, for them, it will be different." Finally, she turned to meet Melinda's eyes directly. "But it never is. Simultaneous destruction; it is the only way."

Melinda's father took the old woman's arm and led her outside. "We'll check on you tomorrow," he said firmly, closing the door.

Melinda leapt up and locked it behind him. A shiver traversed her. Still in a fog, she ascended the stairs to the room she shared with Paige. The familiar snorting breaths of the sleeping child brought a strange sense of normalcy. Early on, she had spent most of her nights diligently clearing Paige's airways with saline and suction, as the nurses had taught her. Eventually, Melinda realized that these actions did little more than prevent both of them from sleeping. Paige's nasal passages invariably reclogged mere moments later.

This time, Melinda walked to her desktop computer and typed in "broch de shlang" in the Google space. Only a handful of entries came up, defining "broch" as curse and schlang as "snake" or, more vulgarly, a slang for penis. Nowhere did she find a site that linked the terms together, although she did find an interesting Yiddish proverb: "A snake deserves no pity." At the moment, it seemed singularly apt.

The familiarity of the room soon lulled Melinda into a state of normal exhaustion. The curse seemed like a distant joke, silliness that dwelt only in the mind of a addled and elderly aunt. Trading her day clothing for pajamas, Melinda performed her evening toilet, then climbed into the double bed she had once shared with her husband, Michael Carson.

She missed him tonight even more than most.

The dream came to Melinda the moment she drifted into sleep, first in blindness, a whisper of sound: "She is dead already, dead from the moment of conception, yet she has ruined your life, your family, for a decade." The words seemed incongruous, wrong, and out-of-place. Melinda rolled, but the voice followed her. "He loves you desperately. He loves you both. He would return, and you would all be happy, if only she had gone where she belonged. Gone from this horrible death within life, gone from a world where she knows nothing, where she can only suffer without understanding why."

Melinda managed a moan, but she could not awaken. A picture of Paige formed in her mind, eyes unblinking, expression unfeeling, like a mindless broken doll. "What kind of mother dedicates herself to a shell while her living, breathing, feeling daughter is forced to lead half a shackled existence that barely resembles a life?

You dedicate everything to this ... this thing, torturing the man and daughter who need you, making them suffer the greatest evil so you can comfort she who cannot be comforted, except by death."

A new image blossomed, a memory of six years into Melinda's marriage. She had awakened to the light touch of Mike, brushing a stray hair from her forehead. He was close, staring at her with an expression that defined devotion. She had asked the time, and he had told her 2:15 AM. He said he often studied her in the dead of night, reveling in her beauty and the unique, natural perfumes that defined her, scarcely daring to believe, even now, that he had won her. It was at that moment she realized how lucky she was to have a man who adored her, who prized everything about her, who gloried in even her most disheveled state.

Mike still loved her, she knew, even after the divorce. It was in his eyes, in the kindness he showed her, so unlike the exes despised by relatives, friends, and colleagues. When others droned on about post-divorce vengeance, she could not complain in turn. Mike listened when she spoke, he never missed a visitation or a support payment, and he spent as much extra time with Kaylee as she allowed. Only one thing stood between reconciliation.

Melinda rose from the bed, opened the trunk, and removed the 12-gauge. Carefully, silently, she eased a round into the chamber. She walked to Paige's bed, an enormous crib with the pillow tacked safely beneath the sheet and the blankets carefully loosened to prevent suffocation. Without a real thought, Melinda pointed the barrel through the slats, directly at Paige's head.

"No one will know," the voice cooed softly. "Everyone understands that she can die any moment, that she should have passed away in her first year."

The words prodded Melinda. She removed the safety. The sight of Paige's familiar, flaccid body, the chest moving rhythmically, the breaths loud and snorting, seemed so normal. Melinda imagined the shot, the roar of the gun, the buck of the stock against her shoulder, the tiny head exploding, brains and bone splattering the walls and ceiling. Blood would pour through the bars, staining the bedspread, the carpet.

The voice grew louder, accusing. "You demon mother! Would you murder your own flesh and blood!"

Melinda staggered backward with a squeal of realization.

"What kind of vicious creature could murder her own daughter? The girl is innocent, her suffering untold and unfair. You have no right to call yourself mother, no reason to live."

Melinda found the gun turning toward herself. Yet logic intervened. A handgun, she could press to her temple, but she saw no means to commit suicide with a shotgun, no way to place it against a vital organ and still reach the trigger. That confusion brought salvation. The voice was not her own, did not even originate inside her. It was an external force, one clearly bent on destroying her. *"Broch de shlang!"* she shouted. "Show yourself."

Something heavy dropped from the ceiling. Melinda tried to dodge, too late. It slammed against her, seeming heavy as piled bricks, pinning her to the ground. The 12-gauge spun from her grip, bumping across the carpet. Before she could move, massive coils swung around her, and she found herself cocooned by a massive serpent. Melinda screamed, then immediately wished she had not. As the air rushed from her lungs, the coils found room to tighten. Desperately, she fought for breath, but only a strangled wheeze defied the serpent.

"Kill . . . me," she gasped out. "Leave . . . daughters . . . alone."

The snake eased up ever so slightly, just enough for Melinda to catch a slight breath. "I can't. It's my job to kill every member of your family I can."

"No," Melinda rasped, struggling. The coils pinned her arms. She could move her legs, but only up and down, in a pointless tantrum. "Spare them . . ." Ruth's words came to her mind, unbidden: *the curse will lift when the* broch de shlang *is killed the same moment as its host.* Melinda no longer doubted. Her own death seemed certain, but she saw no way to end the curse, no means to take the monster with her.

"Mommy!" Kaylee stood in the doorway, clutching the gun with clear effort. Too heavy for the child, it sagged in her arms. Her eyes looked as large and round as half-dollars.

Suddenly, Melinda knew. "Kaylee, shoot it!"

"But, Mommy, I might—"

The snake hissed, coils constricting.

Melinda wasted her last breath on two more words. "Trust me." Then, dizziness overturned thought. Her lungs screamed in agony, her bones seemed to creak and shudder, she felt as if she floated in a sea of pain.

A bang crashed through Melinda's ears. *At last it's over.* The pain vanished in an instant, leaving only a dull ache. As if from a distance, she saw Kaylee collapse from the kickback, the shotgun tumbling from her grip. Melinda appreciated that she saw this much in what had to be the moments just after death. She could not imagine the buckshot penetrating the snake and not her as well.

Yet, the moments before the end seemed to stretch into an eternal, ringing silence. She watched Kaylee throw the gun aside, watched the girl run to her side and reach for her hand. "Don't bother," Melinda said, shocked that she could speak. "I'm—" *I'm what? I'm clearly not dead.* The realization came in a shock; and, to her surprise, it disappointed her.

Melinda sat up, backpedaled from the bleeding snake, and caught Kaylee in her arms. "You were so brave, Kaylee-Kitten. So brave."

Kaylee caught her mother, tears wetting through the fabric of her pajamas. "Mommy, I think Paige . . . I don't hear her . . . sleeping."

Paige. Melinda pressed Kaylee gently to the bed and ran to the crib. Paige lay utterly still, her eyes closed, her expression more peaceful than Melinda could ever remember. A slight smile touched the corners of her scarred lips. She made no snoring sounds, and her chest did not move. "Paige?" Melinda shook her body, limp, as always, but, somehow, more so. "Paige!"

The eyes did not open. The expression did not change. Only then, Melinda noticed the chips on the bars, the holes in the bedding, the single tiny opening in Paige's pajama shirt, at the level of her heart. *She died. With the same shot. At the exact same moment as the* broch de shlang.

Kaylee sat on the bed, talking. "Mommy, I was scared to shoot it, scared I might hit you, too. But then, Aunt Ruthie was here, and you both told me to trust you. And she helped me point the gun just right . . ."

Just right. Melinda stared at the hole in Paige's pajamas; and, suddenly, it all made sense. *I wasn't the host. Paige was the host.* Realization went deeper. *The curse is over. Kaylee is safe. And her children. And their children.*

She wondered if her father would find great-great Aunt Ruth dead, too, in the morning. God bless her ancient spirit.

Melinda ran to Kaylee, catching her into an embrace. "Oh, my brave, brave, dear child. I wasn't the one strong enough to save our family. You were."

Kaylee could not possibly understand. "I love you, Mommy." Her gaze went past her mother. "And I'm so sorry about Paige."

Melinda looked at the massive and bloody snake corpse on the floor, still as stone, clearly dead. "Paige went quickly, without pain." She felt certain of her words. The expression on Paige's face convinced her. "We knew God would take her sooner than later; we had thought much sooner. But she had ten years to live, a whole decade of kindness that only a scarce few with her condition ever get."

Kaylee clung to her mother. "Mommy, can we call Daddy?"

Melinda could use some understanding. Though still shaken from the events, though grief had only just begun to fill her soul, she needed a kindred soul beside her, the only one who could truly share her pain. She lifted the phone and prepared to dial 911. "As soon as I finish calling the police, you may."

"He'll come, you know. Anytime. He loves us."

Melinda spoke words she had not in years. "You know, Kaylee, I believe he truly does." She could scarcely imagine their family coming together again, hated to think that such joy could spring from the death of loved ones. And, yet, she felt certain it would. Once again, they would become a family.

Melinda had often wondered why God had chosen

their family for this trauma, why he had cursed them with such significant handicaps. Now she understood. For, without Paige, there could have been no happy ending. In her own quiet way, Paige, too, had lived and died a hero.

THE WOOLY MOUNTAINS

Alexander B. Potter

Harold bats long eyelashes at me and snuffles my hair. I give his nose a gentle push. "Yes, hair is tasty. No, you cannot eat it."

The llama snorts and stamps, ears twitching. He pushes past me, stops, stamps again. I follow, but he refuses to move further.

Sheep clump to my left in a jostling mass. I scan the pasture. Couldn't be a coyote. Harold would already be kicking the interloper into the next county. A few more feet and a dark blot on the grass up ahead catches my eye. Flies hover over it.

Standing over the remains, only two small clumps of bloody wool identify it as sheep. The rest is eaten beyond recognition. Or possibly attacked with a chainsaw. Lots of blood, lots of bits.

"Hell."

"You're sure it's not normal predation?" Dean settles across from me, stirring his coffee.

"I thought maybe, when I heard about the other attacks, but Harold takes care of coyotes. That's all we've got."

"Thought you said we have bear? Harold wouldn't—" He breaks off, eyes narrowing. "Or were you just trying to scare me?"

"Would I do that? A macho, fearless guy like you?"

"You're mocking me."

"Mock mock mock."

He smacks my hand with his spoon. "So no bear?"

"Actually, yes. Unlikely though. Black bear are shy and mostly after garbage. No one's had any tracks. Normal predators leave tracks. No, I'm thinking Uncanny."

His spoon taps a nervous beat. "Werewolves?" His hand makes an abortive reach for the scars on the left side of his face, then stills.

"I don't . . . think so." Wolves and sheep. He isn't the first to suggest it. But something doesn't ring right. "Werewolves leave tracks, the locals know better than to take livestock, and we're hardly running short of deer, as the garden can attest. Zombies maybe? They don't fall under the Integration Policies. All that shuffling around might wipe out tracks, and sheep have fairly large brains." I catch Dean's arched eyebrows and clarify, "By volume."

"But there hasn't been a zombie alert in Vermont in ages, right?"

"Nine months. Bernie put them down."

Dean grins. "Bernie? For a guy in his seventies, he wields a mean shotgun."

"You better believe it. He offered to teach me when I first got here and he saw I didn't 'have a man around.' And realized I wasn't likely to get one."

"He gets it? Is that why he hasn't assumed we're a couple?"

Our closest neighbor took a shine to me the day I arrived in Vermont a year ago, but hasn't much more than nodded to Dean since he moved in two months back. "He asked about us, but seemed relieved when I confirmed his initial impression."

"Relieved you're a lesbian?"

"Relieved because he likes me, and doesn't trust you."

"What did I do?"

"Showed up with a penis. I don't think he trusts many men. Lot of daughters, remember. Fathers with daughters get cagey around pretty young men like yourself."

"Not like I'd have designs on his daughters."

"I think he figured that out, too."

"Astute."

"Definitely. He used to be part of the Service, you know. Though he wouldn't shoot a werewolf to save his life, even before Vermont instituted the Policies. Always made me wonder . . ." I trail off, but fall short of elaborating on my suspicions in deference to Dean's nerves. "Anyway. Dead sheep."

"Vampires don't make *any* sense."

"Gnomes are out of the question and ghouls don't deal in animals."

"Dragon?" Dean hazards. "They don't pay attention to *any* policies, do they? Could account for the lack of tracks." He mimes an attack from above with one hand swooping down, fingers curved, but I'm already shaking my head.

"Don't be silly, everyone knows there aren't any dragons."

"Oh, right. They're a New Hampshire problem. You told me."

"They've never crossed the Connecticut River yet; I doubt they're starting now." Who the hell knows why, but they don't.

"So what now?"

"Clean the guns." Always an appropriate response. "Visit Bernie. I'll take care of the weapons, if you'll card the merino."

"You get the weapons, I get the wool. Reesa, there's something seriously fucked about our division of labor."

I lead the way through the woods. The midday air hangs still and close, my forearms damp with sweat under the sheaths of the VisiBlades. My Sweet's Harvester rests heavy against my shoulder, the extra clips of iron, copper, and silver dragging at my belt. Since moving to Vermont I gave up arming during daylight, especially since Integration. Feels odd.

Dean tugs the heavy braid hanging down my back. "You sure we shouldn't take the truck?"

"Why waste gas? Enjoy the spring! You bitched enough about the snow in March. Appreciate the exercise. You know how much I *love* exercise."

"Another good reason to drive."

"I may not love it, but I could always *use* it." I slap the full curve of my ass with my free hand.

"You don't either—" he protests, obviously ready to leap into an ode to zaftig women.

"Relax," I laugh. "I'm perfectly happy to be full-figured. The ladies like me *voluptuous*. As do the gentlemen, when I bother with them. The heart still needs exercise. You could do with some, yourself. Too much sitting around knitting and you'll lose muscle tone." I poke his stomach. "Nothing will attack in full daylight."

"You don't know what this is. Maybe it's a day-hunter."

"Dude. Chill."

"I'm just getting a weird feeling."

I choose not to mention that I am, too. My eyes sweep the area but nothing moves. Just an odd sensation of presence . . . watching.

He grumbles. "I signed on to make yarn, not hunt monsters. That's why I came here. You said Vermont had less than its fair share."

"We do! And our Uncannies get along with humans. Mostly. We've still *got* them, and not all signed the Policies. You want monster-free, hop a plane to Switzerland." I freeze, head tilting. Off to the left, sticks crackle underfoot. I whip my head around but nothing moves. Nothing . . . tangible. What did I see?

Branches snap to our right, followed by a heavy thud and a crash. A low hoot echoes from the left then a shrill shriek from the right. Dean's head swivels to follow the noises.

When nothing else stirs, I head off to the left without warning. Dean grabs the back of my shirt. "What are you doing?"

"Stay close." Something shifts like smoke filtering through the air, disappearing even as it materializes.

"What the—"

"You see it?" Swinging the Harvester off my shoulder, I thumb the iron bolt into place, twisting the lock open with a practiced twitch and sighting at . . . absolutely nothing.

The air doesn't shimmer again. I reach the spot I first saw movement. Lowering my Harvester, I crouch beside a snarl of brush. "Keep watch." Scanning the ground turns up no tracks. But something . . . sun catches the smallest sparkle among tangled branches. I reach, but it's gone. No, there again. And gone. Used to finding dropped bits of fiber, I pluck at where it *was* and pull back a tuft of hair.

As I stare, it winks out of sight, only the texture against my skin telling me I haven't dropped it. Then it's back. Silverwhite, it glitters in sunlight like the plentiful red in my brown hair. "Check this." I nudge Dean with my foot.

He tears his attention from the woods. "What is that, hair?"

"Watch." On cue, it disappears. His breath catches when it reappears.

"Bizarre."

"Indeed." I tuck it in my pocket. No noise reaches me beyond the drone of spring insects gearing up to become the bane of my existence for the next few months. Twisting the lock on the Harvester, I disengage the bolt. "Let's go." I move faster.

"Have you seen or heard anything like that?"

"No."

He falls silent and I don't waste further breath reassuring him. We make it to Bernie's in record time. Once out of the woods and crossing his yard I breathe easier, seeing the humor in my brief panic. I still glance over my shoulder as I knock. The bright day gives no indication of anything lurking in the trees.

"Trouble, Reesa?" Classic New Englander, Bernie gets right to the point. Granted, toting a Harvester indicates I'm not over for tea. I set it in the rack by his door and explain about my sheep.

"Kroegers lost a bunch of chickens. Hell of a mess." He shakes his head, walking to the couch. "No tracks, nothing. Bit clean through chicken wire."

I pull the tuft of hair out and sink into the rocking chair. "Seen anything like this?"

He brings it close to his face. The strands waver in and out of visibility. He pulls glasses out of the chest pocket of his overalls. "What the hell . . ."

"It's not your eyes. It disappears." I watch, gauging his reactions.

"If that isn't the damnedest thing," he mutters, rubbing the hair between his fingers. He looks up. "Was it with the sheep?"

"No, we found it in the woods." Does he look relieved? "We heard something, saw movement. Found this."

"You should have heard the noises!" Dean interjects. "There was more than one of . . . it. One hooting and another yelling and crashing around—"

"Hooting?" Bernie's brows draw in and I nod, exchanging a long look with him. He lifts the hair to smell it and grimaces. "Can't smell a thing. Damn sinuses. You?"

Taking the hair, I sniff. "No," I admit apologetically. I always want to be extra-helpful around Bernie. Dean grabs the hair, and I wonder if he suffers the same impulse.

"This thing attacking . . . it's got some sense. Leaves out zombies. Damn fool things. They were my first bet."

"Werewolves might—" Dean starts, but Bernie waves an impatient hand.

"Vermont werewolves have more sense than that."

"Exactly! Smart enough to clear tracks—"

Bernie shakes his head. "Not werewolves."

"But—"

"Not werewolves," another voice speaks. A lovely dark-haired woman in her forties enters, small and fine-boned, with large liquid eyes.

I smile at Bernie's eldest. "Hi, Cathy."

Catherine nods. "I guarantee it's not werewolves." She perches on the arm of the couch, graceful and self-contained.

"How can you guarantee—" Dean stops, eyes widening. He sinks into a chair.

Catherine smiles, unruffled. "The local werewolves assured me."

Dean's face pales. Knowing Vermont has successful Integration Policies is an intellectual exercise. Sitting across from an integrated werewolf is an emotional experience, and likely not a pleasant one given his history in Pennsylvania. Having suspected for a while now, I just hope Catherine won't be offended. I've kept Dean and Bernie's daughters apart without much trouble. Guilt pokes at me for not warning him, but ethics dictate that you just don't imply someone is Uncanny unless you *know*. I couldn't see agitating him by implying werewolves *might* be visiting next door at all hours.

"So, *not* werewolf—" A car pulling up makes Catherine pause.

"Who's that?" Bernie asks. Catherine rises and crosses to the window, politely ignoring Dean shrinking into his chair as she passes.

"Ned," she says, voice clipped. "If you'll excuse me." She tosses her head and leaves the room.

Bernie heaves himself to his feet, limping to the door and opening it before the knock.

"Bernie!" Ned Dietrich bounds up the steps, striding in with a wide grin and a hearty handshake. "You have company! Didn't mean to intrude!" He walks into the living room, flashing blinding white teeth the whole way. I can't help smiling. Hardly my favorite person, he's still hard to dislike. "Reesa! My favorite weaver!"

"Hi Ned."

"And her sidekick!" Ned heads for Dean's chair, hand extended.

Dean leaps up, color returning in a surge, dopey grin breaking across his face. I muffle a snicker. Dean doesn't *like* Ned any better than I do—surprising, given his understandable discomfort around Uncannies could make him sympathetic to Ned's position as chair of the local Society for the Preservation of Human Rights. But Dean's an inclusive sort by nature, and didn't jump on board with SPHR. He distrusts Ned on principle. Like or no, though his response to Ned is a lot more visceral than mine.

Even I can appreciate that Ned's thick black hair, dark complexion, and deep brown eyes make a killer combination. It's an arresting face— "good bones," my mom would say. The semi-permanent five o'clock shadow just adds to the appeal. Tall and rangy, his strong features, ready grin, and infectious enthusiasm mean his more irritating aspects too often get overlooked. I affectionately refer to him as our local Greek god descended to Earth as a used car salesman, though if he has any actual Greek blood, I have no idea. He doesn't sell cars either.

I can appreciate the powerful sensuality he radiates even knowing I'd never touch him with the proverbial ten-foot pole. Dean claims the same. I have my doubts.

Of course, more than enough people are happy to overlook strident politics and a tendency to drink a little too much. Whether or not Ned returns any of the interest is one of our town's big mysteries. A perpetual bachelor, Ned devotes himself to everything in town *but* finding a partner. Which I've noted doesn't stop him from trading on that pure animal magnetism, and he gravitates toward people who respond the strongest. Such as now—

he nods to me but walks directly into Dean's personal space, his grin dampening to a warm, private smile.

I've watched the dynamic since I met him, and honestly believe it's completely unconscious on Ned's part.

Dean accepts Ned's hand before realizing he still has the strange hair and trying to halt the motion. Too late. Ned clasps his hand, releases it, then looks at his own, wiggling his fingers. "What the hell—" Strands of the hair appear and he startles, flicking his hand harder.

Jumping up, I swipe at the hair. "Sorry! We were looking at fiber samples."

Ned's eyes gleam with more interest than fiber samples warrants. "Yeah? Can I see?"

Damn. No polite way to refuse. "Top secret. Don't tell anyone. Proprietary material for String Theory Fiber Arts."

"Hey, you know me! I wouldn't tread on anyone's small business! *Vermont Makes It Special,* after all!"

I groan as I hand him the hair. He does love quoting our state marketing motto. Vermont's emphasis on artisan handcrafts and specialty producers brought me here, but Ned's nonstop boosting gets tiresome. I shouldn't knock it—he's good for the town, the state, and business. Hell, I even agree with him on Vermont secession. If he'd just dial it back a little . . .

Ned stares at the hair with disturbing intensity. "Look at that," he breathes as it disappears. "Hell of a find. Where'd you get it?"

"Business secrets." I snatch it back.

He eyes me, then flashes his genial smile. "Just stopping in to trade news with the Bern-meister! Check on our monster-quest."

Bernie pulls a pipe out of his pocket, inspecting it. "Keep telling you I'm not in the business anymore."

"But you're the man! Our Vermont Shaman! You've got a *way* with monsters. Something goes down, everybody comes to you—"

Dean looks puzzled. "Shaman?" he whispers. "Bernie's Native American?"

"No, 'shaman' isn't actually native, it comes out of Siberia—"

Dean's nose crinkles. "Bernie's *Russian*?"

I open my mouth then close it. "I'll explain later." Ned's attention swings back to us. He gestures at my Harvester racked by the door.

"—prove my point. What brought you over here armed?"

Another reason I don't like Ned. He notices too damn much. I contemplate telling him the weapon isn't mine, but what's the point with clips on my belt and Visi-Blades strapped to my arms. He knows Bernie doesn't rack anything by the door anymore. "Lost a sheep."

"Ripped up? Eaten? No tracks?" His face takes on the fervency that reminds me just how much I don't like certain qualities of his. "Something bad out there," he says with entirely too much relish.

"We were just discussing what it might be," Bernie allows.

Ned brightens. "Any ideas?"

"Not werewolves," Dean says.

Ned laughs. "No?"

"Bernie says so."

"Good enough for me." Ned nods.

"I don't think there's anything for SPHR to be overly concerned—" I start.

"Torn-up sheep? Ankle-deep chicken carcasses? Dead dogs? We're concerned! Who's to say when it'll start on humans?"

"You heard about Kroeger's chickens." Bernie fills his pipe.

"Yessir!"

"Doubt it'll be moving from chicken dinners to people. Not the way these things usually work." Bernie strikes his lighter, holds it to the pipe, and sucks in. When the tobacco glows, he continues. "Sheep, chickens, dog. None of that says 'hunting humans' to me."

"Never know though," Ned says cheerfully. "And even so, it's affecting livelihoods! Hurts the agribusiness. That's our bread and butter! Not good for the state. Especially when we've almost solved our monster problems!"

Bernie nods, placid. "Integration's working out."

"Never let it be said Ned Dietrich can't admit he's wrong! Hate to say it, but it was the best thing for this state. We're a haven. Come to Vermont, where the monsters behave! Didn't trust it, but you gotta believe your eyes. The Policies work and I've shut up."

True. I haven't seen a letter to the editor from Ned in months. He used to be the first to wade into it with Uncannies in the *Brattleboro Reformer* Letter Box. The SPHR now focuses on "monster-monitoring," watching for Policy infractions. They hope to document enough violations to put the Policies back into referendum. In the meantime, I have to admit I don't think monitoring Uncanny activity is such a bad idea. But right now I want to discuss this with Bernie, out of earshot of Ned.

"Some people are talking yeti," Ned says, voice bland.

I wince. Damn the man.

"Thought they were extinct," Bernie returns.

"Didn't we all!"

Dean chokes. "You mean ... *Bigfoot*? The Abominable Snowman?"

"Bigfoot, Snowman, sasquatch, you name it. Gorillas on steroids! Kill you as soon as they look at you!"

Bernie laughs. "You talk like you know, Ned. When'd you meet one?"

"I've seen the torn-up sheep—"

"Seen a yeti tearing them up?" Bernie shakes his head. "Never knew a yeti to hunt farms."

"That's just it, we don't know! They're a mystery. Who's to say what they're capable of? Stories say they've got hellish tempers! Vicious! *They* didn't sign any Policies, however many are out there." Ned glances out Bernie's window as if expecting a horde of yeti to rampage across the yard.

"No, they didn't," Bernie puffs on his pipe. "Well, nothing else new. Reesa's sheep, Kroeger's chickens. Crossed zombies off my list. And no, I'm not going hunting with you."

"But Bernie, you're—"

"—retired."

Ned looks ready to argue, then laughs. "Okay, old man. But don't think I'm done asking!"

"You know what they say. Definition of stupidity is doing the same thing over, expecting different results."

Ned roars, tosses me a salute, then claps Dean on the shoulder. Meeting Dean's eyes, his voice deepens to a confidential purr. "You hear any yeti screaming, you let me know."

Mostly to break Dean out of Ned's spell, I say, "Believe me, I pay too much for my sheep to be losing them."

Ned grins. "Exactly. We've got livelihoods to protect!" He jogs out the door and down the steps, whistling.

"Livelihoods . . . people—what do *you* think he wants to protect most?" Dean asks.

"His career at the Chamber?" I say.

"Don't be too hard on old Ned." Bernie says, then calls, "He's gone."

Catherine reappears, irritated. "Why is he prattling on about yeti?"

Dean frowns. "Did he say they scream?"

"Possibly." I avoid his eyes.

"But that was just Ned being ... Ned. Seriously, they're extinct, right?"

"So people say," Bernie hedges.

When he doesn't elaborate, I sigh. I hoped he'd just come out with it, but apparently he needs a prod. "But they're not extinct, are they, Bernie."

He talked yeti with me frequently last winter. I sat knitting while he described how he felt presences in the woods, found tracks, heard noises right out of the old stories. He gave vivid imitations—hooting, yipping, woofing, shrieking. No reliable sightings for over a century, but Bernie didn't believe them extinct.

He'd seen them.

Having hunted the Uncanny all his life, he had theories. I finished an entire scarf one snowy day listening to how he thought yeti stayed off human radar. He theorized an ability to disappear, something immensely powerful, steeped in magic. Not just fading into the woods and avoiding people—literally *disappearing*, disguising their very existence.

In the depth of winter I listened, amused, thinking him a fascinating old man with a colorful history and a gift for storytelling. Standing in the woods today, feeling something watching, listening to shrieks, staring at disappearing hair ... I'm not laughing. All his stories and theories accumulated in my brain until out there in the woods I just knew.

Fact, not theory.

I expected him to see the hair and open up. Usually, I'd respect his reticence but with animals dying and Ned Dietrich hovering, we don't have time for discretion.

Bernie smokes in silence then finally says, "Not extinct."

"You're having me on, right? This is like the bears. Or unicorns."

"More like the bears," I say.

Dean's widening eyes indicate the dots are connecting. "You're telling me . . . today . . . that really was Bigfoot? Bigfoots . . . Bigfeet . . . more than one?" His voice rises an octave.

"No, likely just one."

Bernie nods. "Common reaction on their part . . . throwing rocks, trying to scare people off."

"That shriek—"

"They can bounce their screams," Bernie explains.

"They *what*?"

"Like throwing your voice," I clarify.

"So, Bigfoot ventriloquists live in our woods and you DIDN'T TELL ME?"

"I didn't *know*!" I did, actually, I just didn't *know* I knew.

Dean glares at me. "And Bigfoots don't leave tracks? I'd think they'd leave pretty damn BIG tracks."

"People only ever find random prints." More facts rise to my brain from last winter. "Bernie thinks yeti take care of tracks, but sometimes get surprised or don't have time. They apparently just don't move very heavily through the world."

Bernie smiles at me, approving. "No need to be scared," he tells Dean. "They're all bluff. It's how they get by. Sweet-natured, really. Not doing this killing, for damn sure."

"You're absolutely certain?" I press. "Nobody but you has talked about yeti to me. Now my sheep gets eaten, a yeti appears in my woods, and Ned Dietrich mentions them, all in one day. Coincidence? Why would someone bring up yeti to Ned?"

"That's what I want to know." Catherine glares at no one in particular. I get the distinct feeling she's glowering at an imaginary Ned. "No matter how big that man's mouth is, he doesn't say things randomly. If he's talking about your yeti-friends, Dad, he's got a reason."

Bernie's jaw sets, stubborn. "Nobody would have reason to point at yeti. I'm *certain*, dammit. They got nothing to do with this. They wouldn't, it's not in 'em. That one in the woods today? Was a travel companion."

"A what?"

Bernie sighs. "It came with the one that's here visiting. They always move in pairs or more."

"Here visiting?" Dean blinks. "Like . . . HERE–here?"

Bernie nods. "The one in the other room."

"Does it know what's going on?" I quell my own surprise in favor of grabbing the opportunity for information. "Do they talk?"

"Oh no. They touch you, then think at you." He waves both hands beside his head as if shooting thoughts at me. "You get it in pictures in your head. Not sure what they know. You showed up before I had a chance to talk to him."

"Will he come out with us here?"

"Think so, if I . . . encourage him." He heads out of the room, pausing to leave his pipe in a ceramic dish on the coffee table that looks like a handmade present from a grandchild. Maybe the yeti doesn't like smoke.

Catherine shoots us an apologetic look. "Might take a few minutes. They're incredibly shy. Took him *forever* to convince them to even be here when one of us was around, and they still won't talk to us. They do *not* like wolves. Hell, they really only like Dad."

I nod. We wait in edgy silence until Bernie reappears, along with an indistinct, opaque shape that is hard to look at. He enters the living room, the strange distortion of air close by his side. My eyes struggle and I realize it must have a large arm draped over his shoulders. Where the yeti touches him, I can see straight through to the wall and furniture behind him.

The air beside Bernie starts to brighten, shimmer. My breath catches in my throat when I realize that gauging the beast's size by the distorted space next to Bernie is ... inaccurate. As it materializes, the yeti rises up on its legs from a bent position, to a full height above eight feet.

A swirl of fine silver hair ripples and settles, catching the ambient light of the room and absorbing it. His head swivels toward us, a dark face standing out starkly in the mass of white hair. Lips pull back, long teeth gleam, and it lunges, screaming.

We fling ourselves backward. My arm whips out, shoving Dean behind me. My other wrist snaps downward in the practiced motion that releases the VisiBlade into my hand. The yeti rocks forward onto its knuckles and charges on all fours, straight for us.

"Don't!" Bernie yells. The yeti swings itself right into my face, teeth bared, and rises upright again, towering over us. Reflex kicks in past all assurance of bluffs and my arm flies upward, blade angled.

"He won't hurt you!" In my peripheral vision, Bernie

limps across the room as fast as he can, one hand reaching out as if to hold the yeti back.

In the next instant Catherine stands between me and the yeti, unflinching. Still in human form, tiny as she is, she tilts back her head and meets the yeti eye-to-eye, silent and still, her arms folded over her chest.

Low rumbling vocalizations fill the air. Just before Bernie reaches him, the yeti lowers back down onto his knuckles. The magnificence of the creature's hair strikes me even in my petrified state. Every shift of muscle sends it swaying, until it takes on the appearance of floating underwater. I long to touch it. I don't know if that's my fiber-fascination talking or if yeti-hair sparks the same urge in normal people.

Bernie's hand settles on the yeti's back. It lifts its hand and pokes one long finger at Catherine's shoulder. When she doesn't move or respond, the yeti tilts its head to one side, withdraws its hand as if satisfied, and hoots softly at Bernie.

"Settle down," Bernie snaps, voice cross. "Damn fool." He points at the couch, and the yeti turns away. "Put that away," he waves at my blade. "He won't hurt anything." He follows the yeti.

Catherine turns to us, rolling her eyes. "You okay?"

I nod, sheathing the blade with fingers that start shaking in reaction. That thing is BIG. "Thanks," I manage, knowing that without her, I could have easily knifed the yeti. That likely wouldn't end well. I look back at Dean to find him chalk-white and shaking, but staring at Catherine with a peculiar expression. Apparently there could be an upside to getting threatened by a yeti and protected by a werewolf.

The yeti continues hooting as he swings himself up

onto the couch in a cloud of glittering silver. The couch creaks under him, and for the first time I notice that it, like the room, is set up to accommodate the movements of something huge, without creating frustration or wreckage.

I return to the rocking chair, happy to sit. Dean positions himself behind it, fingers biting into the puffy back. Catherine stays put. The yeti glances at her now and again, but both seem happy to maintain the distance.

Now that it's calm, I can't keep my eyes off the yeti, thinking about Ned's "gorilla on steroids" comment. The posture, stance, length of arm, and size of hand all say "primate." Hair distribution also resembles the apes, only the face and palms bare. Facial features continue the simian theme, eyes small and close-set under a heavy forehead, nose flatter and broader than a human's. The prominent canines call up images of snarling baboons stalking baby antelope on Nature programs. His fingers pluck at Bernie—now on his hair, now at his shirt—in the manner of apes grooming.

The differences are just as striking. The length and quality of the hair is more akin to a horse's mane or human hair than a baboon's fur. Sheer size and body structure also argues against ape. The yeti doesn't have the swaybacked bulk of the gorilla, nor the comical long-armed, round-tummy look of the orangutan. The body structure most resembles a chimpanzee with longer legs, or ... a human with longer arms.

Even as I mentally set yeti characteristics up against the various great apes, the comparison feels wrong, the same way comparing a werewolf to a standard wolf feels off. The yeti encompasses more than a collection of ape-like characteristics, or even human-like characteristics. The silver-moon glow, the intelligent watchful eyes, the gentle way it looks at Bernie, stroking his shoulder, staying within arm's reach . . . all speak to the "more."

Then there's the invisibility and telepathy.

The yeti returns my regard. The weight of his stare brings back my uneasy feeling from the woods. Despite my statement about yeti moving lightly through the world, his presence is tangible, a heavy aura surrounds him. Bernie is right about the yeti possessing *deep* magic. I'd go so far as "bottomless."

The yeti's hand settles on Bernie's and its head dips toward him. Bernie wraps his gnarled fingers around the long, dark ones and returns the silent, companionable attention. Unexpectedly touched at the image they present, my throat tightens.

Bernie's face darkens. "You best take a listen."

Unsure what to do, I push up out of my chair. The yeti extends his right hand and I walk toward him. His dark eyes meet mine, and the world tilts. It's like a large hand thrusts into my head and *pushes*. Unsteady, I reach for his offered grip. The cool skin surprises me, but not as much as the inherent gentleness. His fingers close on mine and gravity shifts again, sharper this time. I sink to the floor, knees buckling. The massive strength in his one-handed grip supports me down. I hear Dean in the distance, but the scraps of words fall away with my surroundings as night rises up.

Occasional shafts of moonlight shine through the trees, but mostly it's just dark. I can't believe the details in the shadowy recesses of the woods, though, the subtle shading along the spectrum of gray, all discernable to me. Scents fill my awareness, spring itself the most prominent bouquet. Earth like I've never smelled it, deep and dark, crawling with protein. Plants in every scent of green—scent of green? Yes, all the varying greens have their own smells, woody, sweet, bitter. Underneath hangs the reassuring scent of Family.

They slip out of the woods like ghosts. Pale silver-white, dark reddish-brown, or some mix of the two, moving like gorillas, bent forward with knuckles on the ground. Dark faces watch me, intent and serious. They surround me. I shift my weight and the group moves out as one.

I move fast, faster than I've ever run. A cool night breeze sets my hair whipping, silky silver streams flowing over my face. The rhythmic sway of my body surprises me, the impact of my knuckles on the ground nowhere near as uncomfortable as I would have thought. Something *burns,* a hot stone in my chest, dangerous warmth where there should be only coolness. It pulls me forward, disruptive and *wrong,* until I break the tree line and see the houses of the Bare.

Head lifting to the wind, a scent like burnt matches floods me. Furious movement, a dark-on-dark image, and there—the little winged ball of death and destruction. My vision telescopes as my Focus narrows. I watch in exaggerated slow motion as chickens careen from one side of a fenced pen to the other, doing cartwheels in the air as they're flung with astounding strength by vicious jerks from a tiny marauder.

The flat, serpentine head on a long neck snakes around to train disturbing yellow eyes on me. Dark wings spread then fold as it dives, the movement fast even in the slowed perception of Focus. A sharp curved beak drips black with blood. The head darts, beak sinking into a fat chicken with evident relish. It rises into the air and flings the bird to the ground.

Time springs back to full speed as I release my Focus and shriek. The little beast shoots upward then arrows straight for me. Hoots rise into the night. I stand, lifting my arms and shrieking as the thing descends. Family swarms from the trees.

The Winged Death hisses and spits, comes to a dead stop in midair by billowing its wings then twists back on itself and flies away, tail lashing the air. A flash of silver in moonlight makes my Focus snap back, and time slows again, the band of silver encircling the slim neck confusing. The dark sky spins. Stars dissolve, becoming the wooden-beam ceiling of Bernie's living room.

I find myself on the floor, staring up at a worried Dean. "I'll be damned. You were right. It's a dragon."

"—buzzsaw with wings," I sketch the size of the dragon with my hands. "I've never actually seen one. They're so tiny!" I round on Bernie. "Did you know the yeti are the reason why dragons don't cross the Connecticut?"

Bernie nods. "Figured. Dragons are always regional. Had to be something territorial."

"So how did this one get here?" Dean asks.

Bernie rests his hand on the yeti's. "Don't know. They felt it maybe a week ago, so they came looking. They've been tracking it. Most dragons get clear of yeti territory damn quick. This one stays. It knows it don't belong, but won't leave."

"That's never happened before?"

"No. Never seen a dragon in a collar, either."

"That's just bizarre," Catherine states. "No dragon would *consent* to a collar."

I cut to the chase. "How do we take it down, take it out?"

Bernie shakes his head. "Can't kill it without a license. Federally protected. Best thing is to trap it, get that collar off. Can't figure why it's staying if not for that collar.

The two magics—yeti and dragon—don't mix. They steer clear naturally. If the yeti can feel it, the dragon can feel it shouldn't be here."

"It looked happy enough snacking on chickens. Didn't seem perturbed until it dive-bombed me. Er . . . him."

"Dragons are mean sonsabitches." Bernie warns. "Trapping it'll be a job."

"But one we need to do, and fast," I say. "When he showed me what happened at the Kroeger's, he screamed. The others, too, and hooted. That clears up who mentioned yeti to Ned."

Bernie swears. "Kroegers have been here long enough. Probably know some old legends. I just didn't think the yeti'd been anywhere near the killings." He grips the yeti's hand. It becomes agitated, starts to rise, going insubstantial around the edges. He's ready to bolt.

"Don't leave!" I appreciate their desire for secrecy and seclusion, but something tells me yeti-assistance is the only thing that'll bag us a dragon. My brain snags on that. Bag a . . . "Bernie, you've got a NetShot 2500, don't you? I saw one, when you showed me your old gear."

He shakes his head. "1600. I left the Service before they issued the 2500. But that won't hold a dragon . . . not even a 2500. They were only ever for werewolf pups and ghouls. And the occasional gnome that got abusive. Dragons would tear right through 'em, wouldn't matter how you lined the nets. And I only have copper nets."

I study the yeti. "I understand. But if you still have a net frame, we might have something the dragon can't burn through."

Midnight finds us hiding in the woods around the Kilpatrick farm. So far, watching the Kilpatricks' fields has done nothing but spook the Kilpatricks' horses, who keep scenting the werewolves. Calmer—or just stupider—the cows stand in clumps.

Turns out all five of Bernie's daughters have the blood. Four werewolves pace around us as protection, the fifth back at our place with Bernie.

Bernie predicted the dragon would move to the next farm. Only sheer force of Daughters kept Bernie from coming with us, making me grateful they're as stubborn as their father. Time meanders as we crouch in the damp night, the wolves ranging out then returning. Bernie's arthritis wouldn't appreciate the moist chill.

Hanging out in dark woods with a small pack of were-wolves is high on Dean's list of Things Never To Do. I say nothing when he presses close to me.

All remains quiet until just after 3AM when all four werewolves lift their heads in perfect unison. Seconds later, a wolf howl rises in the distance. A feral edge ripples through the pack as four heads swivel in the direction of the howl, and my property.

The pack flows into dark blurs, bounding away, leaving us to jog behind. By the time we stumble into our yard, we're gasping for breath. In the pasture, my sheep race back and forth, wild-eyed and bleating. Herbert snorts and paws. Five wolves fling themselves into the air over and over, trying to reach the dark shape swooping and diving. The yeti crouches, swinging its arms above its head, shrieking. In the midst of the confusion, my eyes find the body on the ground.

"Bernie!" Dean kneels by him. Long claw gouges run down Bernie's chest, the tatters of his flannel shirt and overalls gaping over bleeding flesh. His blistering curses reassuring me, I spin to the Uncanny, bringing the Net-Shot up.

In the stark glare of the outside lights, the yeti becomes even more unearthly, hair whirling, huge shadow dancing in crazy patterns. I sight above his head, knowing it's the best shot at the dragon. Sure enough, despite the snapping teeth of the leaping wolves, the dragon circles his head, feinting, striking. "DUCK!" The yeti crouches lower. The dragon dodges. I fire.

The net shoots out of the launcher barely visible. To my relief, weighted edges spin out just as designed. I've never woven a net for a NetShot. Bernie has, so I trusted his guidance. It glitters, suddenly visible, then winks out; enough to draw the dragon's sharp eye but not enough to warn. In the next instant the dragon tumbles to the ground, wings and limbs tangled.

The wolves circle. It screeches and flaps, trying to writhe away from wherever the yeti-hair net touches its scaly hide. I shoulder aside the wolves to get to it—the netting leaves bright white scorches on it. I don't want to torture the thing, but how to restrain it? "Dean! Get my knitting needle case!"

"WHAT?" His incredulous yell makes a laugh bubble up, but the dragon's pained noises kill it.

"Just DO IT." I gingerly lift the netting away from the dragon. It strikes like a snake, a lancing bite catching my finger. "Dammit! I'm trying to HELP!"

That works. The dragon stills the frantic beating of its wings and quiets. Untwisting the net, I lift, making sure the weighted edges stay flush with the ground. When the net hangs over the dragon like a little tent, it lays panting, baleful yellow eyes staring at me. Blood drips from my finger. The dragon's head shoots out, catching the droplets. I try to ignore it as Dean drops down beside me.

"Put some needles around the edges to hold this up. The net hurts it."

Using size 15s, Dean jams knitting needles into the ground like miniature stakes, twisting the net around the top of each until it forms a net-cage.

"We care that it hurts?" a feral voice growls.

"Your father will."

"Yep." Bernie's voice. Two daughters half-shifted to their intermediary humanoid forms support him.

"It started for the sheep," one rasps. I recognize Laura, the youngest. "Then Dad came out and it went for him. It was after *him*. Didn't even look at me."

Bernie pulls away from his daughters to kneel down, wincing. He widens a hole in the netting, reaching through. His fingers shake but the dragon stays still, and he touches the collar without getting bitten, mumbling under his breath. The dragon's tongue flickers out, licking blood from his fingers.

Bernie's mumbling ends and crackling tree branches bring us around. The dragon hisses, eyes narrowing. Ned Dietrich walks toward us in the jerky, unnatural way I've only ever seen in zombies.

"Dammit, Ned," Bernie sounds cross, but resigned. "Never know when it'll start on humans, eh? Suppose making me the human takes out two birds. You can stop worrying about me talking, and get everyone yelling for Uncanny blood." He releases the dragon's collar.

As if the movement cuts a set of invisible strings holding Ned up, he drops to his knees, gasping. His hand lifts, massaging his chest and throat. A fine leather—leather? no, dragonhide—gauntlet encases his left forearm, like a falconer's glove. A silver bracelet buckles around it, a match for the dragon's collar. Ned glares at Bernie, jaw clenching.

"The guy defending the monsters gets killed by one. That'd turn even the most level-headed," Bernie says, and under his disgust I hear disappointment. "You should know me better. I've never said word one."

Ned looks away but his voice lashes out. "You expect me to believe you weren't just waiting for the best time?" He sneers.

The daughters circle again, closing on Ned. All but Catherine shift back to full wolf, growls rumbling. I gape when Dean pushes into the circle, standing in front of Ned. "Whoa, you're just going to kill him?" Dean says.

Catherine's cold eyes settle on Dean and he quails. Without hesitation I wade in and position myself in front of him. Still, protection doesn't mean agreement. "He tried to kill their dad, Dean."

Without warning, one of the wolves darts forward, catching Ned's pant leg, sinking teeth through denim into the boot and leg beneath. Ned's howl of pain and Bernie's shout of "Jennifer!" doesn't cover the sound of denim and leather rending. A second wolf flings herself bodily at Ned, knocking him flat.

"Heather, don't!"

Despite agreeing, I don't want to be this close. Short women still make for big wolves. Grabbing Dean's arm I haul him out of the circle, stumbling when he digs in.

"No! Think! What happens when he disappears after these attacks, after yeti were mentioned?"

The wolves hesitate.

"He's right," Ned snarls, holding his torn boot together over his bleeding leg. "If I disappear, you just bring it on." He shoots Bernie a dark look, but I can see it's nervous bravado.

The wolves look at each other. "Have him arrested for dealing dragons?" one snarls. I recognize Karen in the cool logic.

"No arresting, no killing," Bernie limps forward, grips Ned's arm, yanks him to his feet. "Me and the yeti are going to chat with Ned." The yeti drifts forward at Bernie's words, reaches out, catches the back of Ned's neck in one large hand, and drags him across the yard to the barn.

"Dad," Karen starts, but Bernie shakes his head.

"No. I promised your mother."

"She didn't mean—"

"It doesn't matter. I promised. No more." He follows the yeti, leaving his daughters simmering with suppressed violence. Dean keeps me between him and them.

I stare at the dragon, wondering what the hell to do with it. Wondering if I'm the only one who noticed, through Ned's torn and sagging boot, the flash of cloven hoof.

Grinning at the armload of yeti-hair, I offer an unconvincing protest. "They don't have to—"

"They want to. You got rid of a dragon." Bernie's eyes twinkle. "Let them. It's important to them."

"They realize as soon as I start spinning this, there'll be an explosion of interest."

"They trust you to guard your business secrets."

I don't need to be told what that means from a species as paranoid as the yeti. I can't wait to start spinning, the silky feel against my hands intoxicating. Weaving the net was sublime. "I didn't do—" I begin.

"You did good." His proud smile is even better than the yeti-hair. "Knew you were special."

Embarrassed, I change subjects. "So. Ned." Bernie hasn't brought it up but I have to ask.

He digs out his pipe, staring at it. "Satyr," he finally says. "Half, anyway. Boy's all kinds of screwed up." He squints past my left shoulder. "You know . . . not many human/satyr pregnancies go to term," he says carefully. "Usually the woman's . . . too traumatized. Understandable. Ned's mother—" He stops, unable to continue, tears collecting at the corners of his eyes.

I suck in a breath as the last pieces fall into place. The product of an Uncanny sexual assault would certainly have some identity issues. He must hate that side of himself. I can't imagine how it happened that Ned's mother chose to carry to term. My heart aches for the unknown woman. "You're the only one who knows?"

"Was. Now there's two of us."

"Great." Not a comforting thought. "Think he intended to kill you?"

"Yep." Bernie shrugs. "Odd man. Not *bad,* really."

"Bernie. He tried to *kill you.* That's bad. Really."

"Desperate people. He wanted his monster war. Probably thought he could push secession through, too, if it looked like dragons were invading. The yeti was just a happy accident."

I remember the yeti dragging Ned like a broken doll. I doubt he considers that accident so happy anymore. "You keep your daughters from killing him because he's a desperate, unhappy man, or because he's Uncanny?"

Bernie chews on his pipe stem. "Don't know."

"You're an odd man yourself, Bernie."

"You'll get odd too, spending time with yeti."

"Think I'll be spending time with them?"

"Let's put it this way. You know how they call me the

Vermont Shaman. None of my girls can inherit the position. Needs a human."

I blink. "Are you saying—"

He puts a hand on my shoulder and meets my eyes, smiling. "I'm saying I'm damn glad you moved to Vermont."

INVASIVE SPECIES

Nina Kiriki Hoffman

My name is Random Delaney. I'm a vermin hunter, but I'm not allowed to use real bullets. Bullets and lasers are a little hard on spaceships, and that's where I generally ply my trade. I have a lot of other cool ordnance, though, some of which I don't understand. I was trained by a Skikka, and you know how those guys are, all about the mystery, you can never see behind the veil, yada yada ping pong. Some of the stuff I use, he didn't even tell me what it was called, which makes it hard to reorder.

There's a bunch of different ways to squik a ship. The best and easiest is the Total Body Squik. If the ship is between trips, you can do the job outside of atmosphere. If everyone's cleared out and took all their junk with them, you gas the whole thing, sonic it to kill all the gas-resistant pests, wander through in your suit and shoot anything else that moves, then open up the doors and vent the atmosphere and everything else not tied down. After that, you scrub every surface with all-purpose pest-end and blast every crack and nook and do it all again.

This is my favorite method, because it's sweet and simple and you get to totally explore a ship—systemworks and living areas and everything in between—at your leisure. I love alone time when I can snoop. People think they've taken everything, but there are stashes that maybe they forgot about, under panels, alongside cables, in conduits, tucked into workings and waste space. I find things. Sometimes not even solid things, but records and memories. It's all treasure. I can swoof the solids out of the ship with a little beacon attached and pick them up later, if it's worth the trip. The memories I store with my own.

Second easiest is to squik the ship while it's in port, though atmosphere complicates things. So many things can survive in atmosphere, we constantly need new bug-stompers. And you have to watch the pesticides harder after you're done with them.

Almost nobody wants the Total Body Squik. Often people discover they have pests while they can't stop what they're doing long enough for a decent all-wash. Most of my jobs involve pest hunting while people are in residence. Cuts down on the poison options a bunch, and requires more finesse, not one of my strong suits.

The *Evander* job looked simple. An in-system run, like most of my jobs—I'm planet-based for now, and maybe forever. I'd need hella big jobs to be able to afford my own runabout so I could go to where the work is, and a fortune would have to fall out of the sky before I could afford to system jump. While I'm waiting for that ship to come in, I get enough routine work to keep the four-year-old daughter in nutriblocks.

The only thing different about *Evander* was it was a luxury run. Big old cruise liner, ferrying rich people around the solar system while they gorge on great food and enjoy the zero-G pleasure rooms, low-G gyms, and all kinds of other entertainments. Never traveled on one of those before; most of my clients were small-time freighters and haulers and the cold-sleep ships that took workers from Terra to Luna, Mars, Titan, other local colonies, and the asteroid belt.

Evander's chief engineer thought the ship had metal mites, so I geared up for that, but I also packed the rest of my armaments, and the most important equipment I own, my suit. Armor, personal climate, propulsion unit, weapons nest, yeah, I feel safer in my suit than anywhere else, and it's got a collapsible carry compartment for Fern, the kid, too.

Usually, when I take away-from-home-port jobs, my side-gran and her partners look after Fern for me, but this time the job came when Gran was on a business retreat. Fern and I live in a room in Gran's enclave. We live in SubTerra, but we have a pipe up to sunlight, and get a spot on the floor most days. Fern's got mirror blocks, and she sets them up sometimes to throw light all over our room.

I didn't have babysitting backup this time, and metal mites didn't sound Fern-endangering, so I loaded the kid on calmers and brought her with me. Goes to show you should never let clients diagnose, and also that I should never have been a mother, but I knew that before Fern was born.

The Skikka had taught me pretty good how to collapse everything into a manageable parcel. They're always surprised at the shuttle port how much mass and how little room my luggage takes. My Skikka taught me how to hide things from scans, too. They didn't stop me at customs.

My ticket didn't authorize Fern, so I had to pay half

for a second one. Maybe I'd get lucky on *Evander* and find pests plus loot.

Fern and me made it up to the orbital station without too much trouble (I put more calmers on her snack stix). I collected my luggage and went to the *Evander*'s dock.

"My stars," said the doorman when he opened the servants' entrance of *Evander* to my buzz. "You're Delaney's Pest Control?"

"Yeah. This is my dwarf assistant."

I showed him my I.D., and he did scans to verify it, then scanned Fern into the system and took a copy of her I.D. bracelet. He frowned. "We didn't budget supplies for two of you."

"Hey, we can eat leftovers. You get those, right?"

"We recycle them."

"She doesn't eat much," I said. "Is there day care on the ship?"

He allowed that there was.

"Come on, Stall-boy, I can't just dump her in the station. She's all the way up here, she might as well come."

He muttered some more about highly irregular and caved, handing me the crew badge that would let me into areas passengers couldn't go.

Our cabin was on the inside, against the core, along with all the other staff and servicepeople cabins. The passengers' cabins were all against the outer walls of the ship; some had TruGlas portholes so the inhabitants could look out and see the actual starfield. The less expensive ones had screens they could program to show what was going on outside, or anything else they liked. (I'd read the brochure.) Even the service cabins had little screens flanked by curtains so we could pretend we weren't locked up in small windowless compartments like machines.

I unfolded Fern's care cage and set her in it with food and water dispensers and the omnigame. She dialed right past all the interactivities, piggybacked the ship's net, and started snooping around. I guess she's seen me do that too many times.

"You okay?" I said.

She frowned at the omnigame and waved a hand at me, like she couldn't be bothered. She's probably seen me do that too many times, too.

I had researched the ship's layout before I left Terra. I geared up, including my suit, in case explorations took me to the outer hull or some of the non-atmosphere parts of the inner workings, though I kept the helmet retracted until needed. I headed down to report for duty.

A lot of things were happening in the engine room. The chief engineer was a human woman named Skeeter Johanson. She had hired me over a comm line; we hadn't met, but she had checked my references. "Delaney. Did I just see you come out of one of the *passenger* lifts?" was the first thing she said to me, and, "What's with the outerwear? Are you *trying* to alarm our guests?" was the second. She tapped the "Delaney Pest Control" logo on my chest, her face twisted into a huge frown.

"Uh," I said, "Yes, I didn't know there was a different lift for crew, and no, I'm not trying to scare anyone. Just want to do my job."

"You need a suit to deal with metal mites? Never mind, we're about to cast off. Get out of my engine room and back to your cabin, and take the crew lift this time. Someone will call you when we need you."

"The crew lift is—?"

She turned her back to me. "Smik! Show this ground-hog where the crew lift is!"

One of the people rushing around checking telltales

and doing engineering stuff broke off and dashed up to me. He had four arms and blue skin, an alien type I couldn't place. I thought we only had contact with Skikka and two other alien races, but I'm not always up on the news. He had kind of a lump for a head, with eye spots all the way around it. "Come," he said in a mushy voice—his mouth was in the center of his naked blue chest—and he trundled out of the engine room, using his lower two arms along with his two legs to locomote. He was hard to keep up with.

He rolled right through a hidden door that led to narrow gray halls toward the ship's core. What do you know, there were three lifts back there. He tapped a button to summon one and didn't wait around to see me get into it.

I played with Fern in the cabin until we were underway, and then Johanson called down and said she was sending someone to take me to the damage sites for inspection, and would I please take off my damned suit?

Since she put it in the form of a question, I decided not to, but I didn't tell her that. Someone else was going to show me around. Maybe Johanson would never find out.

I hung my sampling case off my shoulder and slapped a cloth patch across my Delaney Pest Control logo. Sometimes you want to advertise, and sometimes anonymity is better. The door guard pinged, and I opened it to discover Smik. He looked past me at Fern. "You brought your young?" he asked.

Fern stared at him and screamed. The calmers had worn off, for sure. "That's not the way I raised you, young lady. You be quiet now," I said. It didn't work. She hid her head against the hardshell over my chest and screamed and sobbed.

"Mr. Smik, could you wait outside? I'll be with you in a minute," I said.

"She is perfect," he said.

I couldn't disagree with him more.

The door snicked shut and Fern stopped crying. She pushed away from me and stared into my eyes.

"I have to go to work now," I told her, "and you have to do *your* job, which is being a little kid. In the care cage."

"Okay," she said. I locked her in and she rolled around on the floor of the cage, smashing into the bars, which were cushioned and gave. "You should get a cage, Mama," she said.

"I've got one that walks." I tapped my chest and went out to Smik.

"We must go to passenger territory," Smik said. He had more liquid in his mouth than humans usually did. Some of his words bubbled. "The suit is disturbing."

"We can just tell 'em it's a costume for the ball tomorrow night." Fern had accessed the ship schedule of passenger activities, which had amused both of us. Now I knew what kinds of things rich folks did for fun. "How do they react to you?" I asked Smik.

Smik shook his head lump, and parts of his anatomy between his eyes and mouth swelled up a little. I sure didn't know how to read that.

We took a crew elevator up to the promenade deck. Smik stopped at a storage space and took out a pale robe, which he dropped over himself. It had a maintenance crew patch on the front. It covered the extra arms, and the high collar concealed the fact that he had no neck. The ring of eyes and the smooth blue surface of his headbump were quite odd-looking. He pulled something else out of storage and dropped it on his headbump, and I shuddered. He'd just put what looked like a human head on top of his, complete with short, dark hair. He tapped the collar of the robe, and the new head adhered to it.

"How can you see?" I asked.

"Eye holes," he mushed. The words came from his chest. All right, nobody wanted him talking to the passengers. The upside was that his blue hands looked like gloves, if you didn't look too close and realize his fingers were thin and stick-like and there were a lot of them, kind of clustered.

"Lead on," said I, and followed this spooky-looking dude out into the sacred passenger space.

The decor was like, so two hundred years ago. Furniture was pointy and speckled with spider-like stars, a theme that echoed in the carpet and the light fixtures. The deck was a doughnut shape around the central core of the ship, which had function rooms, like kitchens and laundry, circling the drive shaft.

TruGlas ringed the entire deck so you could look out at the stars, and very occasionally other traffic. Some parts of the glass had magnification insets. A whole section was polarized to block sunlight, and Terra was a huge floating ball, with an edge of Luna beyond.

Where we came out, a lounge bled into a restaurant that bled into a dancefloor, with a couple stages around the edges, and three bars. One of the bars was dark. The other two looked open and ready to get you drunk.

A cluster of passenger lifts opened onto a greeting area between the restaurant and the lounge. A uniformed crew member stood behind a podium there, smiling at passengers as they got off the lift, and pointing out places they could go. At each area, staff members waited to serve. Other than them, it was pretty quiet.

"Come," Smik said, and toddled off. With the robe on, he couldn't use his lower arms to walk, so he looked pretty wobbly.

I followed him over to the dark bar.

Smik lifted a plastic cover and showed me how the bar's pewter-colored edge had deteriorated: it looked like something had chewed off pieces. No metal mites did that.

I got out my sample kit, took a scraping off an edge, and dropped it into the analyzer. Smik and I both watched until the sampler beeped and analysis came up on the readout. The metal identified as allosteel with a decorative fragmented coating. Also present: human saliva.

"No flippin' way," I said.

The sampler beeped again. It had identified four different genomes in the saliva. I stored the results. "Have you had the same passengers for a while? What about staff?"

"The current passengers embarked from Mars Station. Terra is just a stopping point before we head back. The only people we took on at Terra were you, your spawn, and a replacement chef. We lost one chef in an unfortunate flambé accident. All other personnel same since Mars." He was talking pretty good for a bubble-mouth. I could understand almost all the words.

"Are there other damage sites you want me to check?"

"Yes. One we know of." He let the cover fall back into place and contacted the engineering department to let somebody know the bar could be fixed now. We retreated to the crew-ways and took a lift down to the gym level.

The gym had lots of fancy padded equipment with

steel parts that looked to me like torture machines. Some people were already in them, moving things around in the lo-grav. One of the things was a vertical pole, and a woman with long, loose hair was spinning around it, gripping rings. She was scenic.

Smik led me to a cordoned-off shower stall (gravity was slightly higher in the shower room so the water would fall down instead of floating). The stall was brushed steel, only where it wasn't: something had nommed chunks out of it.

I ran tests on the compromised material and got similar results: allosteel, human traces on it, only this time there was a trace of a second, unidentifiable species in the mix. My sampler came up with five more genomes, none matching the earlier ones. It couldn't tell me anything about the alien. Another new species. Then again, I still didn't know what Smik's species was.

"Are there any more sites?" I asked.

"Likely, but we haven't found them."

"You have passenger and crew genomes on file?"

"Purser has," he said.

"I don't know if this is a job for me. If the pests are passengers, you don't want me exterminating them, do you?"

"Humans do not eat metal," Smik said.

So obvious, so true. How did I miss it?

I didn't miss it, really. I was just eeking about maybe shooting people. My Skikka used to dream about the day he could open fire on humans. He'd tell me about this any time I came close to peeking under his veil, which a thing like that can drive you crazy, you know? What could be so terrible? But he never, ever let me see.

I followed Smik back to crew country and up the lift to the purser's office. Her name was Sellis, and she was small, wrinkled, and grumpy. She didn't recognize Smik until he took his fake head off, and she was less than complimentary about my suit, which wasn't fair; my Skikka taught me the suit is the most important thing I own, and I always maintain it, though maybe not cosmetically. She let me use one of her terminals to check genomes, though. I came up with a list of nine names. Two were crew, and seven were among the wealthiest passengers on board, according to the purser, who dropped her other duties and talked to me and Smik when she found out what I was doing.

"These people are doing what?" she asked.

"Munching on metal," I said. "Maybe that's the good news, though. With metal mites, you have a lot of decontamination where I need to shut down whole areas of the ship for several hours while the fumes do their work. These guys are easier to isolate. Gotta figure out what's happening to them, and is it contagious."

"I don't think we can authorize isolation with these passengers," said the purser. "They have too much clout."

"Can we test the crew members?" I asked.

"With the captain's authority." She hailed the captain and talked to him about the situation, then quietly alerted security to round up the two crew members I'd fingered and quarantine them. One was a nurse and the other was a waiter.

While we were waiting to hear back from security, Smik and I camped out in the purser's office, which she wasn't too thrilled about. "Why didn't anyone hear them?" I said. "Must be noisy, chomping on metal. Do you think they all did it at the same time, or were these just random visits to the same spot?"

"How can we know until you ask the beings

involved?" Smik said. I didn't know his body language, but I got the impression he was getting fed up with me.

"Good point." I could talk to the gym staff, see if anybody had noticed anything. Although this wasn't my usual method. I'm not a detective. Analyze and destroy! Then take the money and scamper. "Who spotted the damage?"

"Don't know," he said.

The purser's comm beeped. She spoke to it, then to us. "They've got the two crew in sickbay, isolation room. Now could you get out of here and let me work?"

Smik put his fake head back on and led me down to sickbay, where I met Dr. Pradip and an armed guard. The doctor was friendly, which was a nice change, and the guard was quiet. The nurse and the waiter were inside a glass-sided room. They sat side by side on a med-bed. The nurse was dark-skinned, tall, and muscular. She wore a teal uniform with a medical insignia on the chest. The waiter was shrimpy and wore what all the other crew on the promenade deck had been wearing: black pants, white shirt with creases, gold bow tie. They both sat quietly, too calm for people who had just been rounded up.

"Preliminary scans indicate they are not quite human any more," said the doctor. He was short and dark and had shiny black eyes. "It's very interesting! They have new metallic structures inside—very slender and hard to detect, but I found them."

I wished my Skikka was still around. He was not a people person, but he might have known how to handle this.

"Have you talked to the nurse? Is she someone who works with you?" I asked.

"Yes. She is my assistant. I thought she was a little

strange lately, but I didn't think—a marvel like this right under my nose!" He was all ready to dissect her on the spot. Which kind of put me off, but might be handy in the long run.

"Can we talk to them?"

"Sure, sure." He led me over to a console and pressed a button. "Amara? The exterminator is here. She has some questions."

I did? Again, not my area. "Uh," I said. Both the nurse and the waiter had straightened when the doctor spoke. Their faces still looked blank. "When did y'all start eating metal?"

"Ten days ago," they said together.

"Uh, why?"

"Our systems required it." They were perfectly synchronized in their speech.

"What for?"

"To build—" the waiter began, and the nurse put her hand in front of his mouth.

"To build what?" I asked.

"That is not your concern," said the nurse in a cold voice.

"How could you even bite it? Do you have diamond teeth?" I asked.

"We were given the means," said the nurse.

"Care to explain?" I asked.

"No," said the nurse, but the waiter said, "We produced it from our own selves."

"Quiet!" the nurse said.

"We have the potential to be so much greater," said the waiter. "You can be, also."

"Oh yeah? How?"

"Accept—" the waiter began, and the nurse put her

hand over his mouth again. He struggled a little, then straightened and got quiet.

I lifted my finger from the transmit button and said to the doctor, "Do you know anything about her personal life?" I got that the nurse had changed. I wondered how far, and whether I could come up with some question that would tell us.

He cocked his head and looked at the ceiling. "She has a sister on Mars. Any time anything funny or strange happens on board, Amara always echoes her."

"What's her sister's name?"

"Chika, I think."

I pressed the button again. "Hey, Amara. Did you tell Chika about what happened to you?"

"There is no need," she said. "She will know soon enough."

Well, that was pretty darned vague. I stopped transmitting again. "Doctor, how many tests can you run from here?"

"I have full scan capability, and I already have their blood undergoing analysis."

"I get the feeling taking care of this infestation is more your job than mine," I said.

He smiled. "I like that. Usually, the most exciting thing I do on the ship is prepare hangover cures and treat aphrodisiac misfires."

Smik's comm beeped. "Tell the exterminator we've found another damage site," said the chief engineer's voice. That was when I noticed Smik had his hand on the guard's shoulder, and the guard was just standing there, eyes blank and staring straight ahead.

Smik let go of the guard and tapped his comm. "Received. Where is the site?"

"In the day care center," said the engineer. "How's the extermination going?"

"It is strange," said Smik, and signed off. He stared at me with his fake eyes, and I stared back at his neck where I thought his real eyes were.

The doctor was burbling, weird non-word sounds that might be confusion or joy, staring at a readout on one of his machines. "Alien cells!" he cried. "Unregistered alien cells in their blood! Maybe I can name them after myself!"

"I'll go check the new site, see who else is infected," I said. "Smik?"

Smik's fake head stared at the ground, and then he gave a whole body shrug and led the way out of sickbay.

"I gotta stop at the cabin and check on my kid," I said as Smik headed toward the crew lifts.

"All right," he said. We detoured back to my place.

I opened the door and saw Fern sleeping peacefully on the floor of the care cage. As soon as we came in, though, she sat up, saw Smik, and screamed, even though he was still disguised.

"Mr. Smik, if you would be so kind," I said, and waved at the door. He didn't take the hint this time.

"Purrrrfect," he bubbled in a low voice, darted forward, and reached through the bars of the cage. Fern shrank back from his seeking hand, but one of the fingers shot out and wrapped around her wrist, then dragged her closer. She screamed and sobbed and tried to shove away, with her heels dug into the cage's floor.

I tapped my index finger rocket and shot a rubber bullet at his finger-tentacle. The bullet bounced off and winged me in the chest plate of my suit, leaving a dent. What was this guy made of? I activated a wrist blade and slashed at his hand. Even though I keep these blades supersharp and they're made of titanium alloy, it couldn't hack through him; didn't even scratch the skin.

"What are you?" I yelled, kicked the suit's augmentation hydraulics into play, and launched myself at him. I succeeded in knocking off his fake head and bouncing off his body to whack into the cabin wall, which didn't hurt me, but put a dent in the ship. Meanwhile, he slapped something on the back of Fern's neck, and she screamed even louder.

"Stop messing with my kid!" I screamed. I slapped the side panel on my hip compartment and brought out my big gun, something my Skikka gave me and told me to use only when things were life-threatening. I slapped it down on Smik's headbump, hoping his brain was somewhere nearby, because the alien technology in the Crown of Thorns would send probes digging down into him until they contacted the seat of sentience, no matter how thick and resistant his skin might be, or what they had to go through to get there.

They hadn't met much resistance when my Skikka used the Crown on me, have to say. It took a little longer for them to penetrate Smik's integument. While he was struggling to pull off the Crown, I did an end-run around him and got the care cage's door open. Smik had finally let go of Fern. I grabbed her, ducked into the cabin's bathroom, and locked the door behind me, though I didn't really expect Smik to come after us, not with the Crown working on him.

There were four red spots on the back of Fern's neck. My heart staggered a little, and my eyes squirted. "Baby, baby, baby," I said.

"Mommy, it's all right. I took it off before it could bite me." She showed me a small square metallic thing pinched between her fingers and thumb. It had all kinds of little legs, which were twitching and jerking but couldn't reach around behind it to get at her fingers. Four slender tentacles with bloody tips flopped around.

I grabbed a sample box from a side compartment of my suit and held it out. Fern dropped the thing in and I sealed it shut. Only when I was sure it was immobilized did I hug my daughter.

"Mommy, stop! You have your strength on!"

"Oh, crap! I'm sorry." I opened my arms and checked Fern for damage. She pursed her lips at me and laughed. Not even a bruise.

I don't know everything about my daughter, but I do know she's super tough, like her daddy. Which is a good thing, if you got me for a mother.

My Skikka said there are definite steps to a successful invasion. Infiltrate. Insinuate. Turn the invaded into your own people, and then reproduce with them—harder to fight family. Absorb and colonize.

Pest control works backward from that. If you can interrupt the invasion in its early stages, it's a lot easier to stop.

Once the Crown subdued Smik, I put a whole bunch of restraints on him. I had to take the Crown off and hide it, because it's forbidden tech, or it would be, if anybody else knew about it. But it had pretty well quieted Smik down.

Then I called security.

They found a lot more little colonizers in a hidden pocket nobody knew he had. I found out his species was called A'kla, and there were only a few of them in the solar system. We'd only made contact recently. The chief engineer said he was a great engineer, and she was going to miss him. The doctor was excited by the bug I gave him, and even happier about the collection security extracted from Smik.

The colonized didn't get off so easy. The bugs he slapped on them had worked their way inside, set up residence in the brains, got the bodies to acquire the materials they needed to be comfortable in their new homes. They're all messed up, but it works okay as far as keeping them alive. The doctor is conferring with major medical clinics on Terra, Luna, and Mars to figure out how to treat them, so there's hope. Meanwhile, they are pretty much just weird and creepy shadows of their former selves, and that includes three of the poor kids in day care.

My job was done, and they didn't know how to compensate me, since it wasn't exactly metal mites I fought. Fern and me are taking it out in trade. I finally took off my suit, and now we spend most of our time in passenger territory.

I watch my daughter play and wonder about her daddy, my Skikka, what part of himself he put in her while I had the Crown on my head. She's much more fun than the people the A'kla invaded. But I worry about her teen years.

ABOUT THE AUTHORS

P.R. Frost enjoys attending science fiction conventions in her spare time, where she can be found filking and hanging out with costumers. She and her husband make their home on Mt. Hood in Oregon. They frequently hike on the mountain and in the Columbia River Gorge. They share their home with a psychotic lilac point Siamese. P.R.'s musical tastes are as omnivorous as her reading, ranging from classical to Celtic to new age to jazz, and of course filk. Join P. R. on her Live Journal blog <www.livejournal.com/users/rambling_phyl> and share her latest hiking adventures, progress reports on her books, and gushing over wildflowers.

Jim C. Hines' latest book is *The Mermaid's Madness*, the second in his series about butt-kicking fairy tale heroines (because Sleeping Beauty was always meant to be a ninja, and Snow White makes a bad-ass witch). He's also the author of the humorous *Goblin Quest* trilogy, as well as more than forty published short stories in markets such as *Realms of Fantasy*, *Sword & Sorceress*, and *Turn the Other Chick*. You can find his web site and blog at www.jimchines.com. As always, Jim would like to thank his wife and children for putting up with him. Living with a writer ain't easy.

Nina Kiriki Hoffman has been writing science fiction and fantasy for more than twenty years and has sold more than two hundred fifty stories, plus novels and juvenile and media tie-in books. Her works have been finalists for the World Fantasy, Philip K. Dick, Sturgeon, and Endeavour awards. Her first novel, *The Thread That Binds the Bones*, won a Bram Stoker Award, and her short story "Trophy Wives" won a Nebula. Her middle school fantasy novel, *Thresholds*, will come out in 2010. Nina does production work for *The Magazine of Fantasy & Science Fiction* and teaches short story writing through her local community college. She also works with teen writers. She lives in Eugene, Oregon, with several cats, a mannequin, and many strange toys.

Nancy Holder is the *New York Times*-bestselling author of *The Wicked Series* (with coauthor Debbie Viguie.) They are launching a new vampire series called *Crusade,* the first volume of which will be out in the fall of 2010. She is also the author of the young adult horror series *Possessions* and the sequel, *Possessions: The Evil Within*. She lives in San Diego with her daughter, Belle, their corgi, Panda, and two very hairy cats named David and Kittnen Snow Vampire.

Tanya Huff lives and writes in rural Ontario with her partner, Fiona Patton, and nine cats—one more and they qualify as crazy cat ladies. In 2009, DAW Books published her *Enchantment Emporium* and in 2010 will publish a fifth Torin Kerr space marine book—untitled as yet. When she isn't writing she practices her guitar and complains about the weather.

Jane Lindskold lives in the Wild West and knows many of the resident wolves personally. This does not mean her story is autobiographical. Honest. Lindskold is the author of both the *Breaking the Wall* series (*Thirteen Orphans*, *Nine Gates*) and the Wolf Series (*Through Wolf's Eyes*, *Wolf's Head, Wolf's Heart*). For more titles and some great wolf pictures, see www.janelindskold.com.

Alexander B. Potter resides in Vermont, writing both fiction and nonfiction, painting, and working as an HIV Prevention Specialist at the AIDS Project of Southern Vermont. His published work is primarily in science fiction/fantasy and has appeared in a wide range of anthologies, including ten from DAW Books. He can be visited at www.alexanderpotter.com.

Mickey Zucker Reichert is a pediatrician, parent to multitudes (at least it seems like that many), bird wrangler, goat roper, dog trainer, cat herder, horse rider, and fish feeder who has learned (the hard way) not to let macaws remove contact lenses. Also, she is the author of twenty-two novels (including the *Renshai, Nightfall, Barakhai,* and *Bifrost* series), one illustrated novella, and fifty plus short stories. Mickey's age is a mathematically guarded secret: the square root of 8649 minus the hypotenuse of an isosceles right triangle with a side length of 33.941126.

In the past calendar year, Kristine Kathryn Rusch has won the *Asimov's Reader's Choice Award* and the *Ellery Queen Mystery Magazine Reader's Choice Award*.

She has been nominated for the Anthony, the Shamus, and the Hugo awards. Her short stories have appeared in *The Best Science Fiction of the Year* and *America's Best Mystery Stories*. Her latest novel is *Diving into the Wreck* from Pyr, based on the internationally award-winning story of the same name.

Lilith Saintcrow is the author of the *Dante Valentine*, *Jill Kismet*, and *Strange Angels* series. She currently resides in Vancouver, Washington, with her children, cats, and assorted other strays.

Jeanne Stein is the bestselling author of the urban fantasy series, *The Anna Strong Vampire Chronicles*. Last April, her character, Anna Strong, received a *Romantic Times* Reviewers Choice Award for Best Urban Fantasy Protagonist. The fifth in the Anna Strong series, *Retribution*, was released in August. Jeanne lives in Denver, CO where she is active in the writing community. And no, she doesn't hang out in biker bars to pick fights. Kick boxing is merely a great way to exercise.

Fantasy author Anton Strout was born in the Berkshire Hills, mere miles from writing heavyweights Nathaniel Hawthorne and Herman Melville, and currently lives in the haunted corn maze that is New Jersey (where nothing paranormal ever really happens, he assures you). He is the author of the *Simon Canderous* urban fantasy series as well as numerous short stories. In his scant spare time, he is a writer, a sometimes actor, sometimes musician, occasional RPGer, and the worlds most casual and controller-smashing video gamer. He currently works in the exciting world of publishing and yes, it is as glamorous as it sounds.

Elizabeth A. Vaughan is the author of *The Chronicles o* *the Warlands* and *Dagger-Star*. She still believes that th only good movies are the ones with gratuitous sword or lasers. Not to mention dragons. At the present, sh is owned by two incredibly spoiled cats and lives i the Northwest Territory, on the outskirts of the Blac Swamp, along Mad Anthony's Trail on the banks of th Maumee River.

ABOUT THE EDITORS

Martin H. Greenberg is the CEP of Tekno Books and its predecessor companies, now the largest book developer of commercial fiction and nonfiction in the world, with over 2,100 published books that have been translated into thirty-three languages. He is the recipient of an unprecedented three Lifetime Achievement Awards in the science fiction, mystery, and supernatural horror genres—the Milford Award in science fiction, the Bram Stoker Award in horror, and the Ellery Queen Award in mystery—the only person in publishing history to have received all three awards.

Kerrie Hughes lives in Wisconsin after traveling throughout the States and seeing a bit of the world, but has a list of more travels to accomplish. She has a marvelous husband in John Helfers, four perfect cats, and a grown son who is beginning to suspect that his main purpose in life is to watch said cats and house while his parental units waste his inheritance on travel. Thank you, Justin. She has written seven short stories: "Judgment" in *Haunted Holidays*, "Geiko" in *Women of War*, "Doorways" in

Furry Fantastic, "A Traveler's Guide to Valdemar" in *The Valdemar Companion*. And with John Helfers: "Between a Bank and a Hard Place" in Texas Rangers, "The Last Ride of the Colton Gang" in *Boot Hill*, and "The Tombstone Run" in *Lost Trails*. She has also written nonfiction, including the article "Bog Bodies" in *Haunted Museums*, and has edited two concordances for *The Vorkosigan Companion* and *The Valdemar Companion*. *Girl's Guide* is her eighth co-edited anthology, along with *Maiden Matron Crone, Children of Magic, Fellowship Fantastic, The Dimension Next Door, Gamer Fantastic*, and *Zombie Raccoons and Killer Bunnies*. She hopes to finish the novel she's been writing forever in between getting her master's degree in counseling and working full time for an evil corporation.

Seanan McGuire

The October Daye Novels

"...will surely appeal to readers who enjoy my books, or those of Patrica Briggs." —*Charlaine Harris*

"Well researched, sharply told, highly atmospheric and as brutal as any pulp detective tale, this promising start to a new urban fantasy series is sure to appeal to fans of Jim Butcher or Kim Harrison."—*Publishers Weekly*

ROSEMARY AND RUE
978-0-7564-0571-7

A LOCAL HABITATION
978-0-7564-0596-0

(Available March 2010)

To Order Call: 1-800-788-6262
www.dawbooks.com

DAW 142

C.S. Friedman
The *Magister* Trilogy

Once upon a time...

Cinderella—real name Danielle Whiteshore—did marry Prince Armand. And their wedding was a dream come true.

But not long after the "happily ever after," Danielle is attacked by her stepsister Charlotte, who suddenly has all sorts of magic to call upon. And though Talia the martial arts master— otherwise known as Sleeping Beauty—comes to the rescue, Charlotte gets away.

That's when Danielle discovers a number of disturbing facts: Armand has been kidnapped; Daniellie is pregnant; and the Queen has her own Secret Service that consists of Talia and Snow (White, of course). Snow is an expert at mirror magic and heavy-duty flirting. Can the princesses track down Armand and rescue him from the clutches of some of Fantasyland's most nefarious villains?

The Stepsister Scheme
by Jim C. Hines

"Do we *look* like we need to be rescued?"

DAW 130

Tanya Huff

The Finest in Fantasy

To Order Call: 1-800-788-6262
www.dawbooks.com

DAW 21

Tanya Huff
The *Smoke* Series

Tony Foster—familiar to Tanya Huff fans from her *Blood* series—has relocated to Vancouver with Henry Fitzroy, vampire son of Henry VIII. Tony landed a job as a production assistant at CB Productions, ironically working on a syndicated TV series, "Darkest Night," about a vampire detective. Tony was pretty content with his new life—until wizards, demons, and haunted houses became more than just episodes on his TV series...

"An exciting, creepy adventure"—*Booklist*

SMOKE AND SHADOWS
0-7564-0263-8
SMOKE AND MIRRORS
0-7564-0348-0
SMOKE AND ASHES
0-7564-0415-4

To Order Call: 1-800-788-6262
www.dawbooks.com

Tanya Huff
The Blood Books
Now in Omnibus Editons!

"Huff is one of the best writers we have at contemporary fantasy, particularly with a supernatural twist, and her characters are almost always the kind we remember later, even when the plot details have faded away." – *Chronicle*

Volume One:
BLOOD PRICE   BLOOD TRAIL
0-7564-0387-1 $7.99

Volume Two:
BLOOD LINES   BLOOD PACT
0-7564-0388-X $7.99

Volume Three:
BLOOD DEBT   BLOOD BANK
0-7564-0392-8 $7.99

To Order Call: 1-800-788-6262
www.dawboks.com

DAW 20